The U

By

J.A. Baker

Also by J.A. Baker:

Undercurrent
Her Dark Retreat
The Other Mother
Finding Eva

"*A house is never still in darkness to those who listen intently; there is a whispering in distant chambers, an unearthly hand presses the snib of the window, the latch rises. Ghosts were created when the first man woke in the night.*" – J.M. Barrie

"*Some places speak distinctly. Certain dark gardens cry aloud for a murder; certain old houses demand to be haunted; certain coasts are set apart for shipwreck.*" – Robert Louis Stevenson

August 1980

They stood, watching each other, their dark eyes locked together, both too angry, too resolute to look away. Tension crackled between them like static.

Outside, dusk sluggishly descended. A splinter of sepia light leaked in through the far window, dispersing over the floor and pooling around them, cocooning the two shadowy figures in its fading warmth.

'What are you doing in my house? You've no right to be up here. What a cheek, creeping up my stairs like this. You need to leave.' The voice conveyed authority streaked with a trace of disquiet.

'I don't need to do anything. And I'm not going anywhere. Not yet anyway. I'll leave here when I'm done.'

'I beg your pardon? You'll leave here when I say so. Who the hell do you think you are?'

No answer. Nothing but the sound of their breathing, disjointed and fitful in the slow dying light.

A loose floorboard creaked as one of the figures stepped forward, an arm outstretched, fingers almost brushing against skin.

The taller of the two jumped back as if burnt. 'What do you think you're doing? Get the hell away from me. I said get out!'

'I'm not going to hurt you. Not deliberately anyway. We need to talk first.'

'I've got nothing to say to you.'

'No? Well, for once in your life why don't you just listen because I've got plenty to say to you.'

Their bodies almost touched, outlines and shadows merging into one huge black bulk that swept over the polished floor and trailed down the stairs; an ugly skewed mass of impenetrable darkness.

'I'm not listening to anything you've got to say. You're nothing but a deceitful little liar and if you don't get out this very minute, I'll call the police.'

Laughter filled the air, a sharp acerbic cackle that echoed eerily in the stillness of the empty house. 'Go ahead. Where's the phone? Downstairs? Go right ahead and call them. What are you going to say? That somebody you know is in your house and no, they haven't committed a crime or threatened you, and no, they haven't broken in either, but they're just standing there, telling a few home truths that you're not so keen on hearing.'

For a few seconds there was no response until one of the figures moved. 'You're damn right I'm going to call them. You're not welcome. This is my house and I've asked you to leave. You have refused. In my eyes, that's classed as trespassing. Now get out of my way.'

A hand reached out and with a sharp push, a quick flick of the wrist, the shadow split into two, the huge grey entity ripping apart as one of them fell backwards. With arms outstretched and flailing, fingers grappling for purchase and eyes wide with terror, the lone figure toppled from top to bottom, its body bouncing and snapping as it hit almost every step along the way.

A sharp crack ended the descent as the figure landed, its body twisted and broken, its bulging eyes open and unseeing.

The other person at the top peered over the banister and stared at the grim sight before them. A hush accompanied their journey down as they stopped briefly and stepped over the corpse, avoiding the crimson pool that within a matter of seconds had gathered around the cadaver's head, an unsightly glistening halo that crept and crawled its way over the tiled floor, bleeding into every crack and crevice.

'Good riddance.' The voice was a whisper as the person gently careered around the spreading blood and brain matter. The lone figure slowly made its way towards the back door, careful not to touch anything on the way out.

As they took one last glance around, the door was closed with a light click and the figure snuck out into the clear summer air.

A stout beady-eyed crow swooped down and sat on the fence, the only witness to what had just taken place, the only living being that saw the individual leave. It would be their secret. For almost four decades those few minutes of escape would remain hidden, undisclosed to the rest of the world.

The departing figure turned and glanced back at the house, their eyes narrowed as if deep in thought. They exhaled quietly, smiled and whispered softly under their breath, 'Never thought I had it in me. I'm not sorry though. And you won't be missed.'

One

The reflection

I'd like to say I picked up on it the first time we visited the old place – the sensation that somebody else was around, that uneasy feeling you get when you're being watched – but that would be a lie. I didn't feel anything of the sort. Neither of us did. It was an uneventful morning with no defining memories, nothing we could look back on to say we should have known. The sun shone, birds sang. It was a typical spring day. There were no dark shadows, no eerie moments that made the hairs on the back of my neck stand on end; no signs or indications that anything was amiss. No clue as to what would follow.

Hugh had spent a good deal of the time we were there, itching to visit the basement. It was all he had talked about on the way to view the house. He was full of ideas about how he would turn it into a workshop where he could fix all the bits of broken machinery he had collected over the years. I was less than excited at the prospect of visiting a dank underground room. It held no appeal for me and I urged him to go down there without me.

It was a wise decision on my part. The basement, as it turned out, was much as I suspected it would be – like all basements everywhere, an airless, damp place full of cobwebs, dark corners and echoes. The thought of visiting it filled me with a sense of dread. After a swift glance down, I had stayed in the kitchen, listening to Hugh's voice as it filtered up through the floor where I was standing. I could hear him, speaking to the estate agent in a rapid animated fashion, firing questions at her, his excitement spilling out as he roamed around the concrete floor. He was so keyed up and desperate to purchase the place that excitement practically oozed out of every pore. We were both eager, but Hugh had the edge over me. He radiated pure energy.

The house was a bargain, there was no denying it. Empty for almost two years, it had put most people off due to the extensive renovations that were needed. I'd like to say it didn't faze us one little bit but I don't mind admitting I did feel more than a little overwhelmed at just how much needed doing to the old place. I couldn't complain, however. It was what we had talked about, what we'd wanted for some time. Hugh and I were looking for a project; a property we could pull apart, put our own unique stamp on and then call our own, and Cross House met all our requirements, providing us with something we could get our teeth into.

If only we had known.

I waited in the kitchen while they continued their tour of the basement. I had seen enough to convince me we needed to buy it and didn't feel compelled to go wandering around again. To be perfectly honest, I was starting to feel nervous about such an undertaking. The interior was in a much poorer condition close up than it had looked in the brochure, and if I stared too long and hard at all the flaws and the substantial amount of building work that needed to be done I think my knees would have buckled, so I stayed put and spent the time gazing outside, working out where I could put my bird feeders and how we could best utilise the space out there. The garden was immense. I liked a sprawling lawn and Hugh liked plenty of flowers and border plants, so compromises would have to be made. I could live with that. Arguments about flora and fauna paled into insignificance compared to what we had already been through.

The voices beneath me grew closer, the timbre in their tone altering and changing in pitch as they climbed back up the steps.

I took one last look around the kitchen, opening cupboard doors and peering in even though we had every intention of ripping them out and replacing them with modern units. An island. I really liked the idea of an island where we could gather as a family and chat while we cooked and prepared our food. I had plans for Cross House. High hopes and so many plans.

By the time I had inspected each and every shelf and peered into the darkest of corners, they were back in the kitchen, making their appearance through the tiny entrance next to the old pantry, another feature I planned on disposing of as soon as we moved in. I watched them – Hugh and the slightly frazzled-looking middle-aged lady – as they emerged with their heads bowed. They straightened up and brushed down their clothes, fingers patting and dragging across fabric to remove the dust that clung to their clothes. The look on Hugh's face told me all I needed to know. His mind was made up. He had put an offer in. That didn't disturb me. We had already discussed the financial side of things prior to the visit and pored over photographs of the house online. Before we had even set foot in it, we knew that it was the property we had been looking for. We had outgrown our other home. It no longer felt like a relaxing place to be. We had plenty of reasons to be leaving it behind, none of them pleasant.

I shook hands with the estate agent; the look on her face was one of complete horror as I turned to Hugh and asked him whether the basement contained any dead bodies or rotting carcasses. She must have heard that line and worse many times over in her line of work and eventually laughed when I echoed Hugh's sentiments about loving Cross House and its location. It was in a perfect setting in a tiny village in North Yorkshire with only a handful of neighbours. After what he had been through it was ideal. What could possibly go wrong in such an idyllic place? I then backed up his offer, reminding her that our property had already sold. Estate agents love to hear about buyers without a chain speeding up the whole arduous process. I could almost see the pound-note signs flashing before her eyes as we continued to chat about the charm of the old place and how we couldn't wait to start our renovations once the place was ours.

By the time we were back in the car, both Hugh and I knew that it was a done deal. There was no reason for it not to be. For once, everything would go our way. I could just feel it; the tug of good fortune that I was sure was long overdue. I managed to shut out of my mind all the dated decor and the heavy workload that lay ahead of us and instead focused on the positives. It was far bigger than our current house, was in a rural location and more than that, it provided us with a fresh start, the opportunity to leave those memories behind – all the emotional baggage and stress we were only too keen to forget about.

That's where it all started really. That day in the kitchen when we said yes to the house. That day when we thought our lives would start again, free from terror and fear. We had endured enough. We deserved to sleep easy at night. We deserved some peace of mind and leaving everything behind would afford us just that. Or so we thought.

How wrong we were. The day we bought Cross House was when it all started to go horribly awry. And that's when our story really begins...

Two

The beginning

'You remembered to inform the post office to redirect our mail?' A line of discontent and worry runs down Hugh's forehead. His eyes are narrowed to tiny slits as he stares at me. I've already told him this at least twice but he is so strung out that nothing seems to have permeated his brain. I nod to indicate that I have done it and carry on packing our clothes into the huge suitcase that is laid out on the bed. How have we managed to accumulate so many items of clothing over the years? There are things at the back of the wardrobe I have no recollection of buying – over a dozen scarves in a variety of colours so loud and vile I have no idea why I even considered purchasing them in the first place, and a considerable gathering of handbags so badly dented and scratched they're no longer even recognisable as handbags. Hugh is the proud owner of eight pairs of deck shoes, and even more disconcerting is the fact that he owns fourteen pairs of training shoes, half of which don't even look as though they will fit him.

Scooping them up, I drop them all into a large bin bag one by one, determined to liberate us of the clutter we have lived with for so many years now that we became blind to its existence. We have become used to foraging amongst the rubbish to find our everyday items. The time has come to get rid of it all, to start afresh. God knows we deserve it. It hasn't been a particularly good year. That's an understatement if ever there was one. This has been one of the worst years of my life. I'll be glad to see the back of this house and its recent memories and I'm almost certain Hugh feels the same way. Misery and worry have trailed around in our wake for months now. I won't miss it when we leave.

I hear Poppy and Aiden playing in the room next to us and I am unexpectedly flooded with relief. Even the sound of their voices is enough to shake me out of any state of unhappiness or worry. Hearing the tinkling of their laughter sends goose bumps over my skin. The thought of what could have been makes me wince. I close my eyes and try not to think of it. A few careless mistakes, a past that we didn't know existed, and the life we had worked for, perhaps even taken for granted, nearly came tumbling down around us.

I return to packing and ridding us of as much detritus as I can. Our new house may be much larger but there's so much decorating and refurbishment to be done that it'll be like living in a building site for a good few months. If I can streamline our belongings to make life easier for us whilst we inhabit a house that is covered in dust and stripped bare, then that's what I will do, no matter how difficult or tedious a task it proves to be. After recent events, I am all for keeping things simple.

Hugh drags a large box out of the bedroom, grunting with the effort as he pulls it along the landing and down the stairs. All of our books – more items we have hung on to when we should have really given many of them away – fill the box, causing him to swear and curse as it hits the bottom of the stairs with a solid thump. I smile, knowing he will be rearranging his precious engineering manuals and then looking at the other hardbacks and wondering, as I am, why we kept all this stuff while trying to work out where we will put it when we get there. I also know he is brimming with excitement at the prospect of moving, at the very thought of owning such a large old property; somewhere we can live in and work from and truly call our own; a home where nobody will bother us or terrify and threaten us. We'll be able to go back to normality again, back to an everyday existence. We can return to who we were before our lives were almost torn apart.

I finish clearing out the rest of the wardrobes and cupboards in our bedroom and shout to Poppy and Aiden to help me lift the rest of the bags and boxes down the stairs and into the car. I plan on making one last trip to the charity shop to hand over our unwanted belongings before we move tomorrow.

The kids trudge through, feigning boredom as I hand over yet more sacks of unwanted goods and give them strict instructions to tie them up and then dump them at the front door. I let out a deep breath and run my fingers through my hair before sitting down on the edge of the bed. We're almost done. Just a change of clothes to keep out for the morning, and the duvets and sheets to haul into sacks once we're up and have stripped the beds, and we're ready to go. It's been such a horribly busy time but we've managed it without any major quarrels which is close to a miracle considering what has gone before. I suppose what we've endured has helped us to become more resilient. We have managed to live through the most difficult of times and survived it, so I guess moving house barely registers on any scale when it comes to measuring the stresses and strains of everyday life.

I take one last look around the room, the place Hugh and I have shared for over fifteen years, the place I used to think of as home, and feel no traces of regret at our decision to leave. It was good while it lasted – a comfortable family home – but now it's time to move on.

We spend the remainder of the evening eating a takeaway and squabbling over the only thing we kept out as a way of keeping ourselves entertained for the night – a game of Scrabble. The television has been disconnected ready for the move in the morning so we sit in an almost bare living room and eat with plastic knives and forks since I packed our cutlery away along with all the crockery.

'That's not a proper word!' Poppy's voice reverberates around the empty room as she stares at the board with the word 'poop' on it. Aiden leans back and smiles, his eyes narrow and dark and filled with mischief as he watches her temper take hold. Poppy hates injustice. She also hates losing.

'Okay, you guys, I chime quickly, knowing there is a fine line between fun and frivolity and that slight tipping over the edge into a full-on fist fight and screaming arguments, a point from which there will be no return. 'Time to finish eating and get ready for bed.'

'Bed?' Aiden scoffs loudly, shoving the last of his fried rice into his mouth. 'You're kidding, aren't you? It's only just gone nine o'clock.'

'Not kidding,' I reply lightly. 'We've got an early start in the morning. The van's coming just after seven thirty. We need to be up and ready by then. Quilts and bedsheets to strip off, beds to take apart, furniture to move. Come on, finish off here and let's get washed.'

He stares at me, wondering how long he can hold my gaze, thinking I'll look away before he does. I don't. He drops his eyes after a few seconds, curls his lip and sneers at me. Aiden's transition into a teenager won't be an easy one. At twelve years of age he already has the measure of his younger sister, knowing how to push her buttons, knowing exactly how to wind her up into a frenzy with just one fleeting look or a simple word. He has recently begun trying it on me. It doesn't work. Not at the moment anyway. Give it a few years and he will probably be driving me insane but for now I can manage him, keep him in line with just one glance. I should be enjoying having this level of control. I know from seeing friends with their teenage children how it will all slip away from me and I will be left like a washed-out rag, wondering where he is, who he is hanging around with, whether or not he is drinking or, God forbid, dabbling in drugs. Just the thought of it makes me go cold. Even the idea of his skin sprouting whiskers and being possibly riddled with acne is enough to make me want to snuggle him to my chest and hold him there for as long as I can.

'Come on!' I snap, clapping my hands together briskly.

Hugh catches my eye, winks at me and sweeps his palm across the board, gathering all the tiles up with just one fist. 'You heard your mother,' he says through a mouthful of Szechuan chicken. 'Time for bed now. We've all got an early start in the morning. Places to go, people to see, furniture to shift. Come on now. Chop, chop.'

They both rise out of their seats with a dramatic sigh. Poppy clambers on my knee and plants a wet kiss on my face, telling me she loves me over and over in her squeaky, inimitable voice. Aiden glares at me for a second then relents and gives both Hugh and me a high five. He stopped giving kisses over a year ago, claiming they were for sissies and losers.

I watch as Hugh chivvies them along, threatening Poppy with tickles when she begins to lose impetus halfway up the stairs. I close my eyes and try to take a mental snapshot of the moment. This last year has been exhausting and times like this have been rare. I like to think we have hidden most of our problems away from the kids, protected them from the strain and horror of it all, but I know that's not entirely true. There were times when they were subjected to parts of it, and for that I will never forgive myself. I just hope they have managed to block it out of their thoughts and it doesn't register in their memory banks as a significant event. We did our best to play it all down, pretend that it was the behaviour of a couple of stupid men who didn't know any better. We didn't tell them that our whole family had been threatened by two unrelated individuals whose behaviour bordered on psychotic.

The sound of their voices dies down eventually and I sit and listen to the creak of beds above me as they clamber in, the slight noise of their shuffling feet accentuated in the emptiness of the room. I glance around, suddenly aware of how dark and shadowy the place is, how many eerie unlit corners there are now the soft furnishings and lamps have been packed away. I feel a sudden and overwhelming need to leave the room, to clear away the remains of the food, turn off the light and vacate the place as soon as I can. Too many bad memories here. Plenty of good ones for sure but the bad ones are recent, more cutting and clearer in my mind. Even the images of Aiden and Poppy running around the place, Poppy still in nappies and screaming with laughter as Aiden chases her, are obliterated and blackened by more recent events, charred and ruined by two people who were very nearly the undoing of me.

Standing up, I grab a black rubbish bag, drop everything into it and tie it up. Fatigue bleeds into my bones. It's been a long and exhausting day and I'm under no illusions about how busy tomorrow will be.

I dump the bag by the back door, flick off all the lights and drag myself up the stairs.

In the bedroom, I find Hugh already tucked up in bed. He's spent most of the day humping large boxes around and emptying the garage of all of his tools and gardening equipment so it's hardly surprising he is already asleep. I quickly undress, pull the covers back and slide in next to him, glad of the warmth radiating from his body. Wrapping my arms tightly around him, I snuggle close, grateful that he is who he is: good old reliable Hugh, a strong and buoyant man who refuses to be beaten by life, by the things that we've been through in the past few months. While I wilted and crumpled under the strain, Hugh stood tall – always there, always dependable, never complaining. The stalwart of our little family.

It doesn't take long for sleep to take me. I disappear into a world where everything is skewed and distorted and nothing makes sense. Todd is there along with Jeff and they both stand with ferocious-looking expressions on their faces, shouting to me that everything is my fault. I try to protest that I did nothing wrong, but am only able to grunt, my voice locked in my throat. All that comes out is a protracted groaning sound.

I watch, terrified, as they talk amiably to one another, smiling manically, their features hideously distorted. They turn to stare at me then disappear into the distance, their heads tipped together conspiratorially even though the pair of them are strangers and have never met. Not in my dreams though. In my dreams they plan and scheme together, working out ways they can get to us and hurt me and my family, and it seems I'm powerless to stop them.

When I wake the next morning to the warmth of the weak sun filtering in through the blinds, I am so grateful to be leaving it all behind – Todd, Jeff, the whole sorry debacle. Soon it will be just a dim and distant memory. The fact they still have the ability to infiltrate my thoughts while I sleep makes me angry; firstly and foremost, with both men for what they've put us through and also with myself for allowing the pair of them to climb inside my head when I should have found the strength to finally be free of them.

I shrug off the covers, rub at my eyes to clear my misted vision and pull on my dressing gown, my skin clammy with a mixture of mild dread and excitement at the prospect of what the day will bring. Yawning and shivering, I shove my feet into my faithful old slippers and stand up.

The house is silent. Even Aiden and Poppy, the two early birds, are still sleeping. They too are feeling the fatigue that has us all in its grip. I begin to work out what my tasks are for the day and whether I should wake the kids to help me or leave them be and just get on with what needs to be done.

The decision is made for me as I hear the ruffle and scratch of fabric followed by the light thud of feet on the floor, indicating that Poppy is out of bed in the room next door. I smile, tighten my dressing gown and push open the bedroom door. Time to get started and pack up the remainder of our belongings. Time to leave this place and all its bad memories for good.

Three

Despite my best efforts to keep them away, Todd and Jeff are on my mind as I help Hugh to drag our hefty old bureau out of the dining room and into the van that we've hired for the day. We decided against using a removal firm since a lot of our furniture is fitted into the house and won't be coming with us, but my back is aching and I am hot and tired and now regretting the decision we made to do all the removals ourselves. With the benefit of hindsight, it seems like a rash, ill-thought-out move, but the decision has been made and now we must go with it. It's too late to change our minds.

I realise it', s deceitful running away like this, not giving Todd our forwarding address, but he did some terrible things. He scared me witless and made some awful threats against us. We're doing this, moving house and not telling him, to protect our family unit, to protect what he did his utmost to ruin. As for Jeff, I have no reason to even tell him we are leaving here, let alone provide him with information about our new place. He didn't mean that much to me before it happened and means even less to me now. Jeff hasn't been in touch for probably a couple of months now and neither has Todd. That doesn't ease my worries. They're both still out there. And Todd's previous behaviour tells me he'll be back at some point. Todd always comes back.

The memory of his fist pushing through the pane of glass next to the front door, littering the hallway with splinters of glass and hollering at us that we were a pair of selfish bastards, pierces my brain. It was fortunate that the children were in bed and slept through that particular incident. I dread to think what could have happened if they had been there to witness such a horrific display of anger and violence. And it was horrific. Glass shattering everywhere, his voice booming at us that he was going to kill us all. God knows how they didn't wake, but thankfully they didn't. Poppy suffers with nightmares as it is. Seeing such an event would have caused her untold damage and robbed her of sleep for months.

It was bad enough that she witnessed the drunken visit from Jeff where he called around one evening, completely hysterical, falling in the front door onto the stairs in an ungraceful heap, screaming and calling out for me to leave Hugh and go live with him. We had been sitting watching TV and before we could stop her, Poppy jumped up and answered the knock at the door, despite us telling her not to many times over. Jeff crashed in, tripping over the step, missing Poppy by just a few inches and fell onto the stairs where he lay, sobbing and screaming, his speech slurred as he spewed out a load of drunken nonsense about what a tease I was and how much he loved me.

I block the memory out. I have to. I cannot bring myself to think about it in too much detail. The pair of them harassing us at the same time was more than I could cope with. My flesh still crawls at the memory of it.

The thing is, Todd could have become part of our family if he had acted with a little more decorum and had been polite and civilised, but as it was, he turned up at our home full of fury and hatred. Destruction and anger were his main driving forces and we simply couldn't get beyond them no matter how hard we tried. It was as if he enjoyed being miserable and making those around him feel the same way.

'Right, when I say lift, hook your fingers under this edge and push towards me,' Hugh says as he nods at me to make sure I'm concentrating on the task at hand. How could I not be completely focused when we're lifting one of the heaviest pieces of furniture in the house? Once this one has been moved we'll only have a few smaller items to shift. It goes without saying that we're going to have to lift them all off the truck again when we get to Cross House. I try not to think about it. I'm already exhausted and the day has barely begun. Even if we only manage to get the beds in and assembled then that will be sufficient to see us through until the morning. The van doesn't need to be returned for another day or so. We can take our time unloading it, which I suppose is something to be grateful for.

We successfully lift the bureau and load it without any major traumas or high drama. It was passed down to us by Hugh's wealthy grandma and I am all too aware of its value. Hugh never fails to remind me or the kids every time we pass it with a cup of tea or a glass of juice, that it's a family heirloom. Personally, I think it's an ugly piece of furniture with overly ornate cladding and crudely carved legs, but I am more than happy to let him treasure it and continually tell stories about how his grandfather almost threw it in the skip when they were refurbishing the house. He was stopped at the last minute by his grandmother who returned from a shopping trip, aghast to see its legs jutting out from the piles of rubbish he had put on top of it. I doubt that it's worth half of what Hugh says it is, but if its presence makes Hugh happy, then I'm happy.

'Poppy! Aiden!' My voice echoes throughout every room, bouncing off floors and bare walls, giving the place a sense of being unloved and unwanted. It's just a shell, no longer our home. The new owners won't be moving in for another month. They're coming over from Ireland and couldn't make it here in time so it will sit unoccupied during that period. It makes me feel quite sad to think of this house empty. I desperately hope that if Todd decides to return, he'll see that we have moved on with our lives and realise that he should do the same. We tried with him, we really did, but it was as if he actually enjoyed causing hurt and upset. He didn't come here with the sole intention of being reunited with his long-lost family. I'm almost certain he came here to destroy us.

I listen out for footsteps above me – any sign that the children are around – but I am met with complete silence. Mild fear begins to grip me.

'Come on, you two. We're almost ready to go!' I stare at Hugh outside as he rearranges items in the back of the van. His expression is one of complete absorption. He is locked into his own game of furniture Jenga as pulls out a table and a bedside cabinet and turns them around ninety degrees before jamming them back in again. The children aren't out there with him and they're not in here either. My head throbs. Closing my eyes briefly, I swallow hard. I have to give it one more try. They're here somewhere.

I shout again, this time putting enough force into my tone to let them know I'm not in the mood for any of their silly games. I'm too tired and both Hugh and I are too busy for any of their usual nonsense. Now definitely isn't the time or place for hide and seek.

'Aiden! Stop this nonsense. We don't have time for any of your stupid pranks. Get yourselves down here right now!' He will be behind this. I just know it. Poppy is his puppet, doing as he says, always eager to please her big brother and get on his good side; she will go along with anything he tells her to do. I convince myself that's the case because the alternative is too awful to consider.

I storm up the stairs, ready to holler at the pair of them, but soon realise they're not actually here. Every cupboard door hangs open like a gaping mouth and they are not hiding in any of them. Unless they have managed to pull the bath panel off, clamber in and then put it back in place (which I know for a fact they haven't) then they are definitely not upstairs.

A small slithering thread of fear takes hold and burrows its way into my brain. I think about Todd and his volatile behaviour and threats. And then I think about Jeff and how angry he was the last time we spoke, and before I know it I am racing downstairs, my heart pumping violently as I run from room to room screaming out for Aiden and Poppy to show themselves and to stop being so thoughtless and selfish. For months and months, I've kept a close eye on them both, monitoring where they've been, dropping them off at friends' houses, picking them up again, questioning them both relentlessly about where they went and who they spoke to until eventually I realised that I was scaring them more than any potential kidnapper could.

And now I can't find them. All the doors are open, the house is empty and my children are gone.

I feel light-headed as I check the kitchen, the last room to look in, to discover they're not in there either. I knew they wouldn't be but had to look anyway.

By the time I stagger outside I can hardly breathe. My words come out like rapid gunfire as I almost throw myself at Hugh, tears threatening to spill over any second. 'The kids! I can't find them, Hugh. Where are the fucking kids?'

He holds his hands up in a stance of mock surrender and raises his eyebrows, his nostrils flaring at my swearing, before glancing around at the other houses nearby and then looking back at me. This is a quiet neighbourhood with families who, like us, have young children. People are polite, genteel. Swearing and cursing isn't acceptable. I can't help it. I am beginning to feel desperate. The last year has been like living on a knife edge and I've dreaded something like this happening.

'Calm down, Faye! They can't have gone far. Have you checked upstairs?'

'Yes, of course I've bloody well checked upstairs. I'm not stupid. They're not here with you, are they? Hiding in the back of the van?'

Hugh sighs, arches his eyebrows and then looks at the removals lorry, crammed with all our goods. His lips form a thin tight line as he shakes his head and then stares hard at me as if I'm mad. It would be impossible to fit anything else in there. I can see that; I'm not an idiot. I am however, beside myself with worry and rational thought is no longer playing a part in my thinking. What if they clambered in there before we put the furniture in? What if the pair of them are trapped at the back, hemmed in by heavy items, stuck in the dark and struggling to breathe? What if –

'Oh, I am so sad, seeing you like this! You are actually leaving us today, yes?'

To my right, Irena, our neighbour, steps into view. She reaches out and draws me into a tight bear hug before I can protest and tell her that our children are missing and that I'm becoming desperate and frantic with worry. She holds me there in her big strong arms until I pull away, hot tears pricking at my eyes.

'Georgia and Bianka will be getting so lonely. Nobody to play with! Other children round here very rude and mean. Not like your children, Faye. Your two very lovely little people; you bring them up with good hearts.' She wags her finger at me and gives me one of her jovial smiles that usually never fail to cheer me up. Not today. Today I am teetering on a precipice of angst and exhaustion and may well fall over the edge if my children don't show their faces in the next few minutes.

'They're not at yours are they, Irena?' I half scream.

She widens her eyes and catches Hugh's exasperated expression as she speaks. 'Georgia and Bianka? Yes, they are home at present watching television. Always watching television or computer screen. They will end up with the square eyes!'

'No, Aiden and Poppy. I can't find them, Irena! They're not in the house and we need to get going soon and –'

I feel Hugh tug at my sleeve and shrug him off, furious at him for not taking my fears seriously. I snap my head around to see two figures in the distance, strolling up the street as if they don't have a care in the world. Aiden is dipping his hand into a large bag of sweets and Poppy is sucking on a lollipop then lifting it out and twirling it around in the air like a majorette with a baton. I don't know whether to laugh or cry. I had visions of them sweltering to death in the back of the removal van or being snatched by a psychotic Todd or a lonely, half-crazed Jeff, both of whom are determined to get back at us for turning them away after one desperate and drunken insult too many. I didn't visualise Aiden and Poppy visiting the local shop buying sweeties with their pocket money. My voice is an accusatory shriek as I point at them and then turn to face Hugh, anger boiling up inside me like molten lava. 'Did you say they could go to the shop?'

He frowns and takes a step back away from me. He did. He definitely did. This is all his fault. I can tell by the look on his face that they asked him while he was busy. His mind was elsewhere and he didn't listen to them properly and said yes to their request to get them off his back while he packed things away. I can't decide if I want to run and hug them both, holding them tight until they can no longer breathe properly, or stay put and slap Hugh's smug face.

'Ah, they are here now!' Irena shouts as she raises her hands in the air dramatically, the tops of her arms wobbling about. 'That is important thing. Children all safe now and everybody happy.'

I admire Irena's positivity. I wish I could be more like her instead of the bumbling wreck I always turn into in times of stress. She radiates warmth and an air of perpetual capability and it's always difficult to stay angry or upset in her presence.

I watch as Poppy spots our effervescent neighbour and breaks into a gallop, flinging herself into Irena's big, welcoming arms. 'Children!' Irena shouts, 'I am saying goodbye and will be missing you! You will come and visit us, yes?'

Poppy squeals excitedly and Aiden gives one of his reserved nods, his face almost breaking into something closely resembling a smile.

'Ah, so good of you! I will be telling Georgia and Bianka to expect you soon!'

'You have our new address don't you, Irena? You must come and visit once we're settled,' I say quietly, relief very slowly washing over me. I will miss Irena a lot. She has been a good neighbour and friend, keeping us entertained with her quirky Eastern European customs and her incessant affection and laughter. It was Irena who came to our rescue the first time Todd turned nasty and aggressive. She heard the commotion and came to the door asking if we needed help, saying brusquely that she had already called the police and giving Todd one of her stern glares. She hadn't called them, but it was enough to scare Todd away. He had scurried off down the street wearing a sheepish expression. It didn't stop him coming back though. Nothing seemed to stop Todd. He always came back.

'Yes, we will visit you often! So often you will be wishing you hadn't given me new address.' Her barking laughter fills the air. She carefully extricates herself from Poppy's vice-like grip and gives me another tight hug, then shakes Hugh's hand, his body practically vibrating from the force of her grasp. 'You have nice time in happy new home. Anyway, I am going now or I am thinking I might cry!'

She gives us one last wave and with that she is gone, shuffling away back into her house where chaos reigns supreme. I thought Irena was quite possibly one of loudest, most exuberant people I had ever met, until I was introduced to her children, Georgia and Bianka, who guffaw and giggle like a pair of braying donkeys, and Stefan, her husband, a portly man whose booming laughter can shatter glass.

I turn and glare at Aiden and Poppy, my initial anger rapidly dissipating after listening to Irena's high-spirited speech. 'Next time you disappear anywhere, please let me know first, okay?' I quickly glance at Hugh to let him know that I'm aware of his mistake, then turn back to both of them, my gaze still one of disapproval.

Aiden's mouth opens in immediate protest. We don't give him a chance to come out with a smart retort. Hugh pulls the shutter down on the back of the van, the noise of grating metal filling the air and causing me to flinch. He hooks his thumbs through his belt loops and hitches his trousers up then nods towards the house, his voice just loud enough to catch Aiden's attention. 'You're bringing the rest of the bags in your car aren't you, Faye? Right, Aiden, you're sitting up in the front of the van with me. Poppy, you're in the car with your mum.' For the first time all day, Aiden smiles, his cheeks flushing as he clambers up into the small removals lorry, a flash of gratitude evident in his eyes.

I grab Poppy's hand and head up the driveway into the house where we do one last sweep of each of the rooms, gathering up half-filled sacks and boxes, dumping them in the back of the car and then going back in to check cupboards, making sure they're empty before looking around the place one last time. My eyes rove over every surface, into every corner; all dark and bare. All that remains are a few fleeting memories which in time, will fade and disappear. All gone. Nothing left of us in this place. Time to move on.

I step outside and lock up, then let out a long breath and swallow down the lump that has risen in my throat. I have no idea why I'm so emotional. This house no longer feels like ours. Too much damage has been done in there in the last year for me to feel overly attached to it. Funny, isn't it, how bad memories have the power to annihilate even the happiest of thoughts? 88 Cambian Close no longer belongs to us. All the good things that happened there have been razed to the ground.

I move back and gaze at the upstairs windows, now full of shadows and a sense of coldness. I look at the children's bedrooms where they used to play, then at my bedroom – the place where I spent so many years sleeping next to my husband, the place where our children were conceived. The very same place where Jeff tried to attack me. I shiver and turn away, acid churning, my stomach tightening at the thought of it.

Clutching Poppy's hand, I slot the house keys through the letterbox for the estate agent to collect in the morning, and make my way down the driveway for the final time.

'Come on, Pops,' I say with more conviviality than I feel, 'let's go home.'

Four

It's almost dark by the time Poppy and I get to Cross House. Brackston Village seems even quieter than the last time we visited and I am weighed down by a sudden feeling of loneliness and fear. This is when it really hits me – an unexpected sense of isolation. A voice whispers to me that we don't really belong anywhere. I try to ignore it but it stays put, tunnelling its way into my mind. It's as if we're in some sort of hiatus, suspended between having a sense of security and a lovely place to call home, and freefalling into a deep, dark abyss. I feel like our family is stepping into a cold dark vacuum. Fear and uncertainty nip at me and I can't seem to shrug them off. They're not feelings I'm familiar with and not ones I care for.

The hills of North Yorkshire sit beyond the ridge of the roof tiles, almost obscured by a heavy shroud of murky, ominous-looking clouds that have bubbled up together in an angry portentous mass. It's strange; after the tumultuous year we have had, I expected to feel jubilant with this move but instead I feel a mild sense of dread as I pull up on the gravelled driveway and kill the engine.

Poppy is asleep in the car after an early start this morning. Outside, Hugh and Aiden are already unloading the van, Aiden helping by carrying in the smaller items, a serious look on his face at being given a position of responsibility. I watch him struggle across the gravel and through the front door with a box of books and think how much he resembles Hugh with his mass of dark hair and swarthy complexion. I sit for a couple more minutes watching them both, trying to gather my thoughts, hoping we have done the right thing buying this big old place. It seemed so right at the time; we were buoyant and positive about it back then but now for some inexplicable reason I cannot rid myself of the feelings of doubt. There is no earthly reason for me to feel this way, none at all.

I open the car door, all the while telling myself that I am being ridiculous, and step out, the sound and sensation of walking on the gravel like marching on broken glass. I leave Poppy in the back and stare up at the grandeur of the place. Compared to the modern three-bedroom property we've just left behind, Cross House is positively huge but also horribly dilapidated. Built in the mid-nineteenth century, it has an imposing look to it, with a large oak door and huge sash windows. It has castellations around the side of the old extension and a turret roof at the far end, giving it the look of some sort of neglected fortress.

Once you get inside, however, it is anything but imposing or secure, with large damp patches on the ceilings, crumbling plaster and dated, dirty carpets that have been down for many decades. Even switching the lights on is a health hazard. It's a two-wire system, so we're going to need a full rewire; just another job to add to the ever-growing list of major refurbishments and building work that Cross House needs. No cosmetic paint jobs in this place. Every single bit of work that we will carry out is essential. According to the estate agent, the previous owners barely occupied the place. They only owned it for two years and lived abroad during most of that time, having bought it as a base; somewhere to stay when they came back to the UK to visit their children. It seems like an expensive way to keep in touch with family as far as I can see, but I gather they were a wealthy couple who enjoyed an extravagant lifestyle. I exhale loudly as I survey the exterior of Cross House and think about the decay inside. What a pity they didn't decide to use some of their millions to update this property. God knows how the owners before that managed to inhabit this place in its current state. I visualise an old lady living here – no family or friends, just her alone in this old house, spending day after day sitting in one room until she eventually passed away, her body slowly rotting in an old chair by the fire.

I shiver and tell myself to stop it. This is silly; it's no more than slight apprehension at such a huge change in circumstances. I walk round to the back seat, lift Poppy out and haul her over my shoulder. Even for a slight seven-year-old, she still feels extraordinarily heavy and I almost lose my footing as I make my way over the small stones on the driveway that continually shift under my feet. I stumble into the darkness of the large vestibule and head into the hallway, my feet echoing eerily on the tiled floor.

By the time I get to the kitchen, Poppy is awake, sleep ebbing away from her and a look of excitement written all over her face at the prospect of going off to explore the new house. And there is a lot of it to explore – seven bedrooms, numerous larders and cupboards that Aiden and Poppy will undoubtedly use to hide in, two huge sitting rooms, two dining rooms and a kitchen so large you could probably fit the entire downstairs of our previous house into it with room to spare. Outside, the garden is enormous with numerous outhouses we have yet to even uncover and enter. They are out there somewhere, hidden under years and years of undergrowth that's been left to grow wild for God knows how long.

Poppy slips off my shoulder, her legs buckling slightly, her co-ordination still fogged up by a deep sleep. She bolts into the living room where Aiden is carefully unpacking a box containing old crockery and cutlery that I haven't used in years. Not exactly necessary items at this juncture, but I leave him to it, not wanting to disturb his affable demeanour. Aiden's emotions are in a constant state of flux of late, hormonal changes stamping out and almost obliterating his once cheery disposition.

'I want to help!' Poppy cries as she delves into the box, her little hands ferociously rummaging through its contents. For once, Aiden lets her get on with it and I am eternally grateful that there is no squabbling or fighting to contend with. I am too on edge and far too exhausted to intervene and be the negotiator between the pair of them.

'Faye!' Hugh's voice rattles through the empty hallway, ringing off every wall, floor tile and bare window. 'Come up here, will you? I need a hand with these beds.'

Between us, we manage to assemble every piece of bedroom furniture without either of us getting too fractious, despite being hungry and tired and despite me feeling as if a dark veil is hanging over us all.

Hugh smiles at me as we unpack and fix things together. He keeps my mind occupied, chatting about everyday things – work, the kids, making new friends in the village – until very slowly, I begin to relax, gradually becoming more accustomed my new and alien surroundings. It's time, that's all it is. I know it. I just need more time to rid myself of the lingering demons that are nibbling at me, hissing into my brain that our previous problems will follow us around forever. They won't. They can't. Neither Jeff nor Todd know our new address, and although Jeff's contact has been sporadic over the last few months, there is always the fear that he will reappear at some point and ruin everything – try to rip apart all we have worked hard to keep intact. The whole thing with him was one big ghastly mistake; a blip in my otherwise stable and happy existence. Looking back, I can't quite believe any of it really happened. I couldn't have predicted it. I was trying to be kind and it backfired spectacularly. A finger of ice travels through my insides at the thought of him. I just want to put it all behind me and get on with the rest of my life.

Jeff was furious when I turned down his advances. He had been a friend at work, somebody I chatted to about the everyday banal issues I had had to deal with when Hugh was working away in Scotland: blocked toilets, how to bleed radiators and all other manner of mundane household problems I was left to tackle on my own. I knew Jeff was quite the handyman and often went to him for advice. He still lived with his mother and I honestly didn't see him as any sort of threat. He was a friend, somebody I could go to for help.

Or so I thought.

But then things began to change. He misread the signals, became over familiar and pushy, asking to come around to the house in the evening, sending me endless texts. There was no escape from him. He was a work colleague, seated only a few desks away from me, and everywhere I went, he was there. Eventually, just to keep him sweet and hoping it would stop his continual pestering, I relented and asked him round for supper one evening. Hugh was still working away but the children were there and I had told Hugh all about it. Although he wasn't delighted, he understood my predicament. He had met Jeff a few times at work parties and found him to be a fairly harmless and amenable chap. Affable; that was the word we had both used to describe him. Hugh may have felt differently about it all had Jeff looked like George Clooney, but we both saw Jeff as a lonely, harmless individual, albeit rather needy and desperate. I felt as if I was helping him, being friendly towards a man who was obviously quite fragile and lived a solitary existence.

How wrong we were.

That very same evening after a few drinks, he followed me upstairs and tried to drag me into the bedroom, his hands grabbing at me, his face contorted and twisted with lust and anger. He lunged at me, his hands clamped onto my chest as he tried to kiss me. I managed to drag his hands away from my breasts and pushed his face and drooling wet lips away from me, but he kept on coming, trying to shove me onto the bed, his large hot fingers pawing at me. At one point he somehow managed to get his hand under my skirt and was trying to pull my knickers down. I became frantic. Nipping and scratching at him, I hissed in his ear that I would call the police if he didn't leave. It took a few seconds for my words to sink in, but he suddenly seemed to sober up, a look of surprise on his face as I gave him one final push. He barrelled back and stood up, moving away from me, his skin ashen with shock and dismay. And all the while I was aware of Aiden standing outside the room listening and crying, his gentle sobbing echoing in my ears.

I swore at Jeff, shouted that he was a lunatic and told him in no uncertain terms that he needed to leave. Which he did. But like Todd, he kept coming back.

'Right,' Hugh says, his voice a bark as it filters through my thoughts. 'I'll let you put the sheets on the mattresses and I'll get on with unpacking the rest of the stuff downstairs.'

***

We spend the evening sitting in the kitchen, talking about our plans for the house: which rooms we will decorate first and which room we will have as our shared office. I would prefer to work in separate areas but Hugh seems to think the big old loft conversion will be large enough to house two desks with ample space to spare. He's right of course, but while I prefer a quiet working environment, Hugh likes noise and background music, so we'll give it some time and see how that plan works out. There are plenty of other rooms for me to move into if it becomes too much and I find that I need more solace and silence. Hugh wanted to keep the printers and telephone lines in one central place, so I can see his point of view, but I need that sense of calm around me when I'm getting my ideas down on paper.

After the debacle with Jeff, I opted to go self-employed as a writer. As soon as the first round of redundancies at the local newspaper where I worked was mentioned, I put myself forward and was delighted when I was given a generous payoff. No more commuting into Newcastle city centre every day and more importantly, no more Jeff.

Hugh was also tired of his job; he was sick of having to make the long drive to Scotland in the middle of the night to avoid the early morning rush hour traffic in Aberdeen, and even more sick of being away from home for weeks at a time, never seeing his family. The whole thing was making us both miserable, so after a great deal of soul-searching and repeatedly checking our financial calculations to see if we could afford it, he set up his own business as an engineering consultant and so far, it has all worked out really well.

I say a small non-denominational thank you for our financially stable status to any higher deity that may be listening, and go about making the beds. It was a huge gamble that we took with our careers, but with a lot of dedication and hard work, it seems to be working out for us and for that I am eternally grateful. Having Hugh around more often has helped still my nerves. Not completely. I'd love to say his presence has an ever-calming effect, but it doesn't. I will always fear unexplained shadows that linger behind me, or the sudden appearance of a stranger at the door, but I have to get over it, move on. I refuse to let my worries and dark thoughts spoil the rest of our lives.

I leave Aiden and Poppy to their own devices for the rest of the evening and listen to their pounding footsteps and shrieks of excitement as they explore every corner of their new home. It's lovely to hear Aiden be so animated and childlike again. I don't want to destroy it so I ignore the fact that they are making an almighty racket and very possibly tearing apart what little decent decor the house has left, and just smile because they are happy and safe. That's all I want for them. Funny, isn't it, that when children are born, we parents spend an inordinate amount of time and care deciding which school they should go to so they can achieve the best results and get a fine job and make something of their lives, when in reality, all we want is for them to be happy. It's the simple things in life that make it worth living: listening to birds singing, the smell of freshly cut grass, knowing your family are now safely away from the clutches of insane people who refuse to listen to reason…

As hard as I try to block Todd and Jeff out of my mind, they remain there, obstinately fresh in my thoughts. Frightening events do that to a person – make them forever vulnerable, guessing at possible future incidents, forcing them to tiptoe their way around each and every day. And I'm tired of it. I want them both out of my head. I chastise myself for actually wishing them both dead. I'm not a bad person, but I want my life back to how it was before they came along and ruined it, and knowing neither of them can ever find me again is the only way that can happen. I've dreamt of bashing their brains in on more than one occasion – not to seek revenge but get them out of our lives so we can be happy; be the family we once were. The people who laughed easily and feared nothing.

I blink back tears at the thought of them. No more. I have to be stronger than they are. I have to move on with my life. Still, visualising both men cold and still on a mortuary slab is the only control I have over them and it's pretty empowering I can tell you.

One day, this will all be a dim and distant memory, but for now I have to learn how to overcome it. It's not easy. In fact, it's very fucking hard – the hardest thing I've ever done – but for the sake of my family I have to do it. I bury the thoughts in my head, tuck them away, look around my decrepit new home and carry on unpacking.

Five

It's only later when we're in bed that I finally mention my worries to Hugh. I expect him to brush them aside and tell me I'm being ridiculous, but instead he listens to me as I tell him about my concerns that Todd and Jeff will somehow find us and our nightmare will just go on and on.

'Why do you think that, then? They can't find us; you know they can't. And if they do, then we call the police and end it once and for all,' he says softly, his face full of sympathy and kindness.

'I know,' I reply, the solid lump in my throat making it difficult to speak. 'I mean, they probably could locate us if they really wanted to. I don't think Jeff will go to all that effort, but Todd probably would...'

I gulp hard and swallow down my doubts, then look away to hide my tears. This is exhaustion and stress speaking, but if I don't get it off my chest, it will eat away at me and distract me from what should be an exciting time in our lives. I also feel guilty for mentioning Todd to Hugh. His presence in our lives isn't Hugh's fault – I know that – but he still frightens me. All I want is some reassurance that he won't come here and start bothering us again. I just want to feel safe.

'Look,' Hugh says, running his fingers through his hair wearily. 'I'm really sorry about Todd. He's a bad lad for sure and I'm really sorry that –'

I put my finger on his lips to silence him and plant a kiss on the side of his mouth, my skin burning with regret for making him think he has to say sorry yet again. Todd isn't Hugh's fault and yet he has spent the last year apologising for him. I don't want him to feel any guiltier about the whole thing than he already does. Sometimes

I forget that this entire sorry business has been just as hard on Hugh as it has on me. It wasn't Hugh's fault that a childhood girlfriend he had when he was just seventeen got pregnant and neglected to tell him. A twenty-year-old Todd is the net result of that relationship, the product of a young romance from many moons ago. He turned up on our doorstep last year, wanting to meet Hugh, the father he had never known. I almost passed out on the spot when he arrived and gave us his news, detailing where he had been living, who his mother was and more importantly, who his father was. There was certainly no denying it. He was Hugh's double, with identical swept-back dark hair and a strong jawline. Even their mannerisms were the same – the way they would both tap at the side of their faces when they were deep in thought or how they gave a half smile when relating a funny tale.

Todd's ready laughter didn't take long to stop. After just a few visits his behaviour became erratic and unpredictable, his moods dark and often chilling. He would give monosyllabic grunts to simple questions, his brows knitted together as he sat brooding. He virtually refused to speak to Hugh and me and completely ignored Poppy and Aiden, claiming that they were badly behaved and needed to be disciplined more, even suggesting smacking them to keep them both in line and curb their playfulness and energetic outbursts. That was just the small stuff though; I could have tolerated his black moods and put his comments down to being brought up in a different household by somebody who had opposing values to ours. I even forgave him for what he had said about the kids. When they are in full flow, Poppy and Aiden can be draining and they regularly push me to my very limits, so I fully understand that they can irritate people who aren't used to how loud and spirited they can be. I was more than prepared to put those things behind us and welcome him into our family fold. What I couldn't tolerate or ever forgive him for was what he did next.

It happened when Hugh was away in Aberdeen. Todd turned up one day with his bags in tow claiming he had had an almighty row with his mother and needed somewhere to stay. Needless to say, I took him in. Who wouldn't? He was family now, wasn't he? I wasn't about to let him sleep on the streets.

Over the course of the next few days, he made demands that were breathtakingly rude – banging and stamping his feet on the floor like a petulant toddler when he needed anything, shouting at me that the food was crap and that he was bored and why wasn't there more alcohol in the house. I was furious and told him to leave if he wasn't happy in our little home. At the time I was dealing with Jeff harassing me, and my patience was at an all-time low. What Todd did next will stay with me forever. Without any warning, he stalked over to where I was standing and slapped me hard in the face. I was too stunned to even cry. Aiden and Poppy were upstairs playing, completely oblivious to what was unfolding in the room below them. With shaking hands, I pointed to the door and demanded he get out, saying I would send his things on later. He refused to go. At six feet four inches tall, he cut a hefty figure in our diminutive living room. I made a move to get the phone but he stopped me, grabbing my arm and shaking it violently, his large fingers pressing into my flesh. The look in his eyes at that moment told me all I needed to know – that this young man, Hugh's son, my stepson, was a monster. Something had changed in him; his mask had slipped. All manner of thoughts passed through my mind in those few seconds: that his mother had poisoned his mind against us, or that he was drunk or on drugs or possibly a combination of all of those things.

The next hit almost knocked me off my feet. I fell backwards onto the sofa and looked up to see him leering over me, spittle dripping from his mouth as he spoke in a voice that sent terror racing through my veins. 'I'll leave when I fucking well feel like it, okay? Don't ever threaten me again.'

His pupils were like pinpricks and as black as coal; there was no emotion or empathy within. Dead, dark eyes with a huge void where his soul should be.

That night I rang Hugh from the bedroom, my voice cracking with raw fear, relating everything that had happened. I told the kids they could sleep in my bed as a treat. I wanted them safe with me. I also needed their sense of fun and enthusiasm to get me through what felt like the longest night of my life. They saw it as an adventure, unaware that the man in the room next to them, their half-brother, could walk in at any minute and beat us half to death.

I had taken a sharp knife up to bed with me and slipped it under the mattress. I didn't sleep at all. Every half hour I swept my fingers along the ridge of the bed, making sure I could get my hands on it should I need to. My phone was under my pillow and I had it on silent, ready to call the police if he came anywhere near us.

I needn't have worried. I found him the next morning, sprawled on the sofa, dead to the world after drinking all of Hugh's beer and nigh on a full bottle of whisky. So much for us not having enough drink in the house. The room smelt like an old brewery and I fully expected Todd to develop alcohol poisoning. He didn't. Instead he slept soundly as I set about cleaning up around him, desperate for Hugh to come home. He was due back that evening and his return couldn't come around soon enough.

After I had called Hugh the night before, he texted me continually throughout the day, worried sick about what had gone on in his absence. He was appalled and assured me he would eject Todd from the house as soon as he got back, which was what he tried to do. Todd, however, was like a meek child by the time Hugh spoke to him, full of remorse and apologising unreservedly for his loutish behaviour. He assured us it wouldn't happen again and wept, begging Hugh and me for another chance, telling us he had been homeless once and couldn't face it again. On and on he went, crying and apologising, pleading and imploring with us to let him continue living in our house. Another chance to make things right. That's all he kept asking for. Just one more chance.

And stupidly, we gave him one.

We agreed that he could stay, and with Hugh around for the next few weeks I hoped he would be more pleasant and conduct himself with a little more decorum. Which of course, he did. For a short while anyway. But it didn't last long. Once again, the veil of normality slowly fell away, revealing his charred innermost intentions.

Only a week after hitting me, Todd called Hugh a stupid bastard and took a swing at him with his huge clenched fist, catching him off guard and sending Hugh crashing to the floor where he fell in an undignified heap. Hugh didn't stay down for long. Springing back up, he grabbed Todd's arm and yanked it up his back, rendering him incapable of doing anything except howling out in pain.

All of that violence, all that unnecessary pain and worry, took place because Hugh had wanted to change the TV channel to watch a documentary on the other side. We knew then that Todd had to go. Violence was obviously in his blood and nothing we did or said would change that. He was too capricious and impulsive for us to deal with. We had to think of our young children, of their safety and well-being, and so that day, Todd was thrown out onto the street with all his belongings and told to never come back. It broke Hugh's heart; I know that he had faint hopes of building a relationship with his newly found son, but it was never going to happen. Not under those conditions.

We thought that that was the last of it. Little did we know it was just the beginning. Todd ran what can only be described as a campaign of terror against us, calling at all hours, banging on the door, screaming through the letterbox that he was going to kill us all, that he would steal Poppy and Aiden from school or burn the house down. We should have called the police but every time it happened we hoped it would be the last and didn't want to have the kids involved in interviews or come home from school to be faced with a row of police officers sitting in their living room. So we did what we could to keep Todd at bay, giving him money to pay for a bedsit, begging him to leave us be, but nothing worked. All this as well as Jeff ringing at all hours, rambling on about how we should be together and how I needed to leave Hugh and go and live with him. Sometimes he would even wait outside, hidden around the corner, crouched like a wild animal, shouting and crying at me that I had led him on and now he couldn't live without me.

Eventually, the tense situation we were living in took its toll on me and I had a breakdown of sorts. I lost a lot of weight and had trouble sleeping, convinced that both men were outside whenever I left the house, ready to attack, waiting nearby ready to kill us all. So when Hugh mentioned moving house, I jumped at the chance. We had talked about it on and off over the years but we had never plucked up enough courage to make that leap. Who would have thought that two psychotic characters would be the catalyst for us to pack up and go?

I smile and stare into Hugh's soft, brown eyes. 'You have nothing to be sorry for. And you're right. They don't know where we are. It's just me being overanxious and fretting unnecessarily. Once we start on the building work in here, I won't have time to think about it.'

I hope this is true because I cannot go back to how things were – constantly looking over my shoulder, being on edge, wondering if the children are safe at school or where they are when they're playing out. Living under that kind of stress day in and day out felt like a physical assault on my body. The strain was intolerable. If either of them ever tracked us down and I had to suffer it again, I feel sure I would need yet more medical intervention to help me through.

'And don't forget, I'll be around a lot more. There'll be days when I have to travel to see customers but as you know, a lot of what I do now is using video conferencing and Skype.'

This does make me feel a lot better. Just knowing that Hugh is around gives me a sense of security and makes me feel safer, as well as the knowledge that neither man knows where we live.

Resting my head back on the pillow, I stare up at the myriad cracks in the ceiling, hoping Hugh is right and that after what feels like an age, all the aggravation and fear is finally over.

I close my eyes and sleep swiftly embraces me, taking me off to a world of darkness and weightlessness; a place where dreams are intangible and ethereal. No Todd or Jeff this time, just comfort and rest in the safety of my own bed.

Six

Despite me still feeling ever so slightly ill at ease, the next few days pass by in an uneventful blur. I make sure one of the first jobs we do is to put a secure bolt on the gate in the back garden. At least that way the kids can play out and nobody can get in. With the weather starting to warm up and summer just around the corner, the first thing they want to do when they get in from school is play outside. Much like the house, the garden is also huge, rambling and in dire need of some work, but it doesn't bother Aiden or Poppy who love it out there, hiding amongst the huge, leafy conifers or playing in the ancient, ramshackle summerhouse that contains all manner of useless items from decades ago. Poppy has taken a liking to an old telephone which we think is probably from the 1950s. It's a heavy, black Bakelite model and she plays with it, pretending to be Hugh's secretary, screaming at imaginary customers that he's busy working and they will have to call back later, while Aiden tears around the lawn shooting invisible intruders and practising his commando rolls across the lawn. Hopefully, once we dig out the other outhouses from under the brambles and undergrowth, it will provide them with another place to play, but for now they're more than happy to potter around the dilapidated summerhouse that resembles a cricket pavilion, with its sage green wooden cladding and retro cream coloured windows.

Slowly but surely, I feel the knots in my muscles begin to loosen. It feels strange, being able to relax. I watch the children run about in the sunshine and gaze at the nuthatches and blue tits that tentatively peck at the feeder. A welcome ribbon of heat sits on my back as the sun stretches over the kitchen, dappling the surfaces with spots of deep ochre and wrapping me in its warmth. For the first time in a long while, life seems good. I actually feel free of worry and anxiety, and the weight that has been pressing down on me slowly lifts.

Reluctantly, I turn away from the window and head into the dining room where arrays of overfilled boxes sit, ready to be unpacked. I look around and take a deep, appreciative breath. I really like this room. I love the way the light falls across the dusty floorboards and can't help but admire the sheer magnificence and height of the built-in cupboards that reach the ceiling. This room may be outdated and in need of a few coats of paint but I still feel some sort of connection with it and can see myself spending a lot of time in here. Out of all the spaces in Cross House, it probably needs the least doing to it. We can buff up the floorboards, repaint the cupboards with an eggshell paint, put a fresher, lighter colour on the walls and it just may start to resemble something half decent.

I smile and congratulate myself on not feeling scared and miserable. It feels good and I long for more times like this. Even Hugh visiting a customer two hours away and not being in the house doesn't faze me. On a whim, I spin around with my arms outstretched, only stopping when I'm overcome with dizziness. It is so damn good to be normal again, to not be constantly looking over my shoulder or afraid to answer the phone in case some fucking idiot is on the other end threatening to kill me or trash our home or kidnap the kids on their way home from school.

I let out a long breath from somewhere deep in my abdomen and drop into a nearby chair. This is how life should be. This is how I want life to be from here on in, and there's now no reason why it should be anything but blissful. I stare out at the overgrown garden and laugh. I anticipate and am more than prepared for the problems and arguments that will no doubt ensue once we start ripping this place apart, but those I can handle; threats against me and my family I cannot.

I decide against putting any books in the cupboards and instead pile them all in the space under the stairs. There is so much storage in this house that I am spoilt for choice when it comes squirreling things away that don't yet have a place to live.

It's when I'm searching for paint online that I sense it – the feeling that there is somebody else around. I spin around, thinking Hugh has returned, then walk towards the window and stand looking outside to the sweeping driveway only to see that his car isn't there. I chastise myself for being stupid and having an overactive imagination. Nobody knows where we are. Nobody we don't want to know, that is. It was just a shift in the light filtering in from outside, I'm sure of it, but now my heart is pounding and I feel dizzy and sick. *Here we go again!*

Blood rushes through my head and pounds in my ears. I close my eyes tightly, clench my fists and grit my teeth. Christ almighty. Is this how it's going to be from now on? Am I going to spend the rest of my days looking over my shoulder, thinking somebody is behind me ready to do me harm? I don't think I have ever hated anybody in my life but by God, I hate Jeff and Todd for what they have done to me and my family. This isn't me. I used to be a confident person, happy and carefree, and now look at me. They have both turned me into a nervous wreck and for that, I can never forgive them.

I pace around the room, listening to Aiden playing on his games above me and to Poppy singing at the top of her voice. The door is locked. We are all safe, and Hugh will be back at any time. I have no need to worry. I stare up at the old clock on the wall left by the previous owners, or possibly the ones before them judging by its age, and decide it's perfectly acceptable to pour myself a glass of wine. It's not quite six o'clock but it's after five which sits well with me.

By the time Hugh gets home just before 7pm, I have drunk over half a bottle of Malbec and am unwinding nicely. Poppy is curled on the sofa with me and Aiden is slumped in an old wicker chair eating a tuna sandwich.

'Well, look at you lot,' Hugh says happily as he flings his briefcase on the far end of the sofa and flops down with us, his arms outstretched on the back of the oversized cushions.

'Look at us,' I say with a slight slur to my speech. I smile and wink at Hugh, who looks startled at my peaceful and laid-back demeanour. His face breaks into a wide grin as he gets up and plants a warm, wet kiss on my forehead.

'There's some casserole in the oven, ready to be warmed up,' I say as he moves away and pulls his jacket off. I listen to him clunk around in the kitchen and hear the ping of the microwave as he reheats his meal. Apart from my little mini meltdown earlier, I feel really happy. This is how life should be – all my family together, everyone safe and content.

I take another swig of my wine and savour the taste and essence of it as it melts on my tongue and slowly trickles down my throat.

'Mummy's drunk!' Poppy shouts as I spill red wine on my lap and stagger slightly when I jump up to wipe myself down.

'Really? Well, we'll have to get Mummy drunk more often, won't we?' Hugh says with an enigmatic smile as he sits down next to me. He balances a tray on his knee and leans over to kiss me again.

My cheeks flush hot and I watch as Aiden grimaces. His face twists in disgust and he pretends to stick his fingers down his throat and gag loudly. I let out an embarrassed, awkward laugh and Poppy shrieks with excitement at his comic display.

We spend a pleasurable evening snacking, drinking and generally unwinding nicely. By the time we go to bed I have finished all of my wine and helped Hugh polish off a bottle of Merlot. The stairs practically move under my feet as I crawl up them to get to our bedroom.

I can barely undress myself and giggle uncontrollably while Hugh tries to help me drag my top off. My arms are a tight tangle, wrapped around each other as the sweater gets stuck. I stand there for a few seconds, squirming and wriggling until eventually it springs free, forcing me backwards onto the bed where I land in a slovenly heap. Hugh hoists me onto the mattress properly, swinging me around onto my side then lifting my feet up and placing them under the covers. He tucks me in tightly as if I'm a small child before climbing in himself and wrapping his cold legs around mine. I yawn, let out another barking laugh and immediately sink into an alcohol-induced sleep.

***

The first thing I notice when I wake up is the darkness. It is absolute. After all the wine, my head feels heavy and my throat is as dry as sand. The next thing I notice is the sound of rustling coming from the corner of the room. My pulse speeds up and the bed seems to sway under me. The sound of my own breathing roars in my ears as I pull the covers tight around my face. I close my eyes, my body tense and locked in place. Sheer terror envelops me. The only sense I have is my hearing and it is frighteningly acute. I listen again as the rustling continues. It seems to move about the room and in my state of alarm, I can no longer tell if it's coming from inside or outside. Myriad images balloon in my mind: a manic, dejected Jeff slumped in the corner, slashing at his own skin unless I consent to run away with him. A furious, psychotic Todd threatening to burn the house down or slit our throats, his cold, dead eyes telling me he is beyond any sort of reasoning with.

My breath pumps out in short, staccato bursts and I struggle to think clearly. Fire licks at my brain, blocking out all lucid and rational thought. I try to still my heavy hot breathing and listen again but there is now only silence. The noise I heard seems to have stopped. I lie there for a few seconds, trying to clear my head and think practically. I'm half asleep and slightly hungover. I try to convince myself it was a dream. A horrible buzzing sensation builds up behind my eyes. My skin prickles and burns as heat gathers under the covers. I may be groggy with sleep but I didn't imagine it and I also know I didn't dream it. There was definitely a sound here in this room.

I lie for what feels like hours, unable to rest properly, my body scorched with fear and dread. I dip in and out of sleep until eventually I drop off and slumber soundly until the sun rising through the bare windows wakes me, its watery warmth pooling over the duvet in great waves.

As soon as I hear that Hugh is awake, I sit up in bed and tell him my story, my words coming out in unconnected, barely decipherable chunks. I am horrified to feel the room spin as I start to recount what happened.

He watches me cautiously through narrowed eyes and places his hand on my arm. 'You look really pale, Faye. Are you sure this wasn't just a dream?'

I want to yell at him that it was definitely real, but now, in the cold light of day and on hearing his sober tones, I am suddenly not so sure. Doubt clouds my judgement and a solid pulse hammers at my temples.

'I mean, for somebody who doesn't drink very often, you knocked back a fair few glasses of wine last night, you know.' His voice is steady and reassuring. Not condescending, not full of disdain at my blurry-eyed account, just Hugh doing his best to remain level-headed and calm despite waking up to a half-hysterical wife who looks as if she's been dragged through a hedge backwards.

Hugh always has a knack for being able to cut to the chase without being cruel or callous and now, hearing his words, I am having second thoughts – misgivings about something only hours ago I felt so sure about. I would love to say the sound I heard last night was nothing to do with the drink or my fragile state of mind but with the passing of time, I am beginning to wonder if I did actually imagine the whole episode. It seemed real at the time. I definitely heard something. Or did I? Was it my disjointed, drunken, overactive mind hearing something ordinary and putting a suspicious slant on it after all we've been through?

I rub at my eyes, trying to conjure a clear memory of last night, but all that comes back to me is the raw fear and the certainty I felt that somebody was in the room with us. It had to be a dream or the drink or a combination of the two. There's no other explanation for it, is there?

***

As the day passes and the fog in my head slowly clears, I become less and less sure of what it was I heard, or indeed whether I actually heard anything at all. A headache sits behind my eyes for most of the day and only begins to lift when the kids finally get packed off to bed later that evening.

I tuck Poppy in, giving her so many cuddles I end up hot and dishevelled. I actually manage to snatch a forehead kiss from Aiden once he's in bed and beginning to get drowsy. As soon as they're settled I run myself a hot bath and soak in it until the water begins to cool. Hugh wanders about the house going from room to room, sizing everything up and taking measurements. I am too exhausted to even think about joining him. There's nothing that can't wait until tomorrow.

I dry myself off, grab a glass of water and stagger up to bed, weariness swamping me. I flop down on the mattress and sleep deeply, dreaming of nothing at all, and by the time I wake the next morning, I have convinced myself that the noise in the bedroom was all in my mind, a rogue fear brought on by alcohol and exhaustion and new surroundings. I was drunk and disorientated; that's all it was. I make a mental note to stick to just two glasses of wine in the future, then get up feeling happier and refreshed, and ready to tackle whatever the day may bring.

Seven

With Aiden and Poppy safely deposited at school, I go about emptying the junk and clutter the previous owners left behind in some of the old wardrobes. The kids were delighted when I informed them that they could continue going to their old schools. They're only a twenty-minute drive away and far less hassle than getting them settled in new ones. A twenty-minute drive is still more appealing than the two-hour commute I used to do into Newcastle every day. Working from home has more than its fair share of benefits.

I should be up there in our shared study right now, working on the next chapter of my novel, but I feel like having a break from it. Getting this house up to scratch is our priority so I don't feel too guilty for taking time away from my computer. Hugh is up there, beavering away, his mind totally focused on a major project he has on the go at the moment. I smile and think about how he thrives on those tight deadlines whereas I hate them. They're a reminder of my days at the newspaper and something I don't miss at all. It's probably better that I stay down here and leave him be.

I lean into the huge oak wardrobe that sits in the corner of one of the spare bedrooms and grab a handful of papers and small books that are tucked away at the back in a neat, tight bundle. I noticed them when I decided to store some of our own things, and was intrigued by what they might contain. Dust motes swirl lazily in front of my face and the musty smell of old paper makes me gag slightly as I lift them out into the daylight.

Sitting cross-legged on the floor, I place the books and papers on my knee and leaf through them. They're mainly old newspapers and some small journals, which immediately piques my interest. I place the newspapers to one side and carefully open one of the leather-bound books. The pages are soft with age and ever so slightly worn. The writing is unbelievably neat, like calligraphy, the prose far more detailed and formal than you would usually find in a diary entry. I spread my fingers over the paper and wipe away a thin layer of dust, staring at the words before I begin to read.

4 July 1978

Whatever next? Tammy came to me last night in floods of tears. She was shaking and sobbing and could barely hold herself upright. I sat her down on the sofa and asked what was going on. It took some time to get it out of her but through all the gasping and crying she told me how it had happened again. I went dizzy as she spoke. The last time I hoped she had imagined it but for it to take place again, I just don't think I can...

I hold the journal up to the light but the page is too damaged to make out what the following words are. It looks like splashes of water on the paper and the ink has smudged, making it impossible to read what comes next. My heart starts up an irregular, uncomfortable beat that makes me want to draw a deep breath. I swallow hard and put my hand on my chest to stem the sensation that is making me feel dizzy. This feels like an intrusion on somebody's privacy. I shouldn't be reading any of it. And yet there is something about it that I feel drawn to. I have no idea why. It's not as if I know these people. They're complete strangers to me.

I feel a tension of opposites stir within me as I stand up and gaze out of the window at the village below. Why did they leave it here? Why would anybody leave anything as personal as a diary behind? And why do I feel compelled to read it, knowing it is somebody baring their soul, somebody putting pen to paper when they were very possibly at their lowest ebb?

Outside, a lady pushes a buggy over the road; in the distance a dog runs freely on the village green, its owner following far behind. People stop to chat to one another, their faces tilted to one side as they listen intently to what the other person is saying. I wonder if any of them are familiar with the people who used to live here or maybe even know the person who wrote this diary entry. Brackston seems like a close-knit village; it's so sparsely populated it would have to be. I'll bet it's the kind of place where everybody knows one another's business, which is always a double-edged sword. Perhaps once we're settled I can ask around, see what they remember, see if I can put a name to these words. Not that it matters. They're probably long since gone. I just feel a sudden need to find out more about the people who lived here. If only walls could speak. If only they could release the memories and possible heartache that once took place in this house and give me some insight into what these words mean.

I decide against reading any further. It isn't right to delve into other people's diaries detailing their innermost thoughts and anxieties, and I for one would be horrified if I thought anybody was rooting through my personal papers.

I drum my fingers lightly on my thigh and continue to watch the world go by outside, noticing the slight fluttering of the leaves as a soft breeze ripples through the trees, sending the birds soaring. My eyes are drawn to the tiny creatures as they take flight, swooping through the vast sky searching for insects, their wings spread wide like huge black talons.

Turning away from the window, I stare again at the diary, its contents tempting me. It's true that it is somebody else's private thoughts, but then, if I cared about something that deeply, I would take it with me wherever I went. I certainly wouldn't move home and leave it for the new owners to find. I gaze at the cover and chew at my lip. Technically speaking, this diary now belongs to me. This is my house so anything in it is now also mine.

Sitting back down, I flick through for an undamaged page and start to read again, pushing away the feelings of guilt that niggle at me. Is it any wonder I didn't enjoy working as a journalist? I should be lapping this up, using it as material for my next novel. So why do I feel like an intruder, delving into the life of a stranger, reading things that should remain unread? The guilt doesn't stop me. Instead, my innate curiosity gets the better of me and I feel compelled to read on, the intrigue too great to ignore.

9 July 1978

I can't live like this. The atmosphere in the house is dreadful and I hate it. I just want it back to how it was. Adrian says he hasn't noticed but then he would say that wouldn't he? They sit together, the pair of them, laughing, doing stupid card tricks and playing board games while Tammy and I are ignored completely. Who the hell does he think he is, this boy? He comes into our house and takes over, acting as if he's lived here all his life. This is my house and Tammy's house too. It's not his and never will be. I'll make sure of it. I don't care what Adrian says, Tammy is my priority and I'll do whatever it takes to protect her from that boy.

Taking a deep breath, I press my lips together. This is pretty secret stuff. Whoever wrote this was obviously furious at the time. Hatred drips out of it and I begin to feel pity for this poor young lad, whoever he is. I wonder who these people were and why the person who wrote in this diary loathed him so much. Then I think of Todd and the trouble he caused us and suppress a wave of dread that travels through me. Perhaps I should feel some sympathy for the person who wrote this. After all, I have no idea what the boy did. I know from bitter experience that people can appear to be one thing and yet be something entirely different once the surface is scratched and the real them appears from underneath their carefully constructed façade.

I flick through the rest of the diary but it's almost empty. Just a few sentences about a local choir and some dates for the next book club meeting. Disappointed, I place the journal to one side and slowly leaf thought the stack of local newspapers, the dry yet pliable surface of the paper making me recoil ever so slightly. The date at the top is from the summer of 1980. I scan through the various dated adverts and stories, one of the news articles in particular catching my eye and making my heart flip about my chest. My breath catches in my throat as I read and re-read the headline and then stare at the words underneath it. I feel quite sick and there is an imperceptible movement under my feet as a wave of dizziness washes over me. Heat rushes to my face as I say the headline out loud, my voice echoing around the stillness of the room: 'Woman Falls to Her Death in Family Tragedy.'

Hilary Wentworth, wife of the late wealthy businessman, Adrian Wentworth, was found unconscious at the foot of the stairs in her home yesterday morning by her eighteen-year-old daughter. Emergency services were called to the scene at Cross House in Brackston, North Yorkshire where they tried to revive her. Despite the efforts of the rescue team, Mrs Wentworth was declared dead at the scene.

I can hardly breathe. The room continues to move, the floor sloping wildly as I drop the papers and quickly get to my feet. They scatter around me and for a brief moment I think I might be sick. I reach down and gather them up, setting them on the bed in an untidy pile; the words in the newspaper article scream out at me. Somebody died in my house.

Bustling out of the room, I head out onto the landing and stand at the top of the stairs, gawping down at the spot where she will have lain, this Hilary Wentworth lady, the woman who died right here in my new home. I keep my eyes fixed on the space next to the bottom step, revulsion swelling in my stomach. Just the thought of it makes me want to weep.

Shadows flit about me and dark blotches bounce around behind my eyes, making me woozy. I am still standing there, holding my pounding head in my hands, when Hugh comes up behind me and places his arms around my waist.

'Gotcha!' he shouts, his voice ricocheting off the walls. A wave of annoyance courses through me at his unexpected presence.

I reel around, my skin burning. 'Did you know about this?' I bark at him, his jovial expression dissipating as I storm off into the bedroom, grasp the paper and bring it out to show him. I brandish it in front of his face, my hands shaking as I practically roar at him. 'I suppose you knew all about it, didn't you? I'll bet that estate agent lady told you all about it while you were wandering around the basement together. You probably asked to her not to tell me anything about it given my delicate state of mind...'

I hook my fingers in the air to emphasise the last few words and snatch the paper back. I am breathless with rage and panting by the time I finish. Already, I can see that Hugh is completely baffled by my words. He is the world's worst liar and I would know straightaway if he was hiding anything from me. He knows nothing about this past tragedy, about what went on in our new home. That much is obvious. It doesn't stop me, however. I'm in full flow now, blood pumping through my veins, hot and viscous.

I shouldn't be annoyed but I am. And I know exactly why I'm so angry and upset. The whole sorry episode may have happened almost forty years ago, so long ago it should hardly matter and yet I feel duped, as if I have bought a house in good faith thinking it will be our fresh start and now here I am raking up somebody else's history and seedy family secrets when I can barely cope with my own.

'Faye, I have absolutely no clue what you're going on about,' he says in such a calm and comforting voice that I am immediately flooded with guilt for shouting at him. It isn't his fault and I can't fully explain to him why I am so distressed about this revelation without bringing up our other troubles, which I don't want to do. We need to put those times behind us, not carry them about with us like some hulking immovable object that is forever anchoring us to the past.

I know that I'm completely overreacting but can't seem to stop it.

I am still jumping at shadows that don't necessarily exist and it's a hard habit to break.

'I'm sorry,' I manage to say before I drop down on the top step, an embarrassed flush creeping up my neck. 'I found this in the back of one of the wardrobes.' My throat is tight and my eyes are grit-laden.

I hand the newspaper over to him and watch as his eyes quickly scan the article. He puffs out his cheeks and then his face breaks into a wide smile, the corner of his eyes creasing into tiny, fine lines.

'Well,' he says quietly as he reads it again, 'who'd have thought it, eh? Fancy us moving into a place with a bit of history. Mind you, a house this old is bound to have a few people who died here. This is probably just one of many tragedies. And this one is perfect for one of your books, isn't it? Most writers would give anything for a story like this to have taken place right here where they live.'

He's right. Of course he is. I already thought of that when I read the diaries, but this newspaper article is something more. It's a step up from somebody's private ramblings. Discovering this makes me feel as if I've stumbled upon a crime scene. I shudder. Such a stupid supposition. I know nothing about this person. She was probably an old lady and lost her footing but because of the diary and its contents I've gone and blown it all out of proportion. I also know that Hugh is saying these things and making light of it to allay my fears and stop me going into a meltdown.

He gently rubs my back and helps me up onto my feet. 'I don't think there's any need to get upset or worry about something that happened all those years ago. I'm sure there's been loads of families living here since. Besides which, this place has a lovely homely feel to it, doesn't it?'

I don't answer him. After my fright the other evening when I felt certain there was somebody in the corner of the room with us, I am reticent to reply. What I saw in Cross House on our initial visit was a project – something to throw myself into and help me forget what has gone before and what we had been through. I didn't see it as somewhere particularly warm or welcoming. I have plans to turn it into our dream home, somewhere that exudes happiness and warmth, but it doesn't have it just yet. As it is, Cross House is a large, somewhat intimidating property and each of the unfurnished, dated rooms feels cold and uninviting. At the minute this house has all the appeal and attraction of a mausoleum. I'm hoping once we start on our decorating plans, I will begin to feel more settled, more at home. But I don't feel it just yet. As I told myself a few days ago, I just need a few weeks to settle in.

Hugh insists I put everything back in the wardrobe and look at it another day when I have had time to let it sink in, then we go downstairs together and he makes us a light lunch of tuna salad. We eat it in the garden as we sit listening to the chirrup of birdsong from the treetops close by. I feel like a small child being guarded by an ever-watchful parent. Hugh keeps stealing sly glances at me, checking to make sure I'm okay. I pretend I can't see him and stare straight ahead, chewing on my lettuce like a sullen adolescent.

I look around at the huge stretch of garden and a grand house I would never have thought it possible for us to ever own and try to see the positives. I'm a very fortunate lady. Very fortunate indeed. So why do I feel so on edge?

***

Poppy spills out of the school gates, grinning and brimming with excitement at something. I smile, her upbeat mood infectious as she clambers into the car and tells me she has been chosen to take a starring role in the end of year school play. She continues to chatter, giggling incessantly as we head just a few yards down the road to collect Aiden. He's waiting on the next corner and rolls his eyes as he spots his sister's display of exuberance through the window. He slides in the back seat next to her and scowls as he buckles himself in. It isn't that long ago he showed the same display of raw emotion when he came bustling out of school, but he is now far too cool for such things.

I watch through the rear-view mirror as he shakes his head at her then turns to me, a quizzical expression on his face. 'Are you and Dad millionaires?'

'What?' I splutter as I grip the steering wheel and suppress a sardonic laugh. 'Millionaires? Don't be silly! Of course we're not! Why on earth would you ask that?'

He shrugs listlessly and juts out his bottom lip. 'That's what everyone is saying at school. Bailey Alderson lives in the next village to us and he said our house is the biggest one around for miles and that only millionaires can afford a house like ours.'

I smile and shake my head at him, hoping he hasn't taken a ribbing today. Despite his cool exterior, Aiden is still susceptible to barbed comments, dwelling on them, letting them bubble and fester until it eventually becomes too much to contain and all of his worries and anxieties explode out of him in a sudden burst of anger, closely followed by secret tears that he refuses to show.

'Sweetheart, we are definitely not millionaires. Not that it's anybody's business, but we bought Cross House at a reduced price because of the state it's in. It's been left to rot over the years. Nobody has taken an interest in it. I couldn't tell you the last time any of the rooms were decorated.'

'Like the yellow doors and lime green swirly wallpaper in my room?' Aiden says, his voice lifting a notch.

'Yes! Exactly that,' I reply, nodding my head, our eyes meeting in the mirror as I quickly glance his way. 'When somewhere gets old and really rundown, it isn't worth as much and it puts a lot of buyers off. Often people are too busy working to put the time and effort into doing it up, so the seller reduces the price.'

'But you and Dad are going to do it up, aren't you?' he says, and I laugh at his comment, a thinly disguised attempt at making sure we rip off the ghastly wallpaper in his room.

'Yes, sweetheart, we are going to redecorate it. It might take a bit of time but we definitely have plans to turn it into something pretty spectacular.'

I take a deep breath, wishing I could envisage it all in my head. At the moment I can't see beyond the blackness.

'So will Todd be coming back to live with us once it's all done?' His question catches me off guard. So far both Poppy and Aiden have been less than forthcoming with questions about their older brother. It's as if they know there was a problem and have both decided it's best to stay out of it. We told them Todd had moved back in with his mum and that we may see him again at some point. Whether or not that will actually happen is anybody's guess. I do know that he will not step over my doorstep until he is a reformed character, and even then, I don't think I'll ever feel comfortable in his presence.

I try to keep my voice even as I reply to him. 'Perhaps one day, but not at the moment. He's a grown-up and has his own life and friends.'

The one thing Todd didn't have was a life worth speaking of. He was unemployed, refusing our requests to apply for positions he was qualified for. At some point he had knuckled down at school and passed all his GCSEs and A Levels. Whether or not he had any friends, we will never know. He didn't speak of any, but then he only lived with us for a short while. We wanted to help him, we really did, but it was as if he had his own self-destruct button and his finger was permanently poised over it, ready to hit it repeatedly without thought or reason to the hurt he caused or the consequences of his actions.

'Todd was naughty,' Poppy says softly. 'I heard him shouting at Daddy one day. He called him a rude word and then drank all of his beer.'

I let out a long breath and find myself silently hating Todd all over again. We hoped we had hidden most of his antics from the kids, but with the best intentions in the world, it was impossible to shield them from everything. I refuse to let him get to me any longer and turn up the music on the radio to blot it out. Todd is gone. I hope he isn't sleeping on the streets – I wouldn't wish that on anyone – but I cannot have him back under our roof after what he did. I can tolerate teenage outbursts, even from a twenty-year-old who clearly has delayed emotional development. I even accepted the constant eating, and drinking all the alcohol without asking, but the one thing I could not put up with was the violence. He was impulsive and unstable, the aggression sometimes occurring without any reason, like the time I asked him if he wanted to go to the park with us and he responded by throwing an ornament on the kitchen floor, saying I had insulted his intelligence and that he would sooner pull his own fingernails out than wander round a kids' playground looking like a right fucking dickhead.

We didn't go to the park in the end. Hugh picked the kids up from school and brought them home, where we ate in near silence, and I spent the remainder of the evening picking splinters of glass out of my fingers after clearing the kitchen floor.

There was nothing we could do to help Todd. Out attempts were rebuffed and he chose his own path in life. I tried contacting his mother after we told him to leave and was met with silence and a loud grunt before she slammed the phone down on me. We did what we could for that young man. We did what we could.

Eight

I awake in a startled state. Did I dream it this time? I'm almost certain I didn't but in the darkness of the early hours, and still groggy from sleep, I can't be sure. Breathing. I'm almost certain I just heard somebody breathing next to me, as if they were leaning over me and studying my face close up.

I let out a silent gasp, my body rigid with fear. There it is again; hot breath circling in front of my face. I can definitely smell the faint sour odour of rancid breath wafting towards me. My head feels fit to burst and my entire body pulsates with unabated fear. I want to scream, to turn the light on and wake Hugh, but I am too terrified to move, my muscles locked into position by sheer dread.

My hearing is attuned to every sound and movement in the room, every whisper of wind outside, and yet I cannot hear anything. Not like last time when I heard a rustling sound. This time there is nothing. Terror pulses through me, perspiration stands out on my face.

I try to still my breathing and to remain calm. It was just a dream. Definitely a dream. It must have been. There is no other explanation for it. The smell is simply the stale odour of sleep, the scent that clings to our bodies and emanates from our pores after spending hours and hours in bed. Unless I'm losing my mind, there cannot possibly be anybody else here in this room with us. It just isn't possible. Is it?

Then I feel it again. A small but definite waft of warm air passing over my face. I want to scream, to curl up in a tight ball and hide away under the covers. I want whatever it is to go away and leave me alone. I just want to feel safe.

I have no idea what I should do. If I wake Hugh and say anything to him he will briefly close his eyes, take a deep breath, his nostrils flaring slightly as he exhales, and then speak to me as if I'm a six-year-old child, trying to reassure me that we are all perfectly okay. All the while I'll be secretly worrying that I'm on the verge of a breakdown again. I sometimes feel as if I am being perpetually punished for what Todd and Jeff did to us. I am now not allowed to be concerned or fretful about even the most serious of situations in case my family think I am about to be sectioned. We hid most of what went on with Todd and Jeff from my mother to stop her worrying, and the bits I told Jan, my sister, were met with scorn.

'Why don't you just hit him back and tell him to fuck off?' was her reply when I explained what Todd had done. 'And as for that pathetic little nerd at work, well, I'd report him for harassment and then he'll lose his job. Either that or tell him to fuck off as well.'

Jan has never been one for suffering fools gladly, as her previous two husbands will testify. If anybody so much as gives her a sideways glance, she confronts them, demanding to know who they think they are, looking at her like that. I wish I had just half her courage.

I lie as still as humanly possible, my heart hammering wildly. A well of heat builds up around my face as I sink down under the duvet and gasp with fear. The silence is deafening. The breathing appears to have stopped but I daren't move. I imagine opening my eyes and being confronted with the twisted features of a madman who is waiting to rip me from my bed and hurt me. So instead, I wait for what feels like hours, listening, fighting back the tears, hardly daring to breathe. At one point I fall asleep and when I wake again, I know for sure that what I hear isn't my imagination or me suffering the beginnings of some sort of psychological trauma.

What I hear is real.

Feet very slowly shuffle along the floor, accompanied by deep rattling breaths. I bite down on the inside of my mouth to stop myself from screaming out into the night. The taste of metal slides across my tongue and I feel blood settle on my lips. This can't be happening. And yet it is. This is definitely real. Somebody is here, in the room with us.

My heart tries to burst out of my chest. A sudden wave of lava-like heat covers my skin, running down my neck and over my stomach, dampening the sheets in a matter of minutes. Despite this, I shiver violently. My body threatens to go into some sort of spasm as I do my utmost to lie still and keep myself silent, which is so very difficult when I feel as if I'm about to combust.

The footsteps continue, moving past me and out of the open doorway. The door that I closed last night; the door that I definitely pulled shut. I know I did. Before getting into bed, I distinctly remember the click of the old latch as I pulled it to.

I lie as still as death itself, overwhelmed with sheer dread at the thought of Poppy and Aiden, alone in their beds. It suddenly dawns on me that I need to do something. I can't just focus on my own fear and leave them alone with this person wandering around our house. I have to get to them. Springing out of bed, I run onto the landing and turn on the light, my head buzzing with terror at what I might be faced with.

Nothing. There is nobody there.

Oh God! This person is in their rooms...

Trembling and close to tears, I tear into Poppy's room and grapple with the light switch, my fingers like blocks of wood as I slap at the wall with limited dexterity. My mind is in a whirl and my limbs feel as if they belong to somebody else. I am detached from my own body, fear rendering me numb and useless.

The room is suddenly bathed in an orange glow and apart from my daughter's sleeping body snuggled under the quilt, it's empty. I watch, shaking and sweating with both terror and relief, as she begins to rouse from her deep slumber. Quickly, I flick the light off and back out, my head buzzing and my breath hot and constricted as I gasp and splutter in confusion.

Racing across the landing, I almost fall into Aiden's room, my feet a tangle of uncoordinated limbs as I push at his door and turn the light on. Again, it is empty aside from Aiden's face peeping out from under the sheets. He blinks and starts to sit up in bed, his skin pale and his hair tousled. I whisper to him in a shaky voice that I was just checking to make sure everyone was okay. He starts to murmur something but before he can go any further, I tell him to go back to sleep, then I turn the light off and leave. Outside his room, I listen to the soft muffled movement of bed linen as he once again settles down for the night. I close my eyes to hold back the tears that bite at the back of my eyelids.

Out on the landing, I lean against the wall and try to control my breathing. The light hurts my eyes but I refuse to turn it off. I will stay here all night if I have to. I heard something – somebody – I know I did, and I will sit here until morning, keeping watch. I am not going to wake Hugh. He won't believe me anyway so there is little point. I will do this on my own.

The thought that I need something as protection abruptly jumps into my mind. Creeping downstairs, I head into the kitchen and rummage in the cutlery drawer where I retrieve a small sharp knife. My eyes dart around me – every dark corner, every shadow, every single sound no matter how small or explicable, makes the hairs on my arms and the back of my neck stand to attention. I run my arms over my flesh, shivering as the cold air caresses my bare skin.

As quietly and carefully as I can, I make a detour into the living room where I grab a throw from the back of the sofa and sling it over my shoulders, each creak and sound of the old house echoing loudly around me, accentuating my terror.

I skulk back into the hallway and slowly drag myself up the stairs, using the handrail to lighten the sound of my footfall. The last thing I want to do is draw attention to my presence as I move through each of the rooms. I have no idea who is in here. I'm not sure I want to know.

At the top of the stairs I stop and peer down to the bottom, to that spot – the place where a woman from another era fell to her death. I picture her cold, dead body sprawled out there on the hard floor, her broken corpse lying at a horribly distorted angle, her grey skin mottled by death as decay sets in and nature takes its ugly course, her flesh breaking down and decomposing until there is nothing left but dust and bone.

Forcing myself to turn away, I find a place in a corner where I can sit and have a good vantage point of all the rooms as well as the top of the stairs. I shift to one side slightly so I can see the smaller steps that lead to the attic room. I want to be able to see every single entry and exit point. I refuse to rest until the sun comes up and I know we are all safe.

Wrapping myself up in the fur throw that has seen better days, I sit with my back against the wall, the knife tucked firmly behind me. Every now and again, I lean back and run my fingers over the handle to make sure I can grab it quickly should I need to. I pray neither of the children gets up to go to the bathroom in the middle of the night. They usually sleep very deeply, apart from when Poppy has her nightmares, which admittedly are becoming less and less frequent. I just want to sit here undisturbed and watch over my children, to keep them from harm.

My eyes begin to droop, despite me being uncomfortable and chilly. My backside is starting to go numb and my neck aches but I refuse to move. My skull feels too heavy for my body and I am constantly jolted awake every time sleep tries to seize me and my head drops to one side. I rub my eyes and pinch at my skin to keep myself awake. I can't let myself succumb to sleep otherwise there will be no point in me being here. I have to keep my children safe from this intruder, because there is definitely somebody wandering about this house. I am not going mad; I am not having some sort of breakdown and suffering from hallucinations. Somebody else is here with us, in our house. There is a person wandering around here and I refuse to be told otherwise.

***

I am woken by the sound of a blackbird singing outside and I'm bathed in a warm glow of light that is coming in through the large landing window and spreading over the floor. Snapping my head up, I look around, scanning everywhere with wild, frightened eyes. I throw off the blanket and scramble to my feet. I need to check my kids to make sure they are okay. I look in on Aiden first and am relieved to find him lying on his back, still asleep, his mouth gaping open, a soft purr escaping from the back of his throat.

Next, I go into Poppy's room and feel my legs turn to liquid when I see that her bed is empty. The sheets have been thrown back and there is a small crumpled indent in the middle where her body should be, but my daughter is nowhere to be seen. I bring my hand up to my mouth and suppress the scream that is clawing to come out. The bathroom. She must be in there. Be logical. Please, God, let her be in the bathroom!

I all but sprint there, only to find it is empty. Nausea rises. My vision is hazy, obscured by a film of fear as I hurl myself back to the main bedroom. I have to wake Hugh now. Something terrible has happened, I just know it.

I stop at our open bedroom door, and stare at my side of the bed. Poppy is curled up there, her leg sticking out, her long, fair hair fanned out on the pillow around her. Next to her is Hugh, still fast asleep. I don't know whether I want to roar with anger or weep with relief at seeing her slumbering soundly. I don't think I'm strong enough to do either, so instead I cling on to the doorframe to steady myself. My stomach is a swirling mass of hot liquid and my head is tight with shock.

Saying a little thank you, I breathe deeply and try to focus on what I am going to do next. I refuse to let this situation get to me. I have to stay strong, put on a good show and not let Hugh think I'm struggling to cope. I don't want him to worry about me and I definitely don't want him thinking I'm heading for another breakdown with my talk of night visitors in our new house. I do want to speak to him about it, though, once he gets up. I need to phrase it carefully so he will listen and not think me mad. I won't be talked out of what I heard and no matter how much he protests, I will make sure he listens to what I have to say. I just need to keep my fear in check, to act as if I'm in control when that is the last thing I really feel.

It's a Saturday so I leave them all to sleep while I get a shower. I feel particularly grimy after spending most of the night on the floor wrapped in an old blanket that Aiden and Poppy used to use to make dens. I doubt it's been washed since then and don't even want to think about how often it was taken out in the garden and dragged halfway across the lawn.

I tiptoe across to a pile of clean clothes that is sitting on a chair next to the window and grab some clean underwear, a pair of jeans and a T-shirt. I will be so relieved when this house is finished and we have proper places to put things. At the moment we have one chest of drawers between us and it's crammed full. I long for new bedroom furniture like other women long for expensive jewellery and fine clothes.

Creeping past the pair of sleeping beauties, I close the door behind me with a gentle click, then turn around and let out a sudden, unexpected shriek. Aiden is standing there grasping the knife I brought upstairs a few hours earlier. He is holding it in front of his face, the metal partially covering his bewildered expression. The silver blade glints menacingly in the early morning light, an incongruous sight next to his clear skin and bright innocent eyes.

'I found this over there in the corner,' he says flatly, pointing to the place I spent the night crouching like a frightened, wild animal.

'Right, yes, thank you,' I reply, taking it from him and placing it on top of the pile of clothes. 'I was up early sorting through more boxes and must have dropped it.'

He stares at me as if I am mad, his eyes wide with disbelief. 'Sorting boxes?' He looks at the knife and then back at me. 'Mum, it's only seven o'clock. Why would you be up sorting through boxes so early? You're not even dressed yet.'

I feel myself grow hot under his scrutiny. It's always going to be a problem, having a twelve-year-old who is a particularly bright spark and is able spot a lie from a mile away.

'Yes well, when there's so much to be done, it's best to get started early,' I bark, moving past him into the bathroom, adding a sense of purpose to my movements to detract from any nerves that may be showing. 'And anyway,' I add over my shoulder, 'aren't you the one who is desperate for us to get rid of that awful wallpaper in your bedroom? The sooner we clear all the rubbish out of the way, the sooner we can get started with the painting and decorating.'

He nods and groans as he stares in at his room, screwing his eyes up in disgust. 'Can we start with my room first, please?' he asks with a wry smile. 'That paint and wallpaper keeps me awake at night. It's the colour of snot.'

I laugh and tell him we can, my voice still wobbly with shock as I close the bathroom door. Only when it is completely locked do I let it all out. I want to scream and howl, to beat the floor with my fists, but I'm aware of Aiden's presence outside so instead I sit on the cold tiles and let silent tears roll until there are no more left in me.

Deciding against a shower, I run a bath so hot my skin turns a raw shade of pink. I lie back in it, contemplating what happened last night, trying to work out how best to put it to Hugh without coming across as unhinged. There will be no easy way, I'm sure of that. Whatever I say or however rational I sound, he will go into panic mode and insist I dreamt it. Or he will simply grow tired of me and my neuroses and bringing it up will cause a huge rift between us. Either way, he will think me mad.

I go over it again and again until my head aches, talking myself though it step by step; how I'll broach the conversation, what Hugh's reaction might be. I even try to picture his face and work out how I'll stop the conversation if it starts to turn into something that makes me look like I'm losing my sanity. I let out a low cackle and practically submerge myself under the scalding water. Maybe I am. Maybe I am mad and it is all in my head. After all, how would I know where that fine line between reality and craziness actually is? When I get like this – anxious and fretful – it's difficult to see the demarcation between the two. Because it is a fine line, very fine indeed, and I cross over to the other side of it at my peril.

Only when the water starts to go cold do I eventually get out, dry myself off and get dressed, already weary. Something tells me today is going to be a long one.

∗∗∗

By the time they all arrive downstairs with tousled hair and baggy eyes, I have made a large plateful of toast and am just finishing frying a pan of eggs and bacon. Hugh plants a kiss on my cheek and makes a pot of coffee while I dish out the food.

'Smells good,' he says chirpily, grabbing the milk out of the ancient fridge gifted to us by the previous owners. Or possibly the ones before them. I shudder at the thought and block it out of my mind. The last thing I want in my brain is the image of Hilary Wentworth's dead body lying at the foot of my stairs. I have enough to contend with without bringing her demise into the mix.

'I want toast and marmalade!' Poppy shouts as she sits herself down at the table and holds out her plate for it to be filled.

Aiden pushes the plate of toast towards her along with the jar of marmalade. He passes her a knife and I watch as my young daughter wreaks havoc at the table, leaving sticky, orange drips everywhere and spreading crumbs far and wide.

I place the eggs and bacon down in the middle, feeling satisfied as they all dip in. I opt for coffee, my appetite absent after the horrors of last night. My stomach is in knots and all I can think about is sitting down and telling Hugh about it. Later though. Not here, not now. I step away from the table and busy myself with tidying up and making more coffee.

'Mummy slept on the landing last night,' Poppy suddenly shouts, spitting bits of toast everywhere, 'so I slept in her bed with Daddy! Why weren't you in your bed last night, Mummy?' she asks innocently. I go cold and try to think of a million different things to say that will divert attention away from me. Nothing comes out. My mind is a complete blank.

I watch Hugh carefully, dreading what he will say next. He places his cutlery down on the plate with a sharp clatter and turns to look at me. 'You slept on the landing?' His face says it all. He thinks I'm on a downward spiral. I have to nip this in the bud, take control of this situation and turn it around so I don't appear weak and helpless. I need him to be on my side. I need him to believe me when I tell him about our unwanted visitor. This isn't how I wanted it to be. I'm losing control of this situation and if that happens, I'll never get it back. All will be lost.

'Can we talk about it later?' I ask quietly, my eyes conveying a sense of desperation that this is a private matter and not to be discussed in front of the children. Fortunately, Hugh is on my wavelength and senses the desperation in my voice. He nods, his forehead creased with confusion and worry. He spoons more eggs onto his plate and gives Poppy a playful nudge, his eyes constantly flicking back to watch me. 'So what happened to make you come and sleep in our room then, Pops? Thought it might be more comfortable than your own bed?'

I hear Aiden snort with derision and give him my best harsh glare while mouthing at him to stop it.

'I had a nightmare,' she says quietly, her hands halfway to her mouth as she grasps a large slice of heavily buttered toast with chunks of marmalade heaped on top. 'I dreamt there was somebody in my room with me. They were standing at the end of my bed staring at me and I could hear their breathing all loud and heavy.'

A knot of tension tightens over my head as I listen to her words. I want to scream at them that it wasn't a nightmare and it wasn't all in Poppy's head, that it was real. I don't. That would be a terribly foolish move. Instead I turn away and look out of the window, pretending to be busy at the sink washing pots and wiping surfaces down. My hands are shaking and perspiration has broken out on my top lip. I wipe it away with the back of my trembling hand and listen as Hugh consoles Poppy, telling her it was just a dream and that there wasn't really anybody else in the bedroom with her. There was. There definitely was.

Last night, somebody was walking around our house, skulking in and out of bedrooms and watching us all while we slept.

And I know exactly who it was.

Nine

'Todd knows where we live,' I say to Hugh and watch as he suppresses an eye roll. I expected this. I'm prepared for his negativity.

He blinks hard and lets out a small sigh of annoyance. 'And what makes you think that then?'

'Because what Poppy saw last night in her room wasn't a nightmare, Hugh. It was Todd wandering around our house. I saw him as well. That was why I slept on the landing.'

'Wait, wait, wait!' Hugh holds his hands up and shakes his head. I'm ready for this. I knew what sort of response I would get when I told him what had happened. I knew as soon as I asked him to sit down for a minute so we could talk that it would get his back up. Hugh's time is precious and he has his Saturday all planned out. He wants to get down to the basement and clear it out, ready to turn it into a workshop. Personally, I think our time would be better spent stripping off wallpaper and ripping up carpets in readiness for the electricians and decorators coming, but I've no energy to argue.

'So, what you're saying is that Todd came here last night? He broke in, wandered around for a bit and then left? And you thought what – that by sitting on the landing, it would scare him away?'

Hugh always has a way of turning around the things that I say to make me sound irrational and stupid, and put like that, it does sound crazy. I will not be swayed, however, and will stand my ground on this one. I know what I heard. Last night there was definitely somebody in this house.

'Don't try to make me sound ridiculous,' I snap. 'I know what I heard. And Poppy was right, it was the breathing. It was loud and

63

heavy, as if somebody was exhausted or had been running or had some sort of chest problem. And for your information, I sat out on the landing to make sure he didn't go into either of the kids' rooms.'

'But according to what you're saying, that's exactly what happened, Faye. You're saying he was in Poppy's room. Did you see him go in?' Hugh sits back and waits for my answer, his fingers interlocked across his abdomen, his face devoid of any emotion.

'No!' I shout, my patience waning as he applies every sales technique in the book with me to try to catch me out. These are the rules he applies to his customers to get them to open up to him and buy his ideas and he is good at it. Family and friends have joked on more than one occasion that Hugh could sell needles to a porcupine. 'That is not what happened! I heard him in our room and went out to check on the children to make sure he hadn't done anything.'

'And had he? Was he in there when you went in?'

'No he wasn't, which is fortunate because –'

'Hold on a minute,' Hugh says as he suddenly sits forward, a sharp gleam in his eye. I know what's coming next. I might be upset and frightened but I'm not an idiot. He continues, convinced he can break my argument apart with his words. 'I thought you said it was him in Poppy's room? And now you're saying there was nobody there when you checked? Which is it, Faye? Was he there, in Poppy's room, or wasn't he? I mean, did you actually see Todd last night, or are you putting two and two together and coming up with five?'

'Firstly,' I whisper, gritting my teeth so hard they feel ready to dissolve into dust, 'have you ever considered the fact that he went into Poppy's room before he came into ours? And no, I didn't see him, but I heard him and could smell him.'

'Smell him?' Hugh's eyes bulge and already I regret saying the last part about the prowler's rancid breath. He will now mock me and not give any credence to anything I've said.

'Yes, I could smell him. Look,' I say icily as I scrape the chair back and stand up from the table, anger rising in me. 'I realise you won't listen to anything I say, but answer me this – do you know where Todd is right now? Because he could be anywhere. We don't actually know his whereabouts, do we? He could be back with his mother; he could be living on the streets desperate for somewhere warm to spend the night. Think about it, Hugh... he could be here. Just because you refuse to even consider it, doesn't mean it isn't happening.'

I get up and walk over to the window to watch Aiden and Poppy as they play in the garden. Aiden is tearing around, diving into overgrown shrubbery and generally burning off excess energy, while Poppy is sitting in the middle of the lawn threading daisies together with her small, clumsy fingers. Such innocence. I wonder how small people manage to grow up, then stray so badly from the right path in life and end up like Todd – so full of anger and hatred, filling their body with toxins and generally not giving a shit about anybody but themselves.

I don't turn around to look at Hugh. It hurts when he is so dismissive of me, refusing to take me seriously or to listen to any of my ideas. I'm an educated woman who, until recently, held down a responsible job. Hugh wasn't the one who was stalked and sexually attacked. Nor was it Hugh who took a couple of good, hard smacks to the face from somebody much bigger and stronger. All of those things happened to me and although all of those things took their toll on me, they didn't turn me into an idiot who has nothing of any value to say. I will not back down on this point and if my husband isn't prepared to help me find this person, then I will do it on my own. Come hell or high water, I will find out what is happening in this house.

**

His apology is a bunch of flowers and a bar of my favourite chocolate thrust in my hand later in the day while I am in Aiden's room, dragging dirty laundry out of his basket. They're gratefully received after I spent the morning stomping around the house feeling like an unwanted imbecile. I was tired after not getting any sleep and pissed off at having my argument shot down in flames. I knew it was going to happen but it still hurt.

'Sorry. I can be a bit of a clown at times,' Hugh says as he leans forward and kisses me, his unshaven skin brushing coarsely against my face. I smile and accept his apology. What's the point in staying mad at him? I need him on my side; I need him to believe me. Staying angry and upset simply widens the rift.

He spends the remainder of the day sorting out the basement while I continue rummaging through old cupboards and wardrobes. I have no idea why I'm doing it. My mind isn't really focused on this task. I am more concerned with what I plan on doing while Hugh is out of the way and the kids are busy exploring the garden.

Making sure I'm on my own and everybody else is busy doing other things, I find Todd's phone number on Hugh's phone. I never had any reason to keep Todd's contact details and after he left, I was so upset and furious with him, I probably would have deleted them anyway. I quickly write the number down and slip the phone back into Hugh's jacket pocket, glancing around furtively even though I know I'm alone.

I don't make the call while I'm downstairs – too many distractions, and besides which, Hugh would hear my voice from the basement. Instead I hide away up in our shared study, a large, rambling old room with lots of light and a great sloping roof. Through the huge skylight, I can see Aiden and Poppy in the garden below, running around in circles, kicking a ball and shrieking with laughter.

With hot graceless fingers, I punch Todd's number into my own mobile, sweat prickling me at the thought of speaking to him. I don't want to do this. I really don't, but feel I have no choice. I wait for the ringing to kick in and think how I will react if I hear it echoing somewhere in the house, coming from a cupboard where Todd may be hidden, ready to carry out some vicious attack on us. There is a sharp trill on the other end. I move the phone away from my ear to see it if I can hear it ringing anywhere. Apart from the echoing laughter flowing up from Aiden and Poppy outside in the garden, the house remains silent. The ringing tone continues through the handset as I press the phone back to my face. I'm just on the point of ending the call when a voice comes down the other end. A shard of ice stabs at my intestines as I hear it.

'Hello? Can I help you?'

I am completely taken aback. I hardly recognise the person speaking on the other end. It's Todd; I can hear that it's him, but it's a different Todd, not the one I remember and fear. He sounds clearer, more alert. It's not the half-asleep, monosyllabic tone I had got used to hearing from him. Not the aggressive, slurred speech of somebody determined to ruin us. For a brief moment I'm confused. Perhaps I'm mistaken and it's not him at all, just somebody with the same timbre, the same dialect. I wonder if I've put the wrong number in and start to formulate an apology in my head, then stop myself. It's him. I know it is, but something has changed.

'Todd?' I hold my breath, hoping he doesn't cut me off or slam the phone down. Our last words weren't pleasant. I called him a useless parasite and he responded by telling me to fuck off, yelling that I was a skinny little bitch. My face burns at the memory. Although he is the last person I want to be having a conversation with right now, this is something I have to do. I need to know; to get it all clear in my head.

'Yeah. Sorry, can I help you?' His tone is formal, clipped even. I have to get this right. I don't want him to hang up. All I want is a few minutes of his time. I need to know where he is, that's all. Speaking to Todd right now is the last thing I want to do but I have to know.

'It's Faye. I'm ringing about Hugh, your father,' I say, disturbed at the lies I am about tell him. It's the only way I can think of to keep him on the line. To say that Todd and I didn't hit it off is the understatement of the year, but he did have a bit more time for Hugh despite lashing out at him and threatening him. If I pretend something is wrong with his father, he is possibly more likely to listen to me and answer my questions and not cut me off.

My temples thud and my entire body is shaking as I strike up a conversation with the person who hit me. Terror throbs under my skin, clogging up my veins, but I need to do this.

'My dad?' he says with a slight gasp. 'What about him? What's happened?'

I bite my lip and close my eyes before speaking. 'Look, it's nothing too serious but if you're nearby then maybe you could call round?'

I pray he panics and doesn't take me up on it, but I've got to know where he is. If he is close by then I will know that it was him in here last night. And if not... well, I'll think about that later. It's him. I'm sure of it. Who else could it be? Not Jeff. He was a weak, lonely man who doesn't have the wherewithal to do such a thing. That visit had Todd's name written all over it.

I can hear his breathing through the phone and wince at the thought of him being so close by last night. The memory of it makes me want to vomit.

'Thing is, Faye, first off I need to apologise for the way I went on. I'm clean now, I swear it. A mate of mine took me in and got me into a rehab centre. I'm a dickhead, I know that, but I'm trying to be better, okay?'

There's a brief pause as I let him continue. I don't speak for fear of ruining the moment. Is this really a new Todd or is it just another rotten lie? I suspected his behaviour was down to drugs but couldn't prove it. Ours is often a chaotic household and there were times that money disappeared and we presumed we had moved it elsewhere or miscalculated our spending. Now I know. All that time, giving him cash for a bedsit, and we were inadvertently helping to feed his habit.

'And I'm abroad now. I got a job in a bar in Ibiza. Pay's not great but it's sunny and – look, Faye, I'm sorry for everything that happened and for the way I went on with the kids and stuff. I was a mess and y'know, I can't actually remember a lot of it. If my dad is ill I could borrow some money to get back over there but –'

I cut him off before he can say any more. 'It's fine, Todd. Really, it's not that bad. He just had a fall, that's all. Nothing broken. And I'd appreciate it if you don't mention to him that I called you.' My voice is cold. I try to inject some warmth into it but the memory of what he did to us will never leave me.

'Yeah, no worries,' he says quietly. I don't have to explain why I don't want him to contact us. We both know that some things are best left unsaid.

I'm unsure as to whether or not I should believe him. He has given me no reason to in the past. All I have are his words. For all I know he could be hiding around the next corner with ill intent, a weapon at the ready. A thought springs into my mind. It's my last chance to make sure he's telling the truth and actually is where he says he is, although the ring tone when I called him, has already begun to nag at me. It sounded different somehow so perhaps he really is out of the country. Perhaps for the first time ever, he is actually telling the truth and not waiting nearby ready to hurt us or steal from us or do any number of the dreadful things he threatened us with. I wish I'd taken more notice but I was riddled with panic at the thought of speaking to him and not thinking straight.

'Do me a favour, Todd, will you? Send a picture and perhaps when Hugh is feeling up to it I can let him know that you're somewhere safe and warm and not sleeping on the street.'

I clench my teeth, unsure how he will react to this bizarre request. I'm more than a tad relieved when after an awkward silence he lets out a quiet laugh and agrees to my strange request.

We say our stilted goodbyes and I stand, the phone held tightly in my hand as I wait for his picture to come through. This will be the only evidence I have that he really is abroad. And if I don't receive anything, then I will know that it was just Todd being Todd and telling more lies, hurting those who have done nothing but try to help him. I pray the hunch I had about the different sounding ring tone is correct. After all he put us through, I no longer trust my own instincts. After what he put us through, I no longer trust anybody at all.

Time seems to stand still as I wait for my phone to come to life. When it does, it makes my head thud with anticipation. I almost drop it as I wrangle with the buttons to open his message, hardly daring to look at the screen.

My breath leaves me, exiting my body in a great rush. He has sent a video. I open it and watch as he pans around the beach, taking in the most beautiful scenery of golden sand and a sparkling azure sea in the distance. Todd appears on the video and his appearance causes me to half shriek. He is tanned, healthy looking, and he is actually smiling, something he never did while he was living with us. How had I not noticed how gaunt and pale he was when he was here?

'Hi, Faye, as you can see life here is hard!' His voice is a faint scratch and I watch as he gives a small, embarrassed wave, then bids us goodbye, saying we should visit him at some point in the future to get away from the awful British weather, followed by another mumbling awkward apology.

I drop down onto the nearest chair, my stomach tight with mixed emotions. I'm glad he has sorted himself out, I really, really am, and I am pleased he is somewhere warm and is off the drugs and booze. I'm not sure I can ever forgive him for the way he treated us but at least his life is better and he's trying to make something of himself. But that doesn't solve my problem. I was so sure it was Todd who was creeping around here last night but with this new information I know now that it can't have been and I no longer know what to think.

Tears burn at my eyes as I turn to stare out of the window. By calling Todd, I've solved one mystery and in turn, created another. Spots of rain hit the glass in vertical lines, slashing at it violently, a quick and constant splatter of icy needles gaining momentum. A downpour is imminent. I take a deep breath and watch as Aiden and Poppy dive for shelter under a nearby fir tree.

It definitely isn't my errant stepson wandering around Cross House on a night, I know that now for certain. A solid lump sticks in my throat, making it hard to swallow. I try to control my breathing and end up wheezing painfully as the question rattles around my head, making me feel sick and light-headed.

If it isn't Todd wandering around our house in the early hours, then who the hell is it?

Ten

I can't settle. I keep seeing things out of the corner of my eye – moving shadows and unexplained noises everywhere I turn. Like a cat on hot bricks I pace around the house, trying to organise my thoughts and work out what I'm going to do next. The idea that it may be Jeff roaming around here keeps forcing itself into my thoughts. I dismiss it. He just doesn't seem the type, but then he didn't seem the type to sexually harass me and stalk me and try to rape me, yet that was exactly what he did. Sometimes we think we know people when all we really know is their surface, the veneer they present to the outside world. It's what is lurking beneath that makes a person; the dangerous hidden depths that some people have; the darkness that stirs within them and festers deep in their souls.

Poppy rushes past me, her wet hair trailing over my skin, turning my exposed flesh to ice. Aiden follows closely behind, a stack of games for his console tucked tightly under his arm. They both disappear into his bedroom and I hear the familiar creak of his bed as they climb onto it and get ensconced for the afternoon. I keep waiting for a disgruntled squeal from Poppy when he tires of her company and pushes her away, but fortunately it doesn't happen. In a new village with no new friends nearby just yet, Poppy is all Aiden has for company and I, for one, am thoroughly enjoying the peace and quiet that comes with it – no name calling, no fighting, no tears.

I hold my phone tightly, my fingers white with the strain. Hugh is still in the basement, dragging workbenches about and sweeping up and doing whatever it is he must do to make the place somewhere he can do his manual work in. I stand and look out of the window, at the blurred watery view as rain runs down the glass;

long thin rivulets snaking and merging in a downward motion only to be replaced by more as the weather picks up its furious pace and hammers at the window, angry spatters hitting the glass with force. I trail my fingers over the inside of the window, tracing the trajectory of the water as it runs downwards before disappearing. Each and every pane of glass, every door in this house will need to be replaced. They are old and worn, and weather like this makes me think of leaks and draughts and how cold the place will be during the winter if we don't do something about it now. I should really start ringing for quotes, finding local builders and asking them to call round to give us estimates for the work that needs doing. That's what I should do. I don't. Instead, I take my phone, perch on the edge of the sofa and scroll through the names of old work colleagues, people I considered friends. People I can trust. I read them one by one, keeping some, deleting others – Vera Stanworth, an old busybody if ever there was one. I get rid of her details. Pete Dunwoody – the kind of person who said one thing and meant another. I wouldn't trust him as far as I could throw him. I delete his contact details as well. I ponder over one particular name – Allison Haynes. I could get a decent answer out of her without any problem. We became fairly close at one point, going out for lunch and texting each other out of work time, but then Allison reduced her hours and went part-time after childcare became too difficult and expensive and so we gradually grew apart. We haven't spoken for about six months, possibly longer than that. I could trust her, especially if I told her why I was calling. She never much liked Jeff, saying she found him rather slimy and a bit lecherous. I could see how she would think that, but I felt pity for him and if I had taken a deep dislike to him I would be just another on a long list of people who either didn't care for him or rejected his friendship. So I made the mistake of befriending him, letting him into our home, allowing myself to become his victim.

I chew at a ragged fingernail and stare at Allison's number. Just a few minutes – that's all it will take to find out what Jeff is up to and his whereabouts, and more importantly whether or not he is back at work living a normal life again. After our friendship turned into something from a horror movie, Jeff stopped coming into work on a regular basis. He took some sick leave which finished shortly before I found out about the option to take redundancy. I had hoped he would stay off for longer as the thought of sitting so close to him day in, day out, made me feel ill. The last I heard, he was off work again and apart from sending in repeat doctors' notes, nobody had heard from him.

I call her, hoping against hope she will tell me he's back at work and functioning again. Not that it rules him out completely, but at least I would know that his mental health is on the mend, which makes him less likely to be creeping around my bed night after night.

My heart taps out an uncomfortable, sickening beat in my chest as I listen out for the dialling tone.

'Coffee?'

At the sound of Hugh's voice behind me, I drop my phone onto the wooden floor. It spins around in circles, making an almighty clatter. I bend down and quickly retrieve it, turning it off before Allison has a chance to answer.

'Yes, sorry, I should have made some,' I say, my voice hoarse with barely disguised fright. I reach out and take the steaming cup that Hugh is offering me and sip at it, wincing at the searing heat as it travels down my throat. I clasp the drink tightly. It stops my hands from trembling. I have to appear normal.

'Everything okay?' he asks, and I feel myself blush at my covert secrecy.

I do my best to keep the tremor out of my voice as I reply. 'Everything is fine. How's it going in the basement? Everything shipshape down there?'

He nods and tries to hide the mile-wide grin that emerges every time his new workshop is mentioned. Hugh has spent all of his adult years wanting a space to work in and now he has one that is larger than the entire floor space of our previous house.

'I was thinking,' he says quietly, and immediately I feel my muscles clench. I never know what's coming next with Hugh.

Not since my health took a turn for the worse after what we went through. Not since Todd and Jeff sailed into our lives and almost tore us apart. 'After we've got the house sorted, why don't you and I have a weekend away somewhere?' he continues. 'We'll probably be ready for it after we've finished ripping this place to bits. I can book us in that lovely old hotel in the Lake District. The one we visited before the kids were born.'

I try to smile and give him the nod and look of enthusiasm I know he wants to see. I have mixed emotions on this one. Going away to a plush hotel with my husband sounds like a lovely way to spend a few days and I have no doubts at all that we'll be ready for a break after tackling all the work Cross House will throw at us, but the worry of leaving Aiden and Poppy will gnaw at me. They will probably go to their Aunt Jan's and get spoilt rotten, or Grandma's house and be allowed to do what they want, whenever they want. That doesn't worry me. It's leaving them behind that concerns me. I know Todd is out of the country but I still have no idea what Jeff is up to or where he is. Once I can track down his whereabouts I may feel a whole lot better about it, and I admit that a few days away would be lovely, but for the time being, I want to focus on decorating this place and finding out what or who it is that's stalking this house on an evening.

'Sounds nice,' I say as brightly as I can. I don't want Hugh to suspect anything. He thinks it's all in my head and will try to quash any of my theories. We constantly pussyfoot around my issues for fear of overstepping the invisible mark that will shatter the illusion we have that everything is back to normal.

We drink our coffee in near silence, me staring out at the rain-saturated garden and Hugh staring at me, trying to work out what's really going on in my head.

***

Later that evening, after the kids are settled in bed, we discuss the house; how we want the new kitchen to look, what our budget is, what sort of colours we would like for the hallway and living room, the fact that the electricians are booked in to carry out the work, and for the first time since moving in I feel as if we're making headway.

I snuggle into Hugh and we lie there sprawled out over the sofa watching TV, our limbs intertwined, my head resting on his chest. I listen to the soft purring of his breathing as he slowly slips into a state of complete rest, sleep wrapping itself around him, cocooning him in its warmth.

I think about all that's gone on, about Todd and Jeff and about making the call to Allison in the morning once Hugh has got himself immersed in his work up in the study. He hasn't enquired about my absence from my computer and why I'm not writing. There is most definitely a positive side to being thought of as a fragile flower, a rare orchid that could wither and disappear any second; all the pressure is removed and for the first time in my life, I have no deadlines to meet, nobody breathing down my neck giving me impossible targets and making impossible demands. I am my own boss and it feels rather good.

After leaving the newspaper, I spent a few weeks reshaping a manuscript I'd spent years writing. There was plenty that needed altering and so I set to work, editing and rewriting, often deleting large chunks that had taken me months and months to write. The whole thing was both tricky and cathartic. It helped to take my mind off what was going on with Jeff and Todd but it was also a pretty painful process, getting rid of words I'd worked so hard to write. But it was worth it in the end.

I'd like to say the first publisher I submitted to snapped it up, but that's not how it happened at all. Life's not that easy is it? You get out of life exactly what you put in. So I sat, day after day, sending submission after submission and receiving rejection after rejection, until eventually an agent took me on and within a month had secured a deal for my debut novel.

I'm now working on my second book and am already ahead of schedule so I can rest a little and take some time away, not work myself into such a frenzy that I can hardly think straight. That was how I was when I worked in the city and I don't miss it one little bit. I now have the privilege of being able to take a break from my writing and concentrate on other matters, like this house, getting it into a more habitable state and also dedicating more time to my children. It's been so nice, being one of the school run mums and not having to bundle them off to a childminder every morning. I also have the pleasure of being there for them every evening after school. My children and my family are my priority and from now on, always will be. The only positive thing to come out of the whole Todd/Jeff nightmare was the fact that it made me appreciate my family just that little bit more. Sometimes we forget how precious people are.

We stagger up to bed, exhaustion nagging at our bones, and Hugh is asleep again in seconds. This house, the cleaning of it, his work – it's all taking it out of him and he ends each and every day completely wiped out. I have more trouble sleeping, however. I stare at the ceiling, waiting for something to happen, my nerve endings shrieking at every creak, every breath of wind outside, until in the end I succumb to sleep.

I am both surprised and relieved when I wake the next morning to find I've slept through and not been woken by any strange unexplained noises or terrifying presences. No hot stale breath in my face, no shuffling footsteps, no being gripped by fear so overwhelming I feel as if my entire body has been encased in concrete.

Hugh is beside me, still sleeping. I slip out of bed and shower. Today I will ring Allison and find out how Jeff is doing. Today I will find out what is going on in this house.

Eleven

Despite it being a Sunday, Hugh spends most of the day up in the office. Every so often I hear his voice filtering down from above as he speaks on the phone, his tone clipped and efficient. He is a different Hugh when he's working – not the charismatic, compassionate Hugh that is my husband, not the funny, gregarious Hugh when he is being a father to our two children; just a formal capable man who wants to get the job done to the best of his ability. It's no wonder his business is a success. He gives it one hundred per cent. I can almost guarantee he'll be up there most of the day. His time spent in the basement yesterday will be balanced today by working up in the study until later in the evening. That leaves me plenty of time to call Allison and ask about Jeff. We may have had a night free of noise but for all I know he could still be hanging around, waiting for a time when Hugh is away so he can make his move. The very thought of it makes me gag.

I prevaricate by tidying up and ordering up paint and wallpaper online, and contacting builders, asking them to call round to give us quotes for building work. By the time I pluck up the courage to call Allison, it's almost lunchtime. I know why my nerves have suddenly decided to kick in. What if she tells me that Jeff is fine and functioning normally, or he has moved out of the area? I then have to work out what to do next. How do I find out who our intruder is when I have no information to go on and I'm the only person who has experienced it? Poppy is a child and thinks it was a dream, and I would rather she continues to think that. If she were to find out the truth, she would never sleep again, her terror at an all-time high for fear of another possible nocturnal visit.

I find Allison's number and hold the phone to my ear, telling myself I'll give it five rings. If she doesn't pick up by then, she is obviously busy and I'll have to –

'Hello?' I say breathlessly.

'Faye? Oh my God, Faye, how lovely to hear from you!' The sound of Allison's voice brings a lump to my throat. Why on earth did we ever grow apart? How and why did I let that happen?

'Allison, how are you?' I say through a fog of unshed tears.

'I'm fine, just fine. Ticking along nicely, as they say. More to the point, how are you?' she replies, her infectious tone catching me off guard and hitting me in my solar plexus. How could I have forgotten how lovely and natural Allison is? The sound of her voice makes me tingle with delight, her innate goodness spreading over me like warm syrup.

'Me?' I reply lightly, wondering where on earth I would start if I were to tell her the truth, to inform her of the wreckage that has been the past year of our lives. 'I'm fine as well,' I say as nonchalantly as I can, the lie tripping off my tongue with such ease, it scares me.

'When's the book going to be finished?' she asks with an excited squeak.

'First one is finished and due for publication the beginning of next year.' I swallow, feeling silly and somewhat arrogant. Allison has had a novel on the go for the past few years and has had more rejections than most. The last thing I want is to appear egotistical when I know she is desperate to see hers in print.

'No way!' she half shrieks and I could almost weep at the fact she is excited for me. Many in her position wouldn't be. 'That is so amazing. Let me know the publication date as soon as you can and I'll order my copy.'

We chat for a few minutes about work, our children, schools, until I tentatively ask about colleagues and how everyone is doing.

'Brett got the boot. Long overdue if you ask me,' she says in a drawl, 'and Barbara retired. You remember Barbara from accounts?'

I do remember Barbara very well; she was a caustic bombastic woman who loathed anybody under the age of forty, anybody who was lithe or fit or remotely pretty, or basically anyone who was happy with their lot in life. Jealousy oozed out of her every pore. I had heard she was once engaged to a man who left her for another woman. She never got over it and blamed the world in general for the hand that life dealt her. I doubt she will be missed.

I steel myself and pose the question I would rather not be asking, frightened of the answer I may get. 'What about Jeff?' I enquire, my voice croaky with apprehension. 'What's he up to these days?'

Her reply makes my legs go weak. 'Jeff? Oh God, didn't you hear?' she says in no more than a whisper as if somebody is listening in. 'He did a disappearing act. Went AWOL for a couple of weeks. It was after you left. He was found by the police sleeping rough under the railway bridge a few miles away from his house. All that time his mother had been worried sick, thinking she would never see him again and there he was, close by, living on the streets. He was admitted to hospital after threatening to kill himself. He's still there now, although I have heard he's responding to therapy and making progress. Poor man,' she says in a whisper. 'I mean, he was a bit creepy and everything, but nobody deserves to go through anything like that, do they?'

I feel as if I've swallowed a brick and it's lodged in my gullet, stopping me from speaking properly. Even breathing hurts.

'Weren't you friendly with him at one point?' Allison asks, the innocence in her voice so evident, so obvious, it cuts through me.

'Kind of,' I reply, trying to sound dismissive when I feel as if the earth has shifted off its axis and we are all spinning wildly into oblivion. Jeff is in hospital. Not here. Not stalking me. He is in hospital, probably unable to leave of his own accord.

'I haven't seen him for some time now though. I hope he recovers.' I have no idea how I find the strength to speak. My head feels fit to burst.

'We need to meet for lunch, Faye. There's so much to catch up on.'

I do my best to be attentive, to listen to Allison as she ponders over a suitable date and place for us to eat but my mind is focused on other things. I can't concentrate or hear anything she is saying and have to ask her to text me the venue and time, assuring her I'll be there. By the time I hang up, I can hardly think straight. Jeff is in hospital, not here in this house following me, planning another attack. I'm not sure whether to feel elated or terrified. I have just eliminated the two obvious people who would go to such lengths to break in and frighten me and I now have no idea what to think.

The rest of the day is spent wandering around in a bit of a daze, my mind too tight with fear to focus on anything. The most productive thing I manage to do is make sure the children's uniforms are clean and ironed, ready for tomorrow. Anything else is beyond me.

By the time darkness falls, I have convinced myself it was all in my imagination. Maybe I am actually going mad? Using every rational part of my brain to think it through logically, I feel sure the sounds I heard were a manifestation of my innate fears. Couple that with the move here to Cross House and add a healthy dose of exhaustion and it could easily explain everything. I force myself to think that because, with Todd and Jeff out of the picture, there is no other explanation. I need something concrete to cling on to and right now I have nothing. If I allow myself to think otherwise, to even consider the fact that there is a stranger walking around our house at night, I just know I'll end up making myself ill, unable to sleep or eat. Back to how I was last year. Back to existing in a state of fear and confusion.

***

Bath time is a noisy affair. Poppy shrieks and giggles as Hugh covers her in bubbles and gives her a white foam beard. I pretend to be busy making notes about my current manuscript when in reality I am still thinking about Todd and Jeff and how they have suddenly disappeared from our lives after being such a heavy presence. The pair of them were buried under my skin for so long and now even though they're completely out of our lives, they still manage to infiltrate my every waking thought.

Once we get settled and I can see some signs of progress in this place, I'll show Hugh the video that Todd sent. Apart from our conversation earlier, we don't speak of him that much, but I know he still preys on Hugh's mind. He deserves to know that Todd has finally got himself sorted out. Perhaps underneath it all, Todd is a decent sort of guy. People do terrible things once addiction takes over their lives. I just hope he doesn't lapse and revert back to how he was. Funny thing is, apart from our brief telephone conversation, I've never met the real Todd, the drug-free Todd. I have no idea who he is, what he enjoys doing, what his interests are, who any of his friends are. He is a stranger to me. All I remember is the violence he meted out and the fear I felt when he was around. I don't think that will ever leave me. No matter how pleasant he seems at the minute, I know he has it in him to be a monster. Somewhere deep inside him lurks darkness and destruction. All the drugs and drink did was unlock it and let it all bubble to the surface.

I eventually scribble down a few ideas for the next chapter of my novel and throw my notebook down in frustration. Tomorrow I'll make a clean start. No Jeff, no Todd, just me and my family and this rambling old house. I will stop looking over my shoulder for shadows and non-existent entities, and tonight I will sleep next to my husband, undisturbed, without any fear.

There is nobody around who can hurt me. Those times are behind me. I say it over and over in my head. Our enemies are either locked up in a secure hospital or thousands of miles away. All I have is my fear; that's what is driving me, holding me hostage.

Did I imagine that presence in the bedroom? Part of me wants to think I did. That would make life a whole lot easier. I refuse to delve too deeply into any alternative arguments. Therein lies the road to madness. Today helped me work out where the people are who made our lives miserable for such a long time. They can't get to me. At long last I am free of them. At long last I can sleep easy at night.

Twelve

I am awake and my heart is pounding. Damn Hugh and his ability to sleep so soundly. If only I could do the same. If only I could switch off to everything and everyone; to the creaks and groans that fill this house at night. Then I wouldn't be lying here, my chest heaving, and my ears once again attuned to the noise that seems to boom around me, exacerbated and heightened by my terror and grogginess.

The sound of my own ragged breathing feels too loud, as if I'm drawing attention to my very existence in the room. I move my arm as slowly and quietly as I can and drape it across Hugh's chest in the hope it disturbs him. I want him to be roused enough so he can hear what I'm hearing. Then he would have no choice but to believe me. Then I wouldn't feel so terrified and alone.

And to think I came to bed in a positive frame of mind, having forced myself to believe that it was all in my imagination, and now here I am, alert and fully aware of everything that is going on around me. I wish I wasn't. I wish to hell I were elsewhere – anywhere but here in this house. I know now that I am definitely not imagining things. I know that I am not going mad; I am not mentally out of kilter or having a breakdown. I know all of these things because at this very minute, there is somebody here with us in this room.

Hugh doesn't stir. I want to rock him, to shake him into wakefulness, to scream at him that somebody has just walked past us and onto the landing, but I'm terrified of the figure noticing us and doing something unspeakable. This time, I saw something. It's too dark to see real features, but in the blackness, I saw a shape, a faint silhouette as it slowly shifted past our bed.

I could jump up and turn the light on; I could scream at whatever, or whoever, it is to leave us alone and get out of our house, but my stomach is in knots, my head is buzzing with terror and I truly fear what will happen if I were to do such a thing. I have no idea who I will be faced with and what their reaction will be. For all I know they could be armed to the teeth or high on drugs. A whole host of possible terrifying scenarios run through my mind but I don't get up. I'm not taking any risks. Instead I tap my fingers against Hugh's chest, drumming them lightly on his in the vain hope of waking him. No movement. His breathing is a shallow rasp. I increase my force and begin to push at his shoulder, hoping he rouses. Letting out a small splutter, he turns away from me, rests on his side and lets out a deep, rumbling snore. My entire body shakes as I press the heel of my hands into my eyes and suppress a small sob. Undiluted fear howls at my brain. With more force than I intend, I reach my leg out and push Hugh until his body budges into another position close to the edge of the bed. He lets out a small grunt of protest and I seize the moment to wake him.

'Hugh!' My voice is an urgent hiss as I lean over him, my mouth close to his ear. 'You need to wake up!'

'Fuck sake, Faye!' His words are slurred and he flails about as I tug at his arm and shake him. I quickly turn the bedside lamp on. Light floods the room, blinding us. Shielding my eyes, I sit up in bed and push at the small of his back with my cold bony fingers.

'There was somebody in the bedroom with us. Hugh, you need to get up and check on the kids! Somebody's out there on the landing prowling around.'

Before he can turn on me, yelling that I'm dreaming or losing my mind, I jump out of bed and pull on my dressing gown, putting my finger to my lips to silence him. It was only seconds ago that the shadow passed me. They can't have gone far. I wait for Hugh to follow me, gesticulating that he needs to get up and get out there. His nightclothes are askew and his skin is pale at being woken so abruptly. He staggers out of bed, his feet hitting the floor with a thud. I grit my teeth and close my eyes to blink away my irritation. Whoever is out there now has had a warning that we're onto them and will be making a rapid getaway. Either that or getting a weapon ready to defend themselves. I swallow down my fear and annoyance. I refuse to entertain such thoughts.

'I can't believe I'm actually doing this,' Hugh says wearily as we trudge out onto the large gallery landing. I ignore his words and slap at the wall to hit the lights. I want to scream and curse out loud when I find the place empty.

'Check the other rooms!' My voice is laced with desperation. I know what I saw. I also know what I heard and no matter how much Hugh tries to convince me otherwise, no matter how much I convince myself, I know for certain that there is another person here with us in Cross House.

I watch Hugh drag himself off into each of the bedrooms, his eyes bleary, his hair sticking up at divergent angles. Were it not for the fact this is deadly serious, it would be a comical sight. I don't laugh or smile. I cannot, for the life of me, see any humour in this. I need to find this person, this being, before Hugh becomes convinced I am losing the plot.

He emerges from each room shaking his head, anger building in his expression. I silently seethe. There is no way I am about to let this go. Turning away from him, I race downstairs and flick on every light, open every door, fear and anger pushing me on, electricity coursing through my veins. Again, the place is empty. A small knocking sensation builds in my temples. I rub at my face and briefly close my eyes. When I open them again Aiden is standing next to me, sleep blanketing him. His eyes droop and his skin has a grey pallor to it. 'Mum, what are you doing?'

'Nothing, sweetheart. Just getting a glass of water. Come on,' I say softly, 'let's go back to bed.'

Aiden lets me lead him by the hand, back upstairs. He climbs into his crumpled sheets and I take a certain amount of joy in tucking him in. It's not often my prepubescent son lets me get this close now he's turning into a young man, so I savour the moment, breathing in the heady scent of him and stroking his hair until he grows quiet and drifts off into a deep sleep.

When I get back into our bedroom Hugh is waiting for me, just as I knew he would be. I can't work out what his tactic is going to be, whether he's going to be angry at me or whether he is going to treat me as if I'm a porcelain doll; a fragile and delicate entity who needs to be handled with great care for fear of breaking into a thousand tiny pieces. Turns out it's a mixture of both.

'Right, I'm going to be blunt here, Faye,' he says quietly, his eyes dark with thinly disguised anger. 'You're losing it again and I'm not about to sit around and watch your mental health deteriorate. You're scaring the kids, for God's sake! This is the last time we'll ever speak of you seeing or hearing somebody walking about this house at night. There is nobody here. Nobody. Okay?'

He watches me, waiting for a response. I nod meekly, not wanting to get into an argument with him in the early hours. Maybe he's right. If there was somebody here, where have they gone to? My mind feels as if it's splintering, fragmenting into thousands of tiny pieces and stopping me from thinking straight.

'We all need to be up in the morning, but tomorrow, you and I will have a long talk about what's going on with you. You've taken a step back since moving here and I don't like it. Not one little bit. The idea was, we moved house and left all that shit behind us, yet you seem hell bent on continuing it.' He rubs his fingers through his hair. 'Bur right now, we all need to get some shuteye, so turn the light off and let me bloody well sleep.'

Within seconds Hugh is snoring loudly, his body a deadweight next to mine. I am completely still, my skin burning, my veins throbbing with anger and dread. Did I imagine it all? I can't seem to think straight. I hoped Hugh would help me. The least he could have done was hear me out. He didn't. He chose to bat me away like an irritating insect. I always knew it would come to this. There was no way I could have avoided it if I'm being truthful. It doesn't matter what the issue is; if Hugh can't see that there's a problem, then it will always come back to me and my breakdown. How long is this thing going to hang over me? I had every good reason to suffer because of Todd and Jeff, yet Hugh now seems determined to throw it back in my face every time I show concern or fear over any bloody thing. It simply isn't fair, but I must go along with what he says, or I come across as being even more unbalanced. He is watching and waiting for me to unravel. From here on in, it is going to be Hugh's way or no way.

I sleep fitfully, the snatches of sleep I get punctuated with nightmares about prowlers and ghosts roaming around the house, their faces contorted with fury and rage, their intent obvious as they chase me from room to room, calling out my name.

The sheets are damp with perspiration when I wake the next morning. I'm up before the alarm goes off and showered and dressed by the time Hugh eventually opens his eyes and sits up in bed with a bewildered expression on his face. I've thought long and hard about this while I stared at the bedroom ceiling and listened to Hugh snoring beside me. I may have had problems in the past but I'm over them now. I decided whilst showering that I will play his little game. I will be the simpering dependent wife he wants me to be while he is watching me, and when I am alone, I will carry out my own investigative work, scouring every inch of this house for the person who haunts us at night. I will find our nocturnal intruder without Hugh's help. This is something I am more than capable of sorting on my own. I am not an idiot; I am not losing my mind. I know what I saw, and I know what I heard, and if Hugh has a problem with that, then he can go to hell because I am not giving up on this one.

'Coffee?' I ask as brightly as I can without appearing too light-hearted. It's a hard balancing act, this having to appear normal whilst being something entirely different underneath. Yet a part of me feels empowered by it, like I'm taking back control of my life, of my sanity. I'm doing something positive instead of being the victim, and it feels rather good.

'Please,' Hugh says. His eyes follow me around the room. There is an edge to his voice. I should have expected this. His forgiveness for last night may take some time. Hugh treasures his sleep and is like a grumpy child if roused from it. I am not, however, prepared for what he says next.

'I'm going to give Doctor Schilling a call today and get you an appointment. I think maybe we need to get you back there, don't you think?'

My head hurts. I want to scream at him that I'm not unstable or unhinged, that I am not having another breakdown or suffering some sort of mental relapse, but I also know that my protests will be taken as a sign I am indeed suffering some kind of psychological decline, so I remain silent and as calm as I can and stare at Hugh, hoping he sees my frozen expression as a sign I am anything but mad. I refuse to answer his question. It was purely rhetorical anyway and his decision about my mental health needs has already been made. Instead, I turn my back on him and go downstairs where I fill the kettle with trembling hands, a hot sphere of anger and fury building in me. I fight to control it and have to use every ounce of strength I have to be pleasant to him when he finally makes an appearance in the kitchen.

'I've woken the kids. Poppy's just getting dressed and Aiden reckons he'll be up in a few minutes. Said he's exhausted after last night's carry on.'

This is complete nonsense. We both know it, but Hugh has decided to lay it on thick to prove a point; the point being that I am psychotic and in need of medical assistance. Aiden went straight back off to sleep in seconds. We've had way more disturbed times with Poppy's night terrors and Aiden's refusal to put his games console down than last night's event, but Hugh is going down this route to cement the idea in his head that I am on a downward spiral again.

'I'll put some toast on. Coffee won't be long.' My voice feels detached, as if it's coming from somebody else. I swallow and cough to clear the bubble of air that is wedged in my throat.

Behind me, I hear Hugh sigh. I don't want to hear what it is he has to say. He is so sure he can see inside my head, see my every thought and fear. He can't. I am different now. He has absolutely no idea of how I think, of the sort of opinions and sentiments and ideas that fill my head on a daily basis. He thinks he does, but he's wrong.

If I'm being honest, he doesn't really know me at all and perhaps he never has. Perhaps our marriage has always been one big charade. I shiver and block that thought out.

The silence seems to stretch on and on, but then just as Hugh starts to speak, Aiden and Poppy burst into the kitchen with their usual gusto and energy. I push a plate of toast into the middle of the table and hand Hugh his cup of coffee. He takes it gingerly, eyeing me with more than a touch of caution. It's rather amusing, seeing him trying to assess me, making sure I don't tip over that invisible, intangible edge. It's a difficult juggling act for him too – keeping an eye on his feeble-minded wife, gently dancing around me, whilst also keeping me in line when my ideas get too wild and my behaviour too peculiar. I am his overly sensitive wife, easily broken, often nebulous and in need of constant care. Except, of course, I am none of those things. I am completely in control and somehow, I will prove it to him. I know what I saw and I know what I heard and none of it is in my imagination. It's real. To think I even doubted myself. I almost laugh out loud. No more, however. No more.

We eat as though last night never happened, Hugh laughing at Aiden's awkward attempts at adult humour and Poppy declaring she needs her own phone now we live in such a large house. Hugh tells her she isn't the lady of the manor which Aiden finds hilarious. I fuss around the table, dishing out waffles and scrambled egg then clearing up once everyone has eaten. It keeps me busy and stops anybody from discussing what took place last night. It stops me from screaming at my husband that he should be supporting me not trying to fucking well section me.

I'm not surprised at Hugh's offer to drive the kids to school. After all, I'm in the middle of a major meltdown. I can't be trusted to get behind the wheel and escort my own children to school anymore. He's going to see a customer afterwards and won't be back until lunchtime. This fills me with relief. Funny how just a short while ago, I couldn't wait for Hugh to return home from business meetings and now I can't wait for him to leave. His absence will give me a few hours on my own to think things through, a few hours to begin scouring this big old house, a few hours looking for clues as to who the fuck it was that crept past my bed in the early hours of the morning.

Thirteen

Hugh is as good as his word. He makes an appearance at midday just as I'm rummaging through wardrobes, stacking up more old diaries that I found hidden at the back under a pile of old blankets. The low purr of his engine causes me to stop. I listen to the crunch of gravel as his car pulls up on the driveway and quickly stash the recently found journals in a nearby box which I place at my feet. I'll read them later at my leisure, see if I can get a picture of the people who lived here, see if I can get an idea of this house's history.

Brushing my hands down the sides of my jeans to clear the dust off my palms, I stare outside at the snowstorm of white birch blossom that swirls idly around, littering the pavements and lawns with its small circular leaves, leaving the village looking like confetti has been thrown far and wide. If Hugh becomes overbearing with his talk of doctors and my 'issues', I may take a walk around the local area, become acquainted with its routes and, if I get lucky, some of the people who live here. We've yet to meet any of the neighbours and right now, a friendly face would be most welcome.

I listen to the turn of his key in the door and the brush of his shoes on the old, coconut doormat that has seen better days. I don't rush down to meet him as I used to when we lived at the old house. This is a big place and I have plenty to keep me occupied. Greeting my husband isn't top of my priorities at the moment. A bit of distance between us might be a good thing. I didn't expect Hugh to try to help me with what I heard last night, but neither did I expect him to recommend a doctor. My doctor. The same person who helped me last time I struggled to cope. Struggled to cope. I have a plethora of euphemisms at the ready to explain away my madness, my breakdown, my few months of borderline psychosis. Call it what you will. I ended up seeing a therapist and taking medication to help me crawl out of that fearful dark hole and back into the light again.

I'm busy pushing the bed hard up against the wall after deciding I didn't like where it was, when the silhouette of Hugh's tall frame fills the doorway.

'I've made you a cup of tea,' he says lightly, as if last night was an illusion, as if the words he said that cut into me have never been uttered. I suddenly feel angry; he used me seeing Doctor Schilling as a threat, something he could say to make me snap to attention, to stop me coming out with things that he doesn't like to hear or things he doesn't agree with.

'Thanks,' I croak, my throat suddenly tight with resentment. I don't turn around, but instead take the tea he has placed on the floor and sip at it, steam billowing up and curling in front of my face in wispy ethereal trails. I hold my breath, hoping he takes the hint and leaves. He doesn't. The bed squeaks in protest as he sits on it. I hear the rustle of fabric as he makes himself comfortable and feel my stomach sink. I don't want to talk to him or even look at him. Right now, I don't even like him.

He used my weak spot, insinuated I was mentally ill and brought up my past without any thought for how that would affect me and make me feel.

'You look like you've been busy.' His voice is a thin scratch in the forced silence between us.

I instinctively place my hand on the box of diaries. This is something I found and no matter how hard he tries to control me, I will not let Hugh take them from me. Not that he even knows of their existence, but if he were to find out, he would accuse me of obsessing and tell me such things are bad for my health. He would say it isn't healthy to dwell over events that went before, things that have happened that I can't change.

'Kind of,' I say quietly, trying not to sound angry and resentful when that is exactly how I am feeling. 'I'll be here a while. I'm just going to start clearing out some of the old items they left behind. I'm going to make the place fairly presentable, ready for the electricians and decorators coming.'

'Do you want me to give you a hand?'

My breath stops in my chest. That is absolutely the last thing I want him to do. Hugh will find things he deems to be of no value and throw them in the bin whereas I want to keep them, read through them, immerse myself in the lives of the previous owners. I want to find some sort of thread that will connect me to what is going on in this house, because while Hugh has been out this morning, while I have been taking my time and sifting through more newspaper clippings and journals, I have given a great deal of thought to everything that has happened since we moved in here and I have a theory. I am not, however, about to share it with Hugh. My words would only add fuel to his already raging fire and give credence to the idea he has that I'm in the throes of a complete nervous breakdown. Which I am not.

'I'm fine here, thanks. There's no rush. Thanks for taking the kids, by the way.' I almost add an apology for last night in a bid to smooth things out between us, but the words refuse to come. I have nothing to be sorry for. I just don't like the frosty atmosphere that has suddenly settled on us. We've endured enough worry and misery to see us through to the next decade, we don't need any more. But I am not about to act shamefaced and contrite for something I didn't do, or more precisely for something I know I saw and heard. Soon Hugh will hear it too and when he does, I will be all ears, listening out for his apology for not believing me and thinking I'm on a downhill slope into that lonely, desolate place; the place that I never want to return to. My anger simmers as I wait for his reply.

He mumbles that it's not a problem. I am so tempted to stride over there and place my arms around him, to rid us of this awful feeling, but my stubborn streak stops me. Why should I make the first move? It's Hugh who should be apologising to me for his harsh treatment of me.

He doesn't move. He wants to say something, I can sense it, but instead he sits for a few seconds before getting up, telling me in a hoarse voice that he'll be up in the study if I need anything. I don't reply. I have nothing to say to him at the minute.

The tense atmosphere lightens the minute he leaves. I let out a shaky breath and reach down for the box that contains the diaries. With Hugh working from home, the time I have to read them is going to be limited. I need to grab every available second. Fumbling to open the flaps on the box, I clumsily pull out a small notebook and scan it. It's different from the one I found when we first moved in last week. The other one was a leather-bound book, a proper diary. This is more of a jotter; a child's ramblings. Without a shred of guilt, I open it and begin to read.

It's worse than I thought. He's actually coming to live with us. Mum's right. He doesn't belong here. He's really weird. I hope he doesn't think I'm gonna speak to him cos it's not going to happen. I hate him. I hate his stupid card tricks and I hate him. Dad says I have to be nice and get to know him properly. I just smiled when he said that. Dad doesn't really know me that well, does he? Dad also hasn't seen him do what I've seen him do. If he had, then maybe he wouldn't be so keen to let him live in our house.

I stop reading, my heart breaking for this poor boy, whoever he is. Hatred drips from every sentence of this person's thoughts. I scramble around, looking for the adult's diary. There was mention of a girl in there. I wonder if this is the other girl, if it's her words in this journal. I'm pretty sure her name was Tammy. I can't immediately lay my hands on it so instead I flick through this book, looking for some identification as to the writer of such vitriol.

It doesn't take long. On the back page is a wall of scribbles and graffiti with the name Tammy at the centre of it. Surrounding the name is a series of intricately drawn hearts and childish phrases, one of them declaring her love for a pop star whose name I don't recognise.

I quickly flick through each of the books. Most of the pages are dedications to pop stars and bands of the day – David Soul, Suzi

Quatro, Abba, they all get a mention, as well as The Bee Gees and Blondie. I smile despite feeling unnerved by the level of malice in her words. Over half of one the books is filled with song lyrics and one of the others has been used as a scrapbook with clippings from girls' magazines about the latest fashion and what colour nail varnish a young girl should wear to attract boys. Just as I begin to get irritated at the lack of information, I turn a page and see more writing, more of this girl's thoughts poured onto paper. I sit back and begin to read.

Mum said I can definitely go! My first proper party and I am so excited I can hardly sleep. Abigail's parents are so trendy and fashionable. They might even let us drink! Abigail reckons she's allowed Babycham and her mum once gave her a glass of wine. There is no way mum and dad would let me ever drink alcohol until I'm 18. I need to work out what I'm going to wear. My clothes are so boring. If I ask daddy nicely he might give me some money to get the cheesecloth shirt I saw last week in town. Or I could try on that green trouser suit I really like. Mum says I can wrap him round my little finger.

The tone is lighter on this page. No scathing comments about the boy and how much she loathes him. I continue to flick through; most of it is about fashions of the day and the latest music releases, plus teenage jottings and drawings of love hearts and other such childish scribbles. Only one paragraph catches my attention and sends a chill through me.

I'm going to tell them about him and what he does to me. It's the only way I can think of to get him out of here. Everything is spoilt now. Mum will believe me. Not sure about daddy but mum will see my side and know what I'm talking about. She always does. I've been thinking about it for ages and I know exactly what it is I'm going to say.

Something about those words makes me feel slightly off balance, though I can't quite work out what it is. I turn the page only to find the rest of the diary has been torn out. A yellowing stub at the spine is all that remains of this girl's story.

Feeling out of sorts, I place the books back in the box and stare outside. The village is empty save for a smattering of dog walkers on the village green who are heading out towards the opposite end of the village. I decide to go for a stroll. The weather is fine and I need to clear my head.

Without disturbing Hugh or even bothering to tell him where I'm going, I pull on a fleece and my suede ankle boots and step out into the soft spring air.

Fourteen

The breeze is warm and welcoming as I head over the village green where a couple of benches look clean enough to sit on. The pavement is covered in bird shit from the pigeons that sit in the overhanging branches of a huge nearby sycamore tree, but the benches have somehow managed to escape being splattered with the streaks of black and white bird crap that cover the path.

The dog walkers have disappeared from view and the village is all but empty. One old lady, bent with age, stands at her garden gate and watches me as I pull off my fleece and perch on the edge of the wooden seat. I turn and smile at her. She lifts a frail-looking hand and gives me a curt wave before nodding her head and walking back up the path to her front door. I keep my gaze fixed on her, fascinated by how quickly she moves for somebody who appears to be crippled with arthritis. Only when she gets to the door does she turn again, her white hair shimmering in the glare of the sunlight. I see her mouth break into a slight smile and I quickly return her gesture. I want to be a part of this community, to get to know everybody and work out what their stories are, and if anybody knows anything about Cross House, this lady is very probably the one to go to for answers. I'm assuming she has lived here for many years; long enough to tell me what it is I want to know. I have no way of knowing this, but something about her scrutinizing gaze and the way she was standing watching the world go by gives me the impression she is the hub of this neighbourhood, the distributor of wise words and sage advice. I feel certain she can help me unlock Cross House's secrets.

Out of nowhere, a young mother appears, pushing a toddler in a fancy buggy that looks as if cost as much as an average starter home. She leans down and hands him a bag of sweeties which he delves into with so much enthusiasm they spill out onto his lap. He grabs at them and shovels them in his mouth, small pockets of cream-coloured foam gathering in the corners of his wet lips.

I make a point of giving him a wave and saying a small, non-threatening hello. To my surprise and mild delight, the mother sits down next to me on the bench and retrieves a wet wipe from her handbag. She proceeds to dab around the child's mouth with supreme precision, removing all traces of sugary residue from his face.

'You're new here,' she says quietly as she leans back up and looks into my face, her gaze still and ever so slightly off-putting. Her eyes are the clearest shade of blue and so piercing, I feel sure they could cut glass.

'Yes,' I reply, my voice wavering slightly. 'We've just moved into Cross House, the old, ramshackle –'

'Oh, I know which one Cross House is,' she answers, her tone suddenly stiff and unfriendly.

'I'm Faye.' I hold out my hand for her to shake. I wonder if I've said something wrong and have visions of her standing up abruptly and walking away.

Her tone softens and she reaches out and shakes my hand. 'Sorry, it's been a long week and I've been up all night with this little blighter. He's an absolute sod sometimes and just won't sleep. I think we eventually got off at about three o' clock and then Jonathan, my husband, got up at six for work which woke us all up again.'

I feel like hugging her to convey my sympathy. Aiden refused to sleep and I spent many a long evening pacing the living room with him slung over my shoulder, singing, rocking, doing anything I could think of to get him off to sleep. Nothing worked. He eventually started sleeping once he started school. It gave him structure, got his body clock regulated and put him in sync with the rest of us. I decide to remain silent. A week of sleep deprivation is an awful thing and being told it may go on for years only compounds the problem. Instead, I pat her hand and tell her she looks fabulous despite feeling exhausted. A small platitude I know, but I remember from bitter experience that even the tiniest of words can have a massive effect.

'Thanks,' she says weakly. 'I work shifts at Millview Care Home as well so it's all a bit tricky really.'

'It will get better,' I tell her, hoping she doesn't ask when. The truth is often difficult to take when you're running on empty.

I am about to ask her how she knows about Cross House when the little one lets out an ear-splitting shriek, stopping our conversation and making the hairs on the back of my neck stand on end.

'Sorry,' she says sheepishly as she stands up and begins to walk away. 'Now he's tired. Not at midnight or one in the morning but now, when everyone else is awake.'

'You should get a nap while he does,' I suggest, knowing from past experience that housework will get in the way of any daytime sleeps. I always had an internal battle going on when Aiden was little like this tiny chap – get some sleep or get the ironing done? The ironing almost always won.

I watch her walk away, desperately trying to shush the little one as she pushes him along the path and out of sight. It's only when she finally disappears that I realise I didn't get her name. I sit and wonder where she lives. Did I detect a frosty tone in her voice when I mentioned Cross House or was it because she was genuinely tired? I hope I meet her again. I could do with a friend, somebody who lives locally, somebody that I could chat to.

I continue to sit for a while, my thoughts blank. A sliver of sun appears through a crack in the clouds, pouring heat down on the back of my neck. I look up and close my eyes, enjoying the spreading warmth that gradually covers my face. When I open them again, I discover I am not the only one in the village. On the green is a young couple, walking arm in arm, and behind them is an elderly looking man. The couple are decked out ready to go walking. They're carrying backpacks and are dressed for any eventuality, with heavy sweaters slung around their middles and drinks bottles attached to their waistbands. On their feet they are wearing solid boots that probably cost a small fortune. Their determined expressions and body language suggest they're seasoned walkers.

The elderly man behind them is a different matter entirely. He stumbles along, his body bent painfully at an awkward angle. His arms hang loosely at his sides and he looks decidedly exhausted. It's only as he approaches that I see he isn't actually that old, probably approaching his mid-fifties. From a distance he appeared much older. Time obviously hasn't been kind to him. He has the gait of a ninety-year-old. I think about heading over to him and helping him onto a seat but something tells me he wouldn't appreciate my intervention. His eyes have a slightly glazed expression to them and he seems preoccupied, his mind definitely elsewhere. I watch as he walks straight past me, barely noticing my presence.

The walking couple stop for a drink next to where I'm sitting, their chatter directed at each other, not giving me a second glance or even seeming to see me at all. Just as I'm beginning to feel invisible, a voice comes from behind me.

'Have you settled in then?'

I swing around to see the old lady back at the gate. The top half of her body is thrust forward as she leans on the white picket fence, watching me intently.

'Yes, I guess so,' I say uncertainly. 'It'll take a while. There's lots that needs to be done. So much work.' My voice drifts off at the thought of it.

She nods and smiles and I find myself warming to her. She has a kind face; gentle eyes. Her house is a small cottage, quintessentially English and so chocolate-box pretty it looks almost too good to be true. It has small Georgian-style windows, ivy and climbing roses snaking up the whitewashed walls and a gravel path leading up to the front door.

'I'm Gwen,' she says, nodding behind her, 'and I'm just about to put the kettle on if you fancy a cup of tea?'

I all but jump up off the bench and make my way over to her gate before she has finished speaking. This is exactly what I need. It's what I want to do: to become acquainted with the locals and find out as much as I can about our new home. I also love tea and if I'm being perfectly honest, I'm feeling rather lonely. Hugh's sharp words are still cutting into me, making me feel slightly sick.

The inside of her little home is exactly as I expected it to be. Each room is dark with heavily pattered wallpaper and thick brocade curtains that block out almost all the light. She leads me past a small parlour and into the living room where I sit on an old-fashioned armchair reminiscent of the type my gran used to have when I was a child.

'I'm Faye by the way,' I shout after her as she shuffles through to the kitchen and turns on the tap. A gush of water hits metal and I listen to the scrapes and grating sounds of an old lady busying herself in her tiny kitchen. I'll bet she has an old-fashioned caddy and china cups with saucers plus a crocheted cosy for the pot. The idea both entertains and comforts me and I have no idea why.

The high-pitched whistle of the kettle pierces the momentary lull. There is a faint glug and a rattle and in a matter of seconds, Gwen comes shuffling back inside carrying a small tray with two cups of amber-coloured tea and a plate of arrowroot biscuits. The whole thing is both surreal and perfect at the same time.

She hands me my saucer and I take it, thanking her whilst refusing a biscuit. I watch as she nibbles at hers and gently sips at her tea like a tiny ancient bird.

'Do you know much about Cross House, Gwen?' I decide to completely dispense with formalities and get straight to the point. I have questions that I would like answering, a need for information that is gnawing at me daily, and Gwen may well be the lady who can help me.

Her reaction is not one of surprise but more of acceptance, as if she's been expecting me to ask. She raises her eyebrows slightly and takes another sip of her tea before placing it on a small mahogany table next to her chair. It wobbles precariously before coming to a standstill.

'I've lived here for over fifty years, my dear. I know just about everyone in the village; not all of the young ones who've recently moved in, I grant you, but I know all about their houses and who lived there before them.' She takes a handkerchief and rubs her face with it, brushing away the rheumy film that has gathered at the corners of her eyes and dabbing lightly at her nose. 'So, what is it you want to know?'

All of a sudden, the words won't come. There are so many questions I have to ask, so much curiosity and worry bubbling up inside me, and now I have the chance to air it, I'm not sure where to start. I think of the newspaper clipping and decide that is as good a place as any.

'What happened to Adrian Wentworth?' I ask. I decide to start at the edge of the story, not rush in with Hilary's name. I skirt around the article about the woman who toppled to her death down my stairs and sneak in with questions about her late husband, the wealthy businessman. Who was he and how did he die? I want to know it all but use a softly, softly approach. I can't risk coming across as too pushy.

Gwen shakes her head and I watch as a rapid sadness seems to sweep over her, making her lip tremble. She lowers her eyes and blinks over and over. I am just beginning to wish I hadn't asked when she speaks, her voice now tinged with unhappiness.

'Adrian was a lovely man, a real family man. It was such a terrible tragedy. The whole thing was a horrible ghastly mess.'

I wait, a breath suspended in my chest, desperate to know what this ghastly mess entailed, but she doesn't continue. Her mind appears to have wandered off to another time, a different era, perhaps back to when it all happened. She gazes out of the window as if I'm no longer in the room. How I would love to climb inside her head, see what she saw, get to know all the secrets of this village, all the secrets of Cross House.

'I found an old newspaper clipping about Mrs Wentworth,' I say quietly, afraid of tipping the balance the wrong way. There is a sudden tension in the air, a brittle mood of disquiet that feels ready to shatter any second.

Gwen's eyes narrow as she turns back around to face me. Thin kinked lines stretch out from the corner of her mouth as she speaks. Her expression gives nothing away but her voice is as taut as a bowstring when she speaks. 'The fall? Yes, I remember that as well. Everyone presumed she threw herself down those stairs after Adrian's death. Said she was too distressed to go on.'

'But you don't think that was the case?' I interject. This lady knows things, I can feel it. She has all the answers. Everything I want to know about that house is here, stored inside her head.

She shrugs her shoulders and juts out her bottom lip, the film on her yellowing eyes making me wonder how clear her vision is. 'Let's just say that Mrs Wentworth wasn't the type of lady to grieve for too long.'

'So, what do you think happened then, Gwen?' I blink and suppress a shiver. Time seems to slow down while I wait for her reply. The air feels thick like molasses. I struggle to inhale, my mouth trembling as I suck in more oxygen.

'What do I think?' she says nonchalantly as if we're talking about the weather or an episode of *EastEnders* and not the deaths of two people. Two people who once lived in my house. 'I think she slipped. I don't think there was any real drama about it. People tried to paint her as the grieving widow, somebody who couldn't continue living without her beloved husband, but I think they were all wrong. I think in her condition, she probably just stumbled and fell down those stairs.'

'Her condition?' It had never occurred to me that there could be something else amiss, some disability or medical complaint that made her more susceptible to being involved in some sort of accident. I, too, pictured her as falling into a swoon of despair and toppling from top to bottom, her grief for her late husband too much to bear. I check myself and suppress a half smile. It happened in 1980 not 1880. For some strange reason, the picture I have in my head is of somebody decked out like a Victorian schoolmarm, austere and drab, dressed in black and spending the rest of her days mourning her dead husband. I'll bet the real Hilary Wentworth was nothing like that at all. For all I know she could have been the life and soul of the party, although what I read in her diary gives me the impression she was not like that at all; the old-fashioned prose and style of handwriting puts me in mind of somebody stern and constantly disapproving, somebody born in the wrong era.

'Oh, she was always one for taking to her bed. I suppose her problem made it more difficult for her to cope with the minor ailments everybody else endures without complaining.' Gwen sniffs disdainfully and I find myself wanting to shout at her to hurry up and tell me what it is she knows about these people. I say nothing but am willing her to open up to me. If I'm being honest, I don't even know why I'm so drawn to their story. Had I not found the diaries and newspaper articles, none of this would be of interest to me, but I have been inadvertently pulled into their lives and feel a huge desire to piece together all the jumbled parts of it, until I have the full picture.

'What was her problem then? Was it serious?' I am already feeling sympathy for this woman; this ill lady whose body once lay sprawled and broken at the foot of my stairs.

Gwen's voice pushes through my thoughts, through the image I have in my head of Hilary Wentworth with her dead, lifeless eyes and cold bruised flesh after hitting the floor from such a great height. When she speaks, I feel my chest constrict and half splutter to catch my breath.

'Serious? Well, it was bad enough. She had chronic bronchitis so every little cough or cold just about flattened her. She used to shuffle about that house from room to room trying to clear that chest of hers. You could practically hear the rattle of her breathing from here. She spent most of her time in the back bedroom. She reckoned it was the warmest room in the house and the heat helped clear her lungs. She would sit in a rocking chair in the corner, struggling for breath. It was worse at night apparently. Lying flat choked her chest up with phlegm so she would wander about half the night gasping and grunting. Not a nice thing to have to put up with, but then she wasn't a very nice lady so I never had much sympathy for her.'

My own breathing is laboured as I listen to Gwen's words. My skin feels slack against my frame, as if it's about to melt away from my bones like hot candle wax. Suddenly, I feel a need to get out of this place. The walls are closing in on me and the room is unseasonably hot. Perspiration has coated my chest and runs down the back of my neck in tiny rivulets.

I stand up, my fingers clasped around the back of the armchair for balance. If Gwen has detected the seismic shift in my mood, she is considerate enough to not show it.

'Thank you for the tea,' I say, my voice weak and raspy, 'but I need to get back. Just remembered about an email I have to send.'

She nods, her demeanour unchanged, her expression unreadable.

All the way back home, I tell myself how stupid I'm being, that there is no such thing as spirits or ghosts, that the undead do not roam the earth thinking they are still alive, and yet I can't seem to stop shaking. It's utterly ridiculous, I know it is. My father was a scientist; he taught me and my sister all about how insignificant humans are in the grand scheme of things, how immense the universe is and how the afterlife is a man-made theory, proposed by humans to help us come to terms with the idea of death. Our minds cannot cope with the finality of our demise and therefore we have scrambled around for ways to help us continue our lives and the lives of our loved ones by inventing the idea that there is such a thing as ghosts. I know this. It's just that Gwen's words resonated so deeply with me, reminding me of our nocturnal wanderer, and she caught me off guard. I need to talk myself round, think rationally about it, then perhaps I'll be able to digest everything she told me and put it into context.

I stumble through the door, my legs still watery, and head straight upstairs to leaf through the diaries and search for any clues that might help me work out who the boy was that wasn't wanted, how Mr Wentworth died and most importantly, what the real story is behind Hilary Wentworth's untimely death.

Fifteen

'How do you feel about buying a new property?'
'Excited, terrified, overwhelmed.' My voice is tinny in the sterile environment. It bounces off the windows and bare walls like bullets hitting stone.

'You said earlier that you still often feel slightly paranoid. Can you give any reason for that?'

I didn't use the word paranoid. Or at least I don't think I did, but Doctor Schilling is being paid to label me so I will allow her this one minor indiscretion.

'Perhaps because less than a year ago, I was physically assaulted, threatened and sexually attacked?'

I don't look at her. I know she is staring at me, assessing me, trying to work out what is going on in my head, and if I meet her gaze she will use all kinds of psychologist trickery to see through my flimsy bravado, to get inside my thoughts. I don't want her there. Her presence isn't welcome. I know she is a pleasant enough lady but I'm tired of having her rake around in my head and trying to judge me on its contents. The only thing I have that's my own are my opinions and the things that float around my mind, and I will protect them fiercely. They are mine and mine alone. They don't belong to her or Hugh. They belong to me. It's not as if I even have anything to hide or anything of interest flitting through my brain, but if I open up the workings of it and let the pair of them inside, I will have nothing left that truly belongs to me anymore.

'And you still feel vulnerable? As if it could happen again?'

I see where she's heading with this one. She may be better qualified than I am but her line of questioning is painfully transparent, talking

106

to me as if I'm an errant child, an unpredictable entity who needs to be held down and controlled.

'It could happen to anybody at any time,' I say solemnly. And this is the truth. Pick up a newspaper, turn on the news on the TV or go on the Internet and you will be faced with a plethora of stories about how depraved and vicious humans can really be, turning on each other with very little or no provocation at all.

I let out a heavy sigh, not even pretending to disguise my annoyance and boredom. I'm only here because Hugh made this appointment after that day at Gwen's house when I went home in what he described as a 'complete state'. I wasn't that bad. He exaggerated my condition to justify making this consultation with a doctor who I know cannot help me. Not that I need any help. I am perfectly sane. She did help me once, but that's all behind me. I wish everybody would stop looking for fractures in my mind, splits in my thinking, so they can step in and find a cure for my purported madness.

'You look like you've seen a ghost,' Hugh had said as I made my way upstairs and slumped on the edge of the bed. His poor choice of words had exacerbated my diminishing mood and I had burst into tears, telling him I regretted buying Cross House and wanted to go back to Cambian Close. It was a momentary thing, a fleeting thought brought on by what I had heard in Gwen's living room, but he pounced on it, held it tight and used it against me, calling Doctor Schilling's office almost immediately. It was the opportunity he had been waiting for and I gave it to him willingly. My own husband turned on me when I needed him the most.

'Yes, it could,' Doctor Schilling replies, not seeming to notice my sighing or display of deep irritation. 'Do you think you're at greater risk than anybody else after what happened last time?'

'I am at greater risk.' I drum my fingers on the arm of the chair, making a plastic clattering sound in the sinister silence around us. I see what she is doing here. I felt perfectly fine when I came in and now she is edging me into a corner, using leading questions to rile me so I'll either open up and talk or have a major meltdown.

I won't be sorry to disappoint her. I may feel niggled but she will not tip me over the edge. Her words will wash over me. I refuse to let her inside my head.

'You said earlier that your stepson is out of the country. What about the other chap?'

'Jeff,' I say quickly. 'His name is Jeff and he's currently in hospital, or so I'm led to believe.'

I watch as she scribbles something down on the notepad. I don't try look at what she's writing. I'm not in the least bit interested. She has her thoughts and musings and I have mine and they will always remain separate; I'll make sure of it.

'Yet you still feel exposed, susceptible to another attack?'

I want to roll my eyes, to gnash my teeth and scream at her that I am not delusional or suffering any kind of breakdown, that I am perfectly capable of formulating rational thoughts and functioning on a day-to-day basis without my fears impinging on them in any way, shape or form. I don't. That would most definitely put me in the 'in dire need of medical assistance' category. Such an paradox, isn't it? The more you try to prove your sanity, to show the watching world that you are well balanced, the more insane you appear. The only way to show both Doctor Schilling and Hugh that I am in good mental health is to remain calm and agree with them. Protesting merely exacerbates their fears and theories and in a warped kind of way, makes Hugh feel better about everything. He doesn't want my madness rocking his world or upsetting the delicate equilibrium in his finely tuned tidy little milieu, but when it does, he likes to think he has stepped in and put everything back in place before it becomes too damaged; before I unravel completely and ruin everything we have worked hard for.

I tell her that I do sometimes feel exposed and susceptible. It's what she wants to hear and who am I to disappoint her? If she is half the expert she claims to be, she will know that I'm lying, just saying these things to placate her, but I doubt she is astute enough to pick up on it. I'm the customer. We are paying her to find a solution and she feels a need to provide one for us.

Hugh insisted we pay for a private consultation as waiting for an appointment with the NHS would take forever, and apparently, I need immediate assistance.

By the time I leave her surgery later that afternoon, I feel sure my blood pressure is as high as it's ever been. Resentment and anger build up inside me – at Doctor Schilling's patronising manner and pathetic and predictable line of questioning, at Hugh for making me go to visit her, but mostly at myself for appearing so weak and spineless that Hugh felt I needed to be seen by a psychologist who thinks she knows me, when in reality she couldn't be more of a stranger than if I had just met her in the street.

Hugh is working up in the study when I get home and Aiden and Poppy are still at school. He tried to accompany me to the surgery but I insisted I went alone. He would have tried to come in and put his point of view forward, interrupting me and not letting me talk. I told him that that wasn't the whole point of this session. Talking therapy is all about me voicing *my* inner fears and issues, I had said, and how could I really open up while he was sitting beside me listening, scrutinising my every word and movement? He eventually agreed but spent the entire evening before I went in a sullen frame of mind, like a spoilt child. His mood had improved this morning; he'd gotten up early and made breakfast, even cleaned up the kitchen afterwards and offered to drive the kids to school. If I were the lazy type, I could really milk this 'wilting, fragile flower' business and have him running about after me day and night. I won't. What would that achieve? I need to prove that I'm fit and well and the only way to do that is to keep on as I am: getting up each and every day, taking the children to school, working on my book and updating this house. No talk of ghosts or intruders however. Such words will only infuriate Hugh and in turn I will do my image as a well-balanced, stable woman untold damage.

'Faye? Is that you?'

I'm not sure who else he thinks it could be but I answer him in a cheerful manner, telling him it all went well and that I am about to start cooking for our evening meal when in reality I feel like slapping his self-satisfied little face for putting me through it, for making me visit that place again.

'I'm nearly done up here,' he shouts as he leans over the banister, his hair flopping around manically in front of his eyes, giving him the appearance of somebody who is rather scruffy and unkempt. 'I'll be down in an hour or so.'

'No rush,' I say as I drop my bag on the sofa, actually thinking he could stay up there for the next week and I wouldn't miss him.

I head into the kitchen, trying to visualise what our new units will look like. After a visit from a local company a few days back, we finally got around to ordering everything, and I can honestly say I'm looking forward to seeing these old musty museum artefacts go in a skip or on a bonfire. They are positively hideous and I'll be glad to see the back of them. Somebody must have had a good taste bypass when they chose them. I fail to see the appeal of high gloss, aubergine-coloured doors with matching purple wall tiles and contrasting yellow linoleum flooring. The whole thing gives me a headache and makes me feel even more depressed.

I spend the next hour or so preparing a casserole, losing myself in the cathartic process of chopping and peeling, and immersing myself in the smells that emanate from the pan once I set everything off to slowly cook. I do my best to block out the memory of visiting Doctor Schilling, to keep my mind clear of her clinical esoteric words and probing, pointless questions designed to snare me and label me as unhinged; a failed human being. How dare she? How dare Hugh force me to even go there?

I leave the casserole simmering while I collect the children from the sports clubs they both take part in after school, telling Hugh to keep an eye on it. He is coming downstairs as I get my jacket, ready to leave. He wraps his arms around me and I do my best to reciprocate, trying to loosen my stiff and unyielding frame. I'm still furious with him for having such little faith in me, for treating me like a child and sending me off like that. It's going to take more than any casual hug to make me forgive him.

'I'll have everything ready when you get back,' he says, his hot breath close to my neck. I nod and extricate myself from his grasp, reaching up to give him a dry peck on the cheek. I close the door behind me and wipe my mouth as I leave.

***

Hugh has admittedly made everything perfect for us. We are greeted with a set table and the heavenly smells of chicken and potato casserole when we get back. He has even gone to the effort of squeezing fresh juice and preparing a fruit fool dessert. His conscience is obviously pricking him. It'll take more than this for me to soften towards him.

Aiden hurls himself towards the table and greedily glugs down a full glass of juice while Poppy sits demurely, waiting for her meal. We eat much earlier than normal, chatting about anything and everything, our conversations chopping and changing, going in different directions every couple of minutes. I do actually love it when we're together like this, swapping stories and anecdotes, our voices and thoughts meeting and merging in a cloud of happiness and security. It makes me feel content again; secure and safe.

It doesn't last long. Aiden breaks it with his words. 'Is this house haunted?'

I don't look at Hugh but can feel a hot flush creeping up over my neck, searing my skin as it continues up to my face. He thinks I've prompted him, talked to Aiden about our nocturnal prowler. Obviously I haven't, but yet again, Hugh displays his lack of faith in me as a parent and a decent human being.

'Don't be silly,' I say dismissively. 'There's no such thing as ghosts.' I cast a quick glance at Poppy who is watching us, wide-eyed, her fork balanced in the air, piled high with chicken and vegetables. 'Anyway, how did the football trials go?' I say quickly. And it's forgotten. Just like that. As if he never spoke those words, except he did. I have no idea why he said it but later, when Poppy is in bed, I'll ask him, work out why he came out with that question. Of all the things to ask, why that?

We finish eating and I clear the table, all the while feeling Hugh's eyes boring into me, catching his furtive glances at me, as if I am definitely responsible for Aiden's words. One step forward, two steps back is how this whole thing feels. Just when we start to make headway, we are dragged right back to the beginning.

I give Hugh a watery smile as I pass him, my arm piled high with dirty plates and crockery. I'm met with an icy stare. For what feels like the longest time, he doesn't move or blink, just glares at me, his pupils tiny jet-black pinpricks of rage. Then he finally closes his eyes and when he opens them again, I recognise what is in there, what is going on in his head. He is exasperated. He blames me. I'm the idiot wife who caused this, the depressed woman who refuses to get better. Our plans for a better life here at Cross House are crashing down around us. And as far as I can tell, it's all my fault.

Sixteen

I'm furious with Aiden but have to conceal it. He has stirred up a hornets' nest with his words and he doesn't even realise what he's done. I make a fuss of tucking Poppy in, giving myself time to think about how I will broach the subject with him, what I will say, how I will say it. I don't want to give too much weight to what he said or make him fret, but I must find out why he asked, who it was that put the idea in his head. Despite what Hugh thinks, it definitely wasn't me.

Once she is settled and I've read Poppy her favourite story at least half a dozen times, I head into Aiden's bedroom where he is sitting on the bed, games controller in hand, his eyes glued to the screen that sits on a cabinet next to where he sleeps – another thing I plan on changing when we decorate his room. The screen will be pushed further back, out of sight. Less temptation for him. I'll buy him a bigger bookcase. Anything to take his attention away from those damn computer games.

'Hi,' I say as lightly as I can, hoping he senses me standing there. It's a lost cause trying to pull him out of himself once he is locked into these Xbox games. They are a sensory overload, drawing all of his attention to a fixed point on the screen. Fortunately, he sees me and puts the controller down and then turns the game off altogether. He looks tired, his eyes heavy with exhaustion. Today has been a day dedicated to football and when it comes to sports, Aiden always gives one hundred per cent.

'Hi, Mum,' he yawns, and rests his head back on the pillow.

'That thing you said earlier?' I say tentatively. 'Why did you ask?'

'What thing?' His eyes are closing and he's losing interest, his voice waning and distant with fatigue.

'The thing about this house being haunted.' I almost whisper the words, afraid Hugh is close by and about to come storming in accusing me of scaring the kids and talking nonsense again. I know he won't as he's down in the cellar, doing some last-minute jobs before the electricians turn up and rip the place apart, but just lately he's developed a nasty habit of creeping around. Anybody would think he's determined to catch me out, watching and waiting for the moment when my madness makes an untimely appearance and slices us in two.

Aiden is watching me, his eyes suddenly wide and glassy. There's something. I just know it. Aiden may be slowly turning into a young man, but underneath all the bluff and bluster, he is still my little boy. I know him; I can sense every little nuance in his voice, every tremor and pulse that runs through his body.

'Somebody said something at school,' he says cautiously.

'Oh, okay,' I reply as nonchalantly as I can. 'What was said then? And don't worry,' I add quickly, 'you're not in trouble. I'm just curious, that's all.'

Aiden nods and lowers his eyes. 'It was Bailey Alderson again. He said this house belonged to a family who all disappeared or died. He said they passed away in the house and that it's haunted.'

I don't know this Bailey Alderson boy but I hate him already.

'I told him what you said about the house being old and rundown and that was why we could afford it but then he said that wasn't the reason at all. He said we bought it cheap because it's haunted.'

I want to tell my son that Bailey Alderson is full of shit and that he has my permission to punch him square in the face. My blood is boiling but I can't show it. I have to hold my temper in and be the better person. I'm the adult here and Bailey is a child. A very irritating child who talks utter bollocks, but a child nonetheless.

'Well, first off, he's telling lies and trying to scare you. And you know why, don't you?'

Aiden doesn't reply. He shakes his head, a glimmer of interest evident in his expression.

'This is a big house, sweetheart, probably a lot bigger than the one he lives in. He's jealous, that's all it is. And anyway, if he thinks we bought it cheap because it's haunted, why did he tell you we were millionaires? He's completely contradicted himself there, hasn't he?'

Aiden's eyes fire into life, a spark suddenly present that was absent a few seconds ago. He's already formulating what he'll say to shithead Bailey tomorrow at school. Under normal circumstances I would tell Aiden to walk away from it all, not become embroiled in pointless, stupid gossip, but in this instance, I am prepared to let him say something, to stick up for himself and hopefully embarrass Bailey fucking Alderson and make him look like the stirring little shit he obviously is.

I tuck him in, Aiden now buzzing with excitement at the thought of taking Bailey's legs from under him tomorrow in class, hopefully in front of a gang of friends. There is nothing quite as gratifying as publicly humiliating a bully.

'Anyway,' I add casually as I get up and start to leave the room, 'I'm not sure how Bailey knows all of this. He doesn't even live in the village, does he?'

'He lives in Cobworth, the village next to ours, he said. And apparently his gran used to be the cleaner for the family who lived here years ago. She knew the woman who died.'

I nod sagely. It's all falling into place now. They think they can take ownership of this house because of a tenuous link from many years back. Well, they're wrong. This is our house now and despite not feeling entirely comfortable here, I will defend our home from anyone who tries to disrespect it or use it as a way of scaring my children.

I blow a kiss to Aiden, who catches it. He must be feeling tired and vulnerable. Any other time he would tell me to stop it and hide under the covers away from any shows of affection. Not tonight. Tonight, he is my little boy again.

***

I decide to grasp the nettle and do it while Hugh isn't around to stop me. After going downstairs, I Googled the name Alderson and Cobworth and up it came. I was both surprised and pleased. So few families have their landline number registered in the phone book anymore. For once luck was on my side.

Making the call inside is too risky. Hugh is sure to hear me and intervene or roll his eyes and add it to his ever growing list of my misdemeanours. I head out into the garden where the chill of the spring evening air settles on me like a damp shroud, making me shiver. I keep walking away from the house to the far end of the garden. There are parts of it we haven't even discovered yet. I make a mental note to come out with the shears and start cutting things back this week as I bend almost double to get under the overhanging branches of a gnarled-looking tree that looks as if it could collapse at any time. The bark is falling off and there are signs of older limbs that have been chopped off many years ago. I visualise the Wentworths out here in happier times and shake the picture out of my mind. I don't want to think about them. They're long since gone and we are here now. This is our home. It no longer belongs to them. Despite our troubles and recent arguments, I'm determined to be happy here. I have to be. There's no going back.

Holding on to my phone, I stop and stare around me. This garden is even bigger than we thought; so many hidden corners and overgrown areas. I know that there are some outhouses at the very bottom, concealed by shrubbery and weeds. If sharing a study with Hugh gets too much for me, I could possibly turn them into a writing den depending on how decrepit they are. All I need is some paint and a heater. The idea of it buoys me up, gives me a confidence boost for what I'm about to do. I hold the phone aloft for a better signal and then step into a clearing where the bars on my phone suddenly kick into life. I punch in the numbers scribbled on my hand and wait, my heart starting up an arrhythmic, stuttering beat.

The phone is answered after only two rings. I briefly consider ending the call but something spurs me on: the image of a deflated Aiden at school, surrounded by a group of boys smiling sardonically as this Bailey child spews out a torrent of shit about our family, our home. He has no fucking right and I intend to tell his parents as much.

'Hello? Can I help you?' The voice on the other end takes me by surprise. It's much gentler and softer than I expected. I had a vision of this boy's parents as a pair of hard-faced individuals, the type of people who bring their kids up to speak with their fists and have little or no regard for the feelings of others. The person on the other end of the phone doesn't sound like that at all, but then I suppose it's too early to tell. Give it time. Wait until they hear what it is I have to say about their child, then their tone may just alter and morph into something more aggressive, more ugly and defensive.

'Hi, yes, I'm Aiden Morgan's mum. He's in your son's class. I wonder if I can have a word about a couple of incidents that happened at school?'

There is a slight pause, giving me time enough to wonder what sort of reaction I am going to get. I prepare myself for a backlash of sorts; the kind of protective anger that is hidden deep in all parents and only set free if anybody tries to attack their offspring. I'm not ready for what happens next.

'I'm so sorry. I don't know what he's said or done but I'll apologise in advance.' The female voice cracks slightly and I wonder how bad this kid is that his mother actually says sorry before even finding what it is he's been up to. Surprisingly, I find myself backing down, sympathy for her plight outweighing my anger.

'It's nothing too serious,' I say. 'It's just a few things he said to my son about a house we've just moved into in Brackston. He's got Aiden a bit scared and apprehensive after telling him the place is haunted and that people died here.' I stop just short of telling her the part about his gran being the cleaner here. It could be her mother, who may since have died. At the minute she is on my side. I don't want to lose that connection.

There is a short silence and an exhalation and I picture this poor woman rolling her eyes and wanting to shake her boy for being so tactless and loose with his words.

'God, I am so sorry about that. We told him not to mention anything but Bailey is – well, as your son will probably tell you, Bailey is a real live wire. The kids love him most of the time but then he does something really stupid and oversteps the mark. He isn't a bad lad, really, he isn't.'

'I know that,' I say, trying to inject a degree of softness into my tone. 'And I'm not really complaining.' I close my eyes and think about all the nasty and inventive ways of punishing the boy I have thought of in the last half hour, and am flooded with guilt. 'It's just that Aiden's a bit oversensitive about things sometimes so I wonder if you could just ask Bailey to not mention anything about Cross House?' I am aware we haven't even made any introductions yet and feel the need to get on a firm and friendly footing. 'I'm Faye, by the way,' I add, waiting for her reply.

'Cross House,' she whispers, as if I haven't just spoken to tell her my name.

'Yes, we moved in a few weeks back.' I breathe deeply, wondering what it is she's about to come out with. I swallow and realise I've started trembling. There is no conceivable reason for me to feel scared. I've called this woman to warn her about her son's behaviour, which I've done, and for an apology, which I have received. So why do I feel so horribly nervous as if something dreadful is about to happen? Part of me wants to pump her for information, and part of me wants to put the phone down, too afraid of what she may come out with.

'Right,' she suddenly says, perking up, her voice lighter. 'Well, thank you for ringing and I'm really sorry about Bailey. He's not a bad lad, just a bit of a show-off at times.'

I am keen to catch her before she puts the receiver down. Despite my nerves, I know that this is too good a chance to miss. I may never get another opportunity like this – somebody who has a link to this house. Somebody who could give me some solid hard facts.

'The person who was the cleaner here all those years ago?' I say a little too breathlessly. 'I was just wondering if they ever mentioned anything about the owners of this house?'

The silence only lasts a few seconds before she speaks. I hold in my breath, desperate to hear her what she has to say, frightened of missing anything.

'It was my mum. She cleaned there for years and years. It was before I was born but she talked about it for so long afterwards that I felt as if I knew the place inside out.'

'So, you knew about the Wentworths?' I say, my throat horribly dry with anticipation.

'Only what Mum told me.' She stops at that and it's all I can do not to scream at her to open up and tell me everything, every tiny detail, no matter how insignificant it may seem. I want to know it all.

'Don't worry,' I say softly with a faux laugh. 'I know all about the fall down the stairs, and Mr Wentworth dying before her, so it won't frighten me. I'm a lot tougher than Aiden. He's a real softie.'

'You know about Adrian?' she murmurs, a tone of incredulity in her voice. 'How do you know about Mr Wentworth?'

'Well, I don't know a lot, but I know Hilary Wentworth was a widow when she died so he obviously passed away before her.' My face grows hot at my white lies. In truth, I know nothing, only what Gwen has told me. I do know the content of those diaries, however, and it wasn't that pleasant. Something tells me it's about to get a whole lot grimmer.

'Mum reckoned there was some awful things that went on with that family. Something sinister, she said. But anyway,' she says, breaking away from the conversation, 'it was all such a long time ago, and I don't want to be boring you or scaring you with gossip. It's all in the past. I'm sure there's been loads of families lived there since.'

My neck judders with the force of inhaling. I suck in more oxygen, a dizzy sensation forcing me to sit down on the damp grass.

'You're definitely not boring me or scaring me,' I whisper, trying to keep my frustration in check. 'I've been doing some research on the history of the house since moving in. I used to be a journalist so was thinking of doing a story on it. You know the type of thing – family breathes life into an old crumbling house – so any information on its history would be more than welcome.'

There is a pause on the other end of the line. I wait, my heart hammering, my conscience pricking me at the lies that have rolled off my tongue with such ease. I'm becoming quite the liar lately.

'I'm not sure,' she replies, and it's all I can do not to shriek at her down the phone to stop being so fucking anal and just tell me what she knows. 'I mean,' she continues, her voice now vague and unsteady, 'this is only my mum's thoughts on what happened and I wouldn't want anything going in the paper that could lead back to me. We only lost Mum a few months back and I'm not sure I can –'

'I'm so sorry for your loss,' I break in, knowing my words are just an insincere way of acknowledging somebody else's grief. The phrase itself has become a cliché, but there is little else people can do or say in such times. I am also desperate to get her on my side. I need to smooth the path for a possible meeting. 'I can assure you I would never say anything untoward or defamatory or put anything in it that would upset you. To be honest, the whole thing is in its early stages. All I'm doing at the minute is putting together some ideas. I just need to make sure I have enough to go on, to actually warrant putting the time and effort into making it into a story. I don't really want to spend hours and hours on it only to find I don't have enough to make it worth my while. Sorry, I didn't catch your name earlier?'

'Zoe,' she says, her voice a tad brighter after listening to my reassurances. 'My name is Zoe.'

Seventeen

Nothing can dent my mood. Not even the obvious reminder on Hugh's calendar of my next appointment with Doctor Schilling will cause me to lose my smile. Hugh has questioned me a few times on my buoyancy, his tone hopeful but tinged with mild suspicion. He's praying my session with Doctor Schilling has caused it but I can tell that he daren't pin too much on his supposition in case it all comes toppling down. He has no idea about my meeting with Zoe. For once luck smiled down on me and Allison contacted me postponing our lunch. Her mother was unable to babysit which meant her misfortune was my chance. I contacted Zoe after our telephone conversation and slotted her into Allison's place.

After I spoke to Zoe a few days back, she eventually softened and relented and we swapped numbers. I told her I'd be in touch saying how lovely it would be to meet up sometime. I promised to bring some photos of Cross House along with me which I'm hoping will help her to open up and tell me all she knows. In all honesty, I was initially apprehensive as to what her reaction would be. A couple of days had passed, giving her time to think about it; giving her time to change her mind.

She didn't change her mind and even sounded enthusiastic. I asked her if she wouldn't mind not mentioning it to anyone, especially Bailey. At that point I half expected her to back off, but she didn't. If anything, she seemed to be excited by the idea of a clandestine meeting.

We decided to meet for coffee next week, although I'm not sure I can suppress my happiness for that long, or my curiosity. I can barely sleep for thinking about what she may know. Even

Hugh's suspicious frown and gruff manner won't drag me down. I'm back in charge of my life.

In the meantime, I have busied myself with gathering up all of the journals and newspaper clippings. They're stored in a box under the stairs next to the vacuum cleaner and the ironing board. Nobody uses any of those things except me. That space is mine and mine alone. As soon as Hugh has an appointment, I'll get the box out and sift through the diaries and clippings, put them in date order, see if I can make some sense of them. I'd like to have a few knowledgeable questions to put to Zoe when we meet. I don't want to turn up knowing barely anything. What I want is for Zoe to fill in the blanks, to tell me who the unwanted boy was and why they seemed to hate him so much.

Tomorrow, an army of electricians will be turning up to Cross House, ripping the place apart. I don't anticipate either of us getting much work done in the next few weeks. Hugh has decided to put things on hold until the rewire is complete and I have decided to get out of their way altogether by going to the local library where I can use the Internet and get some research done. Hugh thinks I'm working on gathering background information for my next book. Let him think that. It's easier. I'm researching everything I can on Cross House and the Wentworth family. My book is on hold for the time being. Cross House is my project and will continue to be until I find out everything I can about it and there's bugger all Hugh can do about it.

***

We eat in near silence; not a sharp, uneasy stillness but more of a relaxed companionable acceptance that only comes with years of familiarity. Aiden is tired after yet another day filled with sports events, Poppy is simply ravenous and doesn't stop eating long enough to talk. Hugh and I each have our own reasons for keeping quiet. I know that Hugh is working out how to balance his business needs against those of this house, and Hugh thinks I am ruminating over the minutiae of my next book. I pride myself on fooling him. I'm a proficient deceiver and getting better at it all the time.

'What time will you be back from the library tomorrow?' Hugh asks as I clear the plates away, ready to dish out dessert.

'Not sure. Why, do you need me here?' I ask, my heart in my mouth at the thought of having my plans dashed or worse still, being caught out and confronted over what I'm up to. I don't want his prying to interfere with any of my plans.

'I was just thinking, I might need to nip out for an hour. John Staples from Daltso Engineering called me earlier and wants to speak about that project he's got on the go. He needs to set up a meeting and the old sod won't arrange it over the phone. Has to be face to face. Old school, I'm afraid,' Hugh says, smiling resignedly. 'Won't entertain the idea of Skype. He's only just got his head around emails.'

'No problem. Are you not keen on leaving the electricians here on their own?'

'It's not that,' he replies. 'I just don't know how long I'm going to be. John is a real old gossip and I can never tell how long he's going to keep me. It's at two o'clock and I'm thinking I might not get back before they knock off here for the night.'

I mentally calculate what time I will need to leave the library in order to pick the kids up and be back home in time for the electricians finishing. I doubt they'll even contemplate leaving before 4pm so I've got most of the day.

'No problem,' I say with a smile. 'I'll be back here for just before 4pm. I'll pick the kids up then come straight home.'

Hugh nods gratefully. 'Glad to see you're back working on your book again. I was beginning to think you'd developed writer's block.'

'No, not at all,' I lie. 'I just wanted to get a few things sorted in the house before I started on it again.'

'Well,' Hugh says quietly as he pushes Poppy's plate aside and hands her a slice of lemon meringue pie, 'next time we have a spare moment, you'll have to let me have a read of it. Just like the old times, eh?' He winks at me and I can't work out whether he is genuinely relieved I'm writing again or whether he is testing me. We used to be able to read each other so well but lately it's like trying to work out the thoughts of a complete stranger.

Telling myself I'm doing nothing wrong and that it's none of his damn business anyway, I smile at him and tuck into a large portion of meringue, enjoying the sensation as the lemon sears across my tongue and down my throat. He can ask to read it all he likes. Doesn't mean I'll let him. In case Hugh hasn't noticed, I'm an adult. I'll do as I bloody well please.

***

Yet again I'm the only person awake; the only one who can hear our nocturnal visitor as they creep around with frightening stealth outside our bedroom door. Why am I the only light sleeper in this family? It's like being in a morgue. I'm surrounded by bodies that, once they succumb to sleep, are almost impossible to stir. And I so want them to wake up. This is like a form of mental torture – being the only person who is subjected to the nightly terrors that take place in this house.

Only a matter of seconds ago, a drop of saliva fell on my cheek, warm and sticky like tree sap. I felt sick to my stomach and wanted to cry out but was too terrified to even breathe let alone utter any kind of sound.

I lie here, baking in the heat that has gathered under the covers, too scared to move, too fearful to even wake my husband who sleeps beside me, completely oblivious to the fact that somebody or something wanders our house at night. I envy Hugh's near comatose state and in my blind panic begin to think that he has set this whole thing up so he feels justified in sending me back for therapy. It's nonsense, I know it is, but I am so horrified and so horribly furious at Hugh's ability to sleep through it that all rational thought has flown out of the window. All I have is my fear and right now, it is running amok, telling me this whole thing is one big setup. I have to stop myself from thinking that it actually suits Hugh to have an insane wife who stays at home and doesn't ever question him or argue back.

My hearing picks up on something, sending my nerves into overdrive. I feel as if my body is on fire. My flesh burns as somewhere in the house I listen to a grunt which is quickly followed by a deep, androgynous groan. After that, silence. Just when I think I can't take any more of this terror, there is a sudden bang, as if somebody has fallen. I stifle a scream and grab at the duvet, burying my head under it, the intense heat almost choking me as I gasp for breath. Why the fuck does Hugh always sleep through everything that happens in this house? Why am I always left to deal with it on my own?

My head throbs as I fight for breath. Fury takes over from my fear at the thought of seeing him in the morning, fresh-faced and sparkly-eyed after a full night's sleep. My jaw aches as I sink into a state of pure unadulterated anger. I watch his features, slack with sleep, willing him to wake up, but he continues slumbering on, his breath hot and regular as it pulses in my face. I envisage myself slapping him, punching and kicking him and abruptly stop myself. Jesus! What is going on with me? Is Hugh right after all? Am I actually slipping into a pit of madness? What if I really am imagining these visits...

I am no longer able to stand it. My head throbs with trying to think straight. Slipping out of bed, I pad around the room, my body pulsating with terror, and get my dressing gown, the chill of the air raising my skin into goose bumps. I stop and stare at the clock. 4am. Outside, the distant echo of birdsong starts up, cutting into the soft hush of the room. Soon it will be light and then our nocturnal visitor will no doubt disappear, just like before. I'm not sure whether this pleases me or terrifies me. It certainly confuses me. I know ghosts don't exist, but hypothetically speaking, if it were some sort of spirit roaming around the place, why does it only happen when we're asleep? And if it's an intruder, what are they hoping to achieve? Nothing has been stolen, nobody hurt. Yet. I think of stories about people who have been murdered in their beds and briefly consider climbing back in beside Hugh. I don't. I'm scared, utterly terrified of what is out there, but more than that, I'm weary of feeling this way. I need to find out what is going on, to put an end to it all. I don't think I can continue living this way, permanently on edge, permanently petrified. Permanently worried that I'm losing my mind.

I tiptoe past a sleeping Hugh and out onto the landing. It's empty. I should have known it really. This is the pattern now; it's exactly as I expected. Nobody anywhere. An elusive prowler who roams our house at night.

I wipe away beads of perspiration that sit around my hairline despite the fact the house is cold, and look in on Aiden and Poppy. Both asleep, both blissfully unaware that I am once again on the prowl in pursuit of somebody who may not even exist. Christ almighty, this is utter madness.

I head towards the stairs – the place where it happened all those years ago. For some incomprehensible reason, my skin begins to crawl with dread. The closer I get, the farther away I feel, as if I've stepped out of my own body and am watching it all happen from above.

I can barely bring myself to look at the bottom step. My heart pounds as I stare down into the darkness. I lean towards the wall and flick the light on in the hallway beneath me. A rush of something hot and painful travels over the top of my skull as my eyes move to a fixed point on the floor. I bring my hands up to my mouth to stop the scream escaping into the open. The stairs are a blur beneath my feet and my eyes struggle to focus properly as I stare at something at the bottom, below me.

Holding the handrail tightly, I sluggishly make my way down, each step causing me to wince. My body feels a hundred years old as it pulses with dread and terror. The wall feels soft and pliable under my touch, its rigidity now a movable surface. I stop halfway and lean against the cool plaster for balance, letting it momentarily soothe my burning skin. I need to make it to the bottom without falling. I just have to take a deep breath and swallow down my fear. This is my home. There is nobody here who can hurt me.

Taking each step so slowly I wonder if I will ever reach the bottom, I start again. It's a painstaking process but I get there. I stand on the bottom step and look at the mark that is there before me on the floor tiles. I don't need to get any closer to see what it is. It's patently obvious that the small wet mark is blood. Not a lot of it, but enough to make me feel woozy and sick. Enough to send a streak of terror hurtling through my veins.

I stand for what feels like an age, unsure what to do, the dark stain on the floor taunting me with its presence. With leaden legs, I stumble through to the kitchen where I grab a handful of kitchen roll and run it under the tap until it's soaked through. I don't have the nerve to look behind me or search any of the rooms. I'm running on autopilot, my senses on shutdown. I cannot allow myself to feel anything. If I do that, I'm almost certain I would lose control completely and end up a gibbering wreck on the floor. And then what? I know fine well what the next step would be: Hugh would find me, I would get sedated, probably hospitalised, and my life would then be in the hands of the mental health team. It would be the end of me as I know it. Other people are allowed to worry, to fret, to ask for support or help and admit when they can't cope with their lot in life. But not me. I have to keep it all tucked away; every negative feeling that I have, I must now deal with on my own. All because of Todd and Jeff and what they put me through. And that is why I can never forgive them.

Ignoring the shadows that lurk in each and every corner, I head back into the hallway where I mop up the blood. There's no sign of any more. As far as I can see, this is the only stain. But there again, I haven't checked the rest of the house. There could be gallons of fresh blood in the other rooms, a whole host of injured or dead bodies. There could be somebody crouching in the darkness, waiting to strike.

I close my eyes and try to control my breathing. How long can I go on like this? If Hugh and Doctor Schilling don't get me sectioned, I may just end up doing it myself. I've got to get some level of control back, but it's so damn difficult when I have no idea what is even going on in my own house.

A steady pulse starts up in my neck, a rhythmic reminder of the terror raging within me. Standing up, I hold the wet material aloft as if it's contaminated and walk back to the kitchen where I hastily drop it into the bin. I rinse my hands under the tap, dry them and turn the light on.

I'm not sure whether to feel relieved or disappointed. Everything is the same as when we left it before going to bed. Despite feeling sick with fear, I force myself to go into all of the rooms, flicking on the lights, checking every corner, every hiding place. All empty. Nothing has changed.

Except for one thing.

It catches my eye just as I'm about to leave the dining room. A vase has been knocked over. It sits in tiny pieces on the windowsill at the far end of the room. Water is pooling on the sill and dripping onto the floor, a constant trickle of liquid making the gentlest of sounds as it hits the carpet with a slight wet *tap*.

I'm not going mad. This is tangible evidence that somebody has been in here. I can't breathe properly. Gasping, I make my way over there, the floor creaking ominously under my feet. The hairs on my arms prickle as I reach out and trail my fingers into the pool of cold water. Looking around, I can't see anything to mop it up so reluctantly tiptoe back into the kitchen. There's nobody around. I know that and yet I have the strongest sensation that somebody is watching me. My stomach clenches into a tight knot as I grab a towel and stalk back into the dining room. I bunch it together in my fist and angrily wipe the water up, tears now flowing freely. Suddenly it all seems so unfair. A childish reaction I know, but enough is enough. I don't believe I deserve to be subjected to these visitations night after night. Have I not suffered enough in the past year?

I throw the wet towel down, sweep the broken pieces of glass into my open palm and throw everything into the bin. Were it not for the fact that everyone is sleeping, I would shout out into every room that I am done with it all, that whoever is here needs to show themselves. As things stand, they have all the control, skulking around, making me lose sleep, subjecting me to nightly bouts of pure terror. This prowler has the upper hand. All I have is my fear and I'm not sure I can take much more of it. Living through this is like being subjected to physical abuse.

By the time I get back into bed, I am experiencing such a mixture of emotions, I feel sure I'll never get back to sleep: anger, terror, frustration, even paranoia, but most of all I feel defeated. It consumes me. It would seem that I'm in this thing on my own and at this point, I cannot see a way out of it.

I eventually drop off, my dreams marred by ghosts and spirits – the previous owners of this house who wander the place, torturing me with their elusive ways. They are the undead who refuse to die.

Eighteen

The library is relatively quiet after the mayhem I left behind at Cross House. The electrician and his mates turned up just after we'd finished clearing the breakfast pots away, their equipment littering the hallway and their loud voices sweeping through the house in booming echoes. I said goodbye to Hugh with the promise I'd be back before the gang of workmen left. According to the man who appeared to be in charge, they wouldn't be leaving until after five o'clock as they wanted to make the most of the lighter nights and get as much done as they could.

I dropped the kids off at school and only then did I feel myself begin to relax after last night's drama. I waved them off and got straight back in the car, determined to make the most of every single minute available to me.

Knowing the library wouldn't be open at that early hour, I went for a coffee and sat for forty-five minutes, enjoying the solace.

Today I am going to use every bit of strength I have to find out something about Cross House; anything that might help me understand its story. I ignore the thoughts that nibble away at me, telling me it's all in my mind and that I'm slowly but surely becoming unhinged. I am somehow convinced I'll find something today, some piece of evidence that will help me come to terms with what is happening.

I sit at a computer and place my notebook beside me. I only have a two-hour slot so will have to make the most of that time. If it's not enough I will move on somewhere that has a good signal and use my phone. I'll do whatever it takes to get to the bottom of it all.

I begin by searching the name Adrian Wentworth. It seems as good a place as any to start and since he died first, I figure it may just help me put things in order.

There are dozens of Facebook profiles and a smattering of ancestry sites with that name but nothing with any local interest. I narrow it down and type in 'Adrian Wentworth Brackston'. Nothing, but then the information I'm looking for happened long before the Internet came into being. I refuse to give in to the disappointment that niggles at me and change my wording. Determined to find something, I type in 'Cross House Brackston' and wait while the results load up.

There are plenty to see as the page finally springs to life. I read through the array of pub names and guest house websites that are on the first page until one at the bottom catches my eye. It's a private site set up by somebody to outline the contents of old wills. Intrigued, I click on it and scroll down until I see those magical words – Wentworth, Cross House, Brackston. Air expands in my chest and I feel euphoria take hold, lightening my mood. I swallow and tell myself to get a grip. This is only the first piece of information and it may lead nowhere. Still, it's better than nothing. I'm finally being presented with something concrete, something real that could very possibly lead on to more information; material that could prove even more revealing. This is better than sitting worrying day after day. I feel like I'm getting some level of control back, and it's a good feeling.

I open the folder and watch as magical words unlock part of the mystery. Scribbling furiously, I jot down the contents of Adrian Wentworth's will. It would appear he died in 1979 and left behind a hefty sum of money to his wife, Hilary. Over £250,000 to be precise. I read further. It's the total sum of his estate so I presume it takes into consideration the value of the house. It's still a lot of money even given the fact it was almost forty years ago. I click on a money rates and calculator site and am astounded to find out that in today's terms, it would amount to over a million pounds. That's a sizeable sum.

Tapping my pen on my paper, I try to work out how he could have amassed such a large amount of money. I change my search. Hilary died only a year after he did. If his will is online, then surely hers will be there as well? I type in 'Hilary Wentworth Cross House Brackston', and wait.

It comes up in a matter of seconds. The same site, detailing her will. The sum is similar. The only downside is there are no details as to who inherited it. I wanted names. I need to know if that poor unwanted boy got any of Hilary Wentworth's estate. My instinct tells me not, but my instinct also tells me he is the reason for the sinister goings on that Zoe spoke about on the phone.

Shifting my position on the narrow seat, I look for 'Tammy Wentworth Brackston'. She is probably in her forties or fifties which gives me more of a chance of finding her. A woman of that age is bound to have some sort of online presence. The computer whirrs before bringing up a whole host of Facebook profiles plus a few names on LinkedIn. I have no idea what she even looks like so will have to hope she still lives locally and is naïve enough to have her settings on public so anyone can see her posts.

It soon becomes apparent that none of them are her, unless she's moved out of the area. Or has married. I quickly bring up a number of websites that allow free searches for births, marriages and deaths and type in her details, guessing at an approximate year of birth.

The results that come up are all from America. I narrow it down to the UK only and am astounded to see that there is only one result. One result. My fingers feel hot and numb as I click on the link.

I sit for a few seconds, trying to work out if it's her or not. Why are ancestry websites so frustratingly abstruse? The year seems to fit, stating she was born in 1963, as does the area. She is listed as being born in Yorkshire, North Riding, which also matches. What it doesn't tell me is the names of her parents, just her mother's maiden name which is Smith. If I were to begin tracing all the marriages of every Hilary Smith in the UK, I would still be here tomorrow morning.

I try a different search and instead look for the marriage of Tammy Wentworth. Nothing. I allow for various different spellings, even using the name Tamsin. I draw a blank. Either she married abroad or didn't marry at all. Something dawns on me. I search again, only this time I look for the death of a Tammy Wentworth.

I feel like slamming my hands down on the cheap pine desk as the results come up once again with absolutely nothing. How the hell can somebody just disappear like this? Everyone can be traced. Everyone. I'm just not looking in the right places.

I spend the next half hour looking for Tammy, using the words 'Cross House' next to her name or 'Brackston' but still there is zero information on her.

'Everything all right there?'

I turn around to see a concerned-looking librarian peering over my shoulder. My scalp prickles with unease and embarrassment. I hope I haven't been too vocal with my growing displeasure at the results I've come up with.

'Kind of,' I murmur as I gaze at her face and clothes. She's a far cry from the librarians I remember as a child. Dressed in tight black jeans and a shirt that accentuates her ample bosom, she looks more like a glamour model than somebody who spends their days holed up in this dark building, organising and filing books and helping useless researchers like me. 'Well actually, not really.' I point to the names on my notepad and explain my situation, more to unload my frustrations than to seek any form of assistance.

'Have you tried the local newspaper archives?' she says, pointing to a large cabinet behind me that contains row upon row of huge leather books. They're stacked in chronological order with the name of each newspaper underneath; dozens and dozens of them. I could jump up and hug her. All this time and the archived news stories have been sitting so close by I could have reached out and touched them. The journalist in me wants to scream out loud at my own stupidity. I'm obviously losing my touch; not that I ever really had it to begin with.

'The stories for Brackston Village will probably have been covered in *The Northern Echo*. All you need is the date.' She smiles at me as if I'm a child struggling with a particularly difficult concept, then leaves me to get on with my search.

I double-check the date of the will and decide to backtrack from that point. It's a lengthy drawn-out task and takes longer than the two-hour allotted slot I had booked for the computer. At various times, the young librarian comes over to see how I'm getting on, pity for my plight evident in her expression.

'Most of the newspapers are gradually transferring their archived stories onto the Internet, but it takes such a lot of time and they work back to when the paper was first established. You'll probably find articles from the early 1900s online but not the later stuff.' She doesn't move as I skim-read story after story after story, glancing at headlines before turning onto the next page. 'Anyway, you know where I am if you need any further help.'

I glance at my watch, hunger gnawing at me, and am shocked to see it's after one o'clock. I know that the library has a strict no eating regulation and quickly work out whether or not I should pack up and quickly pop to the café over the road or stay here and plod on with my search. It's all feeling pretty fruitless. I've found absolutely nothing and my stomach is empty and my throat is dry. I'm just beginning to feel rather despondent and considering packing everything away for the day when I find it. The headline jumps out at me. A bolt of excitement hurtles through me as I read it.

Local businessman found dead on moors

The search for Brackston businessman Adrian Wentworth has been called off after a body found on the North Yorkshire moors was formally identified as Mr Wentworth.

The local businessman had been missing for five days prior to the body being discovered by ramblers. His car was found the day after he disappeared, over four miles away from where his body was found. The police have yet to issue a formal statement about the circumstance surrounding Mr Wentworth's death.

My eyes mist over as I read it again and again. I glance at the date – 29 November 1979 – and think of how cold it would have been on the moors at that time of the year. Five days in the wind and rain and plunging temperatures. The moors can be brutal in midsummer never mind the dark nights of winter.

I nibble at my lip, tugging at loose pieces of skin. Why was he there? Was he a walker and simply lost his way in the fog?

Flicking back, I look for stories leading up to it. Five days prior. That's all I need to look for. Just five days.

It doesn't take long to locate it. According to the local newspaper, Adrian Wentworth left his home on the morning of Saturday 24 November 1979, telling his wife he was going to town to buy himself a new coat. She reported him missing later that evening when he failed to return home. Next to the story is a small grainy picture of a man I guess is probably in his late forties. He's wearing glasses and a reserved, forced smile.

I stop and think things through. There's nothing mentioned about his personal life. Like all newspaper stories, it only states the facts regarding his disappearance. I can't work out whether it was an accident or whether he had no intention of ever returning home. And if he didn't want to return home, why not? More frustration grips me. What in God's name went on in that house?

I spend the next hour going through each and every page, searching for more stories about him; looking for information on this poor man who left his home never to return. There doesn't seem to be anything of relevance until a thought crashes into my head, almost knocking me off kilter. How did I not think of it before? I quickly leaf through the classified section of the paper and focus on the columns listing the deaths for each day. It appears nearly two weeks after the newspaper reports stating his body had been found. I read it through, trying piece it all together in my mind.

Wentworth, Adrian Peter
Late resident of Brackston Village. Much loved husband of Hilary,
dear darling daddy of Tammy and father of Peter. Private funeral for
close family and friends only. No flowers or cards, thank you.

So little said and yet so much to take in. I don't think I've ever come across such a concise notice for a death. Whilst working at the paper in Newcastle, we came across families who would spend hundreds of pounds on placing the most elaborately worded notices, telling everyone how adored the deceased was, how much they would be missed and how life would never be the same without them, but this? I read it again, shocked at the sharpness and brevity of it. And who is Peter? Why was Adrian Wentworth a dear daddy to Tammy but only a father to Peter?

I sneak a glance over at the librarian. She is busy chatting to an elderly man who looks completely bewildered by her long and convoluted explanation. She points over to the far corner and I watch as he shakes his head. It looks like she's going to be busy for some time.

Grabbing at my phone, I surreptitiously place it over the page and take a photograph of the death notice, then do the same for the other two articles outlining Mr Wentworth's initial disappearance and the finding of his body, before slipping it back in my bag.

I all but skip out of the building, thanking the lady behind the desk as she struggles to direct the old man to wherever it is he wants to be. She gives me a brief exasperated smile and I return it with a mild chuckle, letting her know I fully understand her predicament.

Thinking of my stomach, I head over to the café that is aptly named RumbleTums and grab a coffee and a prawn sandwich to take away.

Sitting in the car, I sip at my coffee, feeling quite smug at finally discovering something about the Wentworth family. It's taken some doing but I'm making headway at long last. When I meet up with Zoe, I'll at least be armed with some background knowledge and her words will then mean something to me. At long last, I'll be able to piece together the history of Cross House. The only thing that niggles at me is this Peter character. Why was he on the periphery of the family? What did he do that was so bad, he barely got a mention in his father's death notice?

I finish eating and drain the remainder of my coffee, by which time it's just after 2.30pm. I apply a quick slick of lipstick, slip the empty cup into my bag along with the sandwich wrapper, put the car into gear and head off for the school. I'll be early but at least I'll get a parking space.

I can barely keep the smile off my face as I turn left and then right onto the main road. Today's trip has been extremely worthwhile. Last night's carry-on is a dim and distant memory. I turn the radio up and listen to the dulcet honeyed tones of George Ezra, then put my foot down and drive, my worries about my returning madness far from my mind.

Nineteen

The house is in pieces when we get back. The team of electricians show no signs of packing up and it appears we will have no electricity for at least another hour, possibly longer. Hugh is still out and I have no idea when he'll be back.

John, the lumbering man who is sweeping up chunks of plaster, tells me they'll work as fast as they can but it's a big place and they've come across many problems.

'Loads,' he says with a shake of his head, as if I'm to blame.

'But you're still on track for getting it finished by next week?' I ask, more than a little anxious as to what his answer will be. I don't want bad news. I have enough to cope with at the minute. I just want it to be over. Rubble crunches under my feet as I step out of his way. I stare at the channels on the walls where they have dug out the plaster to get to the ancient wires underneath and wonder what we were thinking of, buying a house this old and neglected. We must be mad.

'No idea,' he says dismissively. 'Best ask the boss.' He nods over his shoulder to the small, older-looking man standing in the doorway of the kitchen. He has his arms crossed and is surveying the area carefully, his face giving nothing away.

'Hi there,' I say as cheerfully as I can. I think I've done a pretty good job of appearing positive considering my house looks like a building site. A wrecking ball couldn't have done much more damage.

He nods at me and smiles, his eyes creasing at the corners. 'Don't worry, we're on track for completing it next week. John here is a right misery guts, aren't you, Johnny boy? Always loves to cheer the customers up.'

I can't resist a smile as John grunts his acknowledgement and gathers up a pile of rubble and plaster, dumping it in a large black sack next to his huge feet.

'Takeaway?' I say to Aiden and Poppy who all but leap up and down at the suggestion. Brackston doesn't have anything remotely resembling a chip shop or a Chinese takeaway but the village next to ours has an Indian restaurant who I've heard do the best Chicken Jalfrezi for miles around.

They answer the phone, which I find surprising since it's not even five o'clock, and I order our food. I arrange to collect it at 6pm. Hugh should be in by then so it will save me having to bundle the kids in the car, Aiden grumbling that he's old enough to look after himself for an hour, which he quite obviously isn't. After ordering our meal, I go about helping John tidy the place up.

By the time Hugh gets in, they're loading the van and are ready to leave. I quickly tell Hugh that I'm off out to pick up our meal. He smiles appreciatively and declares that he's starving as I rush off, leaving all the mess and mayhem behind me.

The drive doesn't take long. It gives me time to think about my research today. My next move will be to investigate the Wentworth children. They're probably alive somewhere. Not that it matters at all. Not that any of it matters actually, but I've invested time in the research now and am not about to give it up. It's been a good while since I've felt this animated and interested in something. Todd and Jeff sapped me of every little bit of strength I had and our recent night-time visitor has done a fine job of finishing off what they both started. It feels good to be thinking about something else. It just feels good to be busy again.

I stop at a cash machine, pick up the curry and head home, the smell of the food increasing my hunger a hundredfold. My appetite has returned and I find myself looking forward to sitting down and eating with my family later.

The electricity is back on and the rubble all but gone when I get back. Hugh is in the kitchen clearing away the cups and plates left by the electricians. He's whistling and seems to have a spring in his step.

'Ask me what happened today,' he says, unable to conceal his joy.

'Okay,' I say cautiously, 'what happened today?'

'Daltso Engineering want me to oversee their latest project; the one with the specialist machinery. We've agreed a hefty consultation fee and as soon as I get the nod, we're good to go.'

I give him a tight hug. I'm genuinely pleased for him. This has been hanging over his head for a few months now and he was almost certain he'd lost it to a bigger company who could do the job for a lower price. Hugh may be many things – stubborn, unseeing and dogmatic – but the one thing he is, is incredibly hardworking.

We celebrate by opening a bottle of bubbly with our meal and filling our glasses to the brim. The house is a bomb site but it doesn't bother me in the least. Aiden appears to have had a good day at school. Poppy declares she has lines to learn and doesn't want to be disturbed once she's eaten. Hugh and I suppress our laughter and drink more bubbly, the alcohol taking effect almost immediately.

By nine o'clock I feel so tired, I can hardly stand up. Hugh is still on a high and running on pure adrenalin. He stays downstairs watching TV. I shower and slip between the cool sheets, exhaustion enveloping me. I feel myself sinking deep into oblivion and welcome it. Deep, deep into the darkness…

***

His voice shatters my dream, cutting through it like a rock being hurled through glass, rupturing the calm of my slumber.

'Faye! Wake up.' Hugh's voice is a violent grunt in my ear. His hand rocks my shoulder back and forth. I feel my flesh grow cold as I gradually emerge from a deep sleep. My head thuds and it takes a couple of seconds to register what is actually happening.

'Don't move!' he whispers, his breath hot and clammy on my neck as I drag my eyes apart and attempt to sit up. I feel Hugh's palm push me back into a horizontal position. I try to question him but he quickly places his other hand over my mouth. For one awful gut-sinking moment, I think he's gone mad and is about to attack me. All of the arguments and disagreements of the past few weeks, and the thought of having to live with an unstable wife have pushed him to the brink and he has lost control. The sensible part of my brain knows this isn't true, but in my slow and unsteady frame of mind, I just can't think straight. All lucid reasoning has taken a back seat and my brain is unable to process anything. It's a cauldron of fear and confusion, bubbling and spitting, keeping me from working out what the hell is going on.

Wild images fill my thoughts as I lie completely still. A drunken husband, bereft of compassion and empathy; dead children, murdered in their sleep. My children. I gasp for breath and push Hugh's hand away. He doesn't stop me; his arm is suddenly lifeless as he sits up next to me, his body a rigid silhouette in the darkness. What he says next freezes my blood.

'There's somebody in the house. I heard them walking about.'

Once my fear-addled mind allows me to make sense of his words, I'm not sure whether I want to shriek with relief or laugh out loud. At last. I'm not going mad. I'm not imagining it. This is real. Hugh has heard it too. We're now in this thing together, whatever this thing is. All I know is I now feel vindicated in my belief that we are not alone in this place. Now he understands.

'What did you hear?' I whisper, my heart battering against my ribs with such strength, I feel certain I could go into cardiac arrest any second.

'Breathing,' he says quietly. 'I heard deep breathing out there on the landing, then footsteps. I'm going to go and take a look. Stay here.'

There is no way I'm staying put. Not a hope in hell. I've spent so long now worrying and fretting over this; it's eaten away at me, leaving me feeling wiped out, empty and even doubting my own sanity, so if Hugh thinks I'm about to let him go out there and investigate without me, he's sadly mistaken.

I swing my legs out of the bed and stand up, ignoring Hugh's hushed pleas for me to stay in the room. I push past him, desperate to get down there, to see what is causing this. The thought of Hilary Wentworth struggling for breath right here in this bedroom fills me with dread. I don't want to stay here on my own. My father's voice fills my head.

No such thing as ghosts.

Hugh is with me as I step out onto the landing, our cold bodies next to one another. I can feel the slight tremble of his hand as we make our way to the top of the stairs. We silently head down, me behind Hugh, both of us avoiding the creaky boards beneath our feet. Once we reach the bottom, he flicks the light on and practically runs into the living area, his eyes scanning every corner of the room. Turning to me, he places his finger over his lips to indicate that I need to stay silent. Not that I had any intention of speaking anyway. I've been here before. I know the drill. It's Hugh who's the novice.

I should be leading the way.

We creep out of the empty living room, turning lights on as we move about the rest of the house. By the time we reach the kitchen, I can see that he is both confused and exasperated. We've been in every area and there is nobody here.

I watch as Hugh suddenly sprints around the house, pulling at cupboard doors, yanking them open with more force than is necessary. By the time he's finished, sweat is glistening on his face and his skin is a sickly shade of grey. He runs his fingers through his hair wearily, bemusement etched into his every pore.

'I heard something – somebody, Faye. I fucking heard it!'

'I know you did,' I reply softly. 'I know exactly what you heard, Hugh. I've been hearing it since we moved in here. Welcome to my world.'

I don't need to say any more and if he detects the sarcasm in my voice he doesn't show it. He doesn't answer me, but then I don't expect him to. It's the early hours of the morning, we're tired, disorientated, confused. What is there to say? What can either of us say to make all of this any better?

I look around. The walls have been dug out, old wires hang loosely, the floor is grey with plaster dust. Everything is shit. And here we are chasing ghosts, invisible intruders who refuse to reveal themselves. My deep desperation to prove that my sanity is still intact is overtaken by doubts of my possible insanity. None of this makes sense. There is nobody here, yet we have both heard it, felt it even. The memory of the blood and saliva looms in my mind. I close my eyes against it, blocking out the powerful images and sensations that are still fresh in my thoughts. I should have kept the towel as proof. But then, what good would have come of it? It wouldn't give us any clues as to who it is that stalks us, or any indication as to where they disappear to when we try to find them.

Besides, I don't need any hard evidence to convince me that what we are experiencing is real. I know that it is happening, that it is all very real. I just don't want it to be. I want it all to go away.

'Come on,' I say as I reach out for Hugh's hand, our fingers touching slightly, 'let's go back to bed.'

He takes me by surprise, snatching his hand away. There is a look of concern and such ferocity in his eyes that it feels like a punch to the gut. My knees buckle as I notice the look he has on his face. Hugh is normally a calm individual, a man of measured movements and reactions; somebody who always thinks things through before acting. But not at this moment. At this very moment in time he is full of fire. He is in fighting mode, indignant and furious at being duped by an invisible entity.

'Back upstairs,' he hisses, a look in his eyes I've not seen before. It's a look that I don't care for. I don't want the children to be woken by him tearing around upstairs like a frenzied maniac.

'Take it easy,' I whisper. 'Let's just sit down for a minute and think this through.'

He acts as if I haven't even spoken, turning his back on me and heading back upstairs. I follow him, switching lights off behind me, my stomach clenched in trepidation.

I sigh and try to still the quiver that is pulsing through me. This is what I wanted, isn't it? I've wished from the very beginning for Hugh to hear what I've heard and now he has. Now we're in it together whether I like it or not.

Twenty

'Upstairs,' Hugh says gruffly, pointing to the smaller set of stairs that lead up to our shared study. I gulp, inwardly cursing myself for my stupid oversight. I had never even thought of going up there in search of our nightly visitor. The steps are around a corner and hidden in the shadows. Not easy to spot, unless you're looking for them, that is. I feel horribly sick.

I follow Hugh, my breathing erratic and feverish. We've searched everywhere else. This is the only place left.

I reach out and tap Hugh's shoulder. 'We need something for protection, just in case.' I half expect him to tell me to stop being so ridiculous but he nods and stops for a second to gather his thoughts.

'Here,' I gasp, handing him a small baseball bat that's sitting on top of a pile of Aiden's sports equipment, the same equipment I nag him about tidying away every day. For once, Aiden's slovenly ways have worked in our favour.

Hugh grasps the bat tightly in his fist and we both climb up the stairs. I can't stop shivering despite feeling hot. My insides are churning as we make our ascent. I try to calm my nerves but it seems the harder I try, the more scared I become. By the time we get to the top, my legs are buckling under me. I should feel less frightened with Hugh around but for some unfathomable reason, I feel more nervous than ever. Maybe this is it. Perhaps that's the reason for my fear: knowing our intruder could be above us and we are about to be faced with something dreadful, something unspeakable. I am frightened at what Hugh is capable of at this moment in time. I've never seen him so angry.

'If I say run, you need to get downstairs as fast as you can and call 999,' Hugh says in such a deep guttural tone, it turns my blood cold.

I can't speak. I just nod that I understand and watch as he turns on the light and runs into the room, his face contorted and twisted with anger and anticipation. His eyes are wild and his skin is slack and pale as he whirls around, trying to take it all in.

Nothing. There is nothing here. The room is eerily calm and empty.

'What the fuck?' Hugh shouts as he spins around, the bat raised over his head, ready to crush our purported intruder. His expression is alight with fury and he scares me, the strength of his rage filling the room, morphing into something unrecognisable. I don't identify with this anger I see before me. Right now, he is a stranger to me.

'Where the fuck are you?' he suddenly roars. Without warning I fall, the ground coming up to meet me. My knees hit the bare boards with a sharp crack as I slump onto it in an ungainly heap.

I feel the floor bounce and watch as Hugh rushes over to help me up. I resist his attempts to pull me upright. I don't have the energy to stand. My bones ache and my head hurts. I feel sapped of all strength.

'Please, Hugh,' I say quietly, my voice muffled. 'I just need a minute. Give me some space. I'll be fine. I just need a bit of time to clear my head.'

He doesn't say anything but I feel him move away from me. I can hear his breathing over my head and imagine him scanning the room, trying to work out what the hell is happening. Now he knows how I feel. At least he might cut me some slack now he has an idea of how chilling and frustrating it is, trying to find something that refuses to reveal itself. This has been my life since moving here. And now it's Hugh's too. Now he knows. Now he has an idea.

The floor creaks with his movements. I feel him flop down next to me and reach over to take his hand. He locks his fingers in mine and we sit there in silence for a minute, each of us too stunned, too dumbfounded to say anything.

Eventually Hugh shuffles closer and turns to face me. 'I'm sorry,' he says quietly, his anger softening. 'I saw it, Faye. Whatever it was you saw, I've seen it too. There was a figure in the bedroom, a shadow. I saw it as it moved past our bed. At first I thought it was one of the kids but then I heard something and I knew it definitely wasn't Aiden or Poppy.'

'What did you hear?' I ask, almost too afraid to hear the answer.

'Hard to explain really,' he whispers. 'Like some sort of grunting sound. A deep, throaty sort of sound.'

'Like somebody struggling to breathe properly?' Air is trapped somewhere in my abdomen and I have to focus on controlling my own breathing as I wait for his reply.

'Yeah, I suppose that was it. It was a bit like a gasping sound. Too distorted to tell if it was male or female.'

I can't take it all in. My mind is too fogged up to think, my limbs too heavy to move. We sit like that for a little while longer, our bodies gradually cooling in the chill of the early morning air, both of us too weary to say any more.

Finally, Hugh nudges me with his forearm. 'Come on,' he says, his voice croaky with exhaustion. 'Let's get back to bed. I'll come back up here in the morning.'

I don't ask why. I have visions of him tearing the place apart looking for hiding places. The thought of that along with our gang of electricians makes me want to scream and cry. I'll make myself scarce again. I also want to tell Hugh not to waste his energy searching for hiding places and concealed entrances. I don't believe our nightly visitor needs any. Even as I think it, I know it sounds ridiculous. I never thought I would ever entertain such ideas. It's ridiculous, yet I can't think of any other reasons as to why this is happening. Try as I might, I cannot for the life of me work out what it is that's going on in this house. It's all beyond my comprehension. All my life, I've dealt with facts; growing up as a child I was taught to think logically, to separate emotion from reality and what we know to be true, and yet here I am, living in this huge house, daring to consider the fact that it might just be haunted. Dear God, put like that, it does sound insane. But what are the other options? Night after night I have searched this property and found nothing. What am I supposed to think? I feel as if I'm slowly but surely going mad. It seems like the theory I had about these visits a few weeks ago, is proving to be correct.

Hugh warms up much faster than I do once we're tucked up in bed. My flesh feels like I've been subjected to Arctic conditions. I cuddle up next to him, glad of his body heat that radiates towards me. Sleep is swift and peaceful, like a warm bath, wrapping me in its soft silky heat.

***

Our morning routine is thrown into complete chaos after we oversleep. The electricians turn up before we're even dressed. I apologise after greeting them at the door in my pyjamas, and quickly shower and change, shouting to the kids that they need to hurry.

After a flurry of manic activity, I manage to get Aiden and Poppy in the car, Aiden still munching on a slice of cold toast as he slips into the seat and buckles himself in.

The drive to school is a subdued journey. Poppy is still bleary-eyed after being unceremoniously hauled from her bed by an exhausted mother whose patience was at an all-time low, and Aiden is reading one of his superhero books, his concentration fully focused on the words and story. I, however, have my mind full of other things. Things I would rather not have to think about. Things that I don't understand.

'Have you got your book bag?' I ask. Poppy nods and shakes the blue satchel sitting at her feet.

'Swimming kit?' I say, eyeing Aiden up in the rear-view mirror. He raises his head and nods before going back to his book.

The traffic is light and we make it in record time. I let out a heavy sigh and rest my head back as I watch them saunter up the road, Aiden taking a right turn to the secondary school farther up the road once Poppy has entered the primary school gate safely.

I decide to make myself scarce today. I don't want to go back to the library but by the same token, I don't want to be in the house while there is so much work going on. The electricity will be erratic so the chances of getting anything done are fairly slim. I peer out of the window as I drive and decide it's fine enough for a walk. I can amble through the village, take my time, ruminate over what took place last night.

My skin itches with tiredness and frustration as I put my foot down and weave through the overgrown country lanes that lead back to Brackston. If anybody was hiding out in Cross House, a team of noisy workmen would soon find them. There's no place to go to once they start drilling and digging out lumps of plaster, but my uncontrolled imagination is already telling me that what we have roaming about in our home needs no proper hiding place, no dark deep cupboard in which to remain concealed, because our nocturnal wanderer isn't of this world. Spirits don't need to stay safely out of sight, do they? They have the best hiding place of all, disappearing into the emptiness around us.

I find myself being thankful my father isn't alive. He would give me a stern talking to, throwing science and cold hard facts at me as to why ghosts are a physical impossibility. But he never had to witness what I've witnessed, did he? He never had to tear around the house night after night chasing shadows, mopping up blood and cleaning up broken objects. All those things have been real. How would he explain those events to me?

By the time I get back to Cross House the drilling is well underway and white particles fill the air, swirling and billowing in a thick grey haze. Coughing, I flap my hands about to clear the dust away as I make my way past an apprentice, a callow youth with his hands slung in his pockets and a dark, suspicious frown on his face.

Hugh is in the kitchen making a pot of tea for everybody, the clink of the crockery drowned out by the growl of drills and hammers. We haven't had time to speak about last night and with all the noise and disorder around us, I doubt we will for some time to come.

I lean over, plant a kiss on his cheek then grab my notebook, phone and pen. I shout over the unearthly noise that I'm going out for a walk before slinging my sweater around my shoulders and heading outside where the sound of subtle sweet birdsong greets me.

Stopping for a few seconds, I inhale the heady smell of lilacs that are just coming into bloom and find myself grateful for the warmth that sits on my back as the sun makes its early ascent into a cloudless sky. At times like this, the problems of Cross House feel unimportant, a million miles away.

Heaving a contented sigh, I make my way over to the bench next to the village green. I can sit there undisturbed and add to my notes, work out what my next move is going to be. If I can get a decent enough signal, I'll see if I can do a search on Peter Wentworth since his sister proved to be so elusive. I feel a desire to know more about him, to work out what his story is. Without knowing anything about him, I already feel him tugging at my heartstrings, evoking a maternal instinct in me that didn't seem to be present in Hilary. Somebody has to be on that poor boy's side.

The bench is empty, as is the entire green. I settle myself down, content just to be, relieved to be out of the house away from the noise and grime. The sun continues to rise, emitting a weak warmth with the promise of more to come as the day progresses.

I scribble a few thoughts down, then turn around as I hear a sound behind me. It's Gwen. She has got her back to me and is on her hands and knees, her backside raised in the air. I watch as she drags at something and shoves her head down out of sight. Standing up, I can see that she appears to be looking for something in the shrubbery growing next to her front door.

'Everything okay over there, Gwen?' I shout as I start to walk towards her. She has her head ducked low and doesn't appear to hear me. I reach her gate and wait until she has extracted herself from the bushes and then speak again. 'Doing a bit of gardening?'

As she turns to face me, the expression on her face is a combination of shock and something else that I can't quite put my finger on. It's only as I watch her shuffle off away from me and slam the door without even acknowledging my presence that it dawns on me what it was that I saw in her eyes: contempt.

My mouth hangs open as I stand for a few seconds, my brain unable to process what I've just witnessed. I briefly consider knocking on her door then think better of it and instead head back over to the bench where I sit and write, my day suddenly darker than it was a few minutes ago. I feel completely bewildered and upset and thought Gwen was a decent lady, the sort of wise person who is kind to others. I hoped she would help me with my research. I hoped that in time, she would become a friend.

An unexpected lump rises in my throat, borne out of weariness and defeat more than anything else. I blink away tears, a sudden feeling of loneliness washing over me. Tomorrow I'm meeting Zoe for coffee. Things will seem better then. This is just a passing phase. Tomorrow everything will look brighter.

I pick up my phone and tap away at it, continuing with my research, all the while completely unaware that I am being watched.

Twenty-one

Peter Wentworth proves to be just as elusive as his sister, Tammy. I try various permutations with my search, but each and every time come up with nothing. A big fat zero.

Above me, a blackbird chirrups merrily and a pigeon coos, the sound echoing over the empty stretch of grass, accentuating how alone I am.

My neck aches and my eyes are gritty as I throw my notepad down on the bench and tuck my phone into my pocket. It all feels so pointless – so completely and utterly futile. Even though I spend my days trying to fathom what is taking place inside that house, spending every spare minute researching its past, nothing has changed. My nights are as disturbed as ever, filled with fear and confusion and to top it all I'm worn out, so dreadfully tired and weary. The house is currently in pieces and the best plan I can come up with is to sit on a park bench Googling scraps of information I've managed to come up with. I must look a sorry sight – a solitary figure, crumpled with fatigue and not even worthy of acknowledgement from an elderly neighbour.

I suddenly feel horribly conspicuous, sitting by myself, as if the entire village is watching me from behind their curtains, judging me, thinking how stupid and naïve I am for falling for such a trick, for buying an old house on the cheap when all the while they knew it didn't want us. Here we are, throwing thousands and thousands of pounds at it when in truth, we should have walked away, left it for another family. Let them be eaten up by the misery Cross House will undoubtedly throw their way.

Standing up, I gather my things together and turn to look at Gwen's cottage. A shadow quickly shifts out of view, sending an unexpected chill across my exposed flesh. I step closer, hoping to get a better view but all I'm confronted with is a clear pane of glass. Something is wrong. My prevailing instinct is to go over there, march up the path and knock on her door, but a small part of me, a silent sense hidden deep within my brain, holds me back, telling me it's a bad idea. I can't be certain but I don't think it was Gwen at that window. The shape didn't fit her tiny frame. It was somebody larger; a mysterious shadow that didn't want to be seen.

I swallow down my unhappiness and move away from the house feeling more than a little troubled at Gwen's rejection. If she doesn't want to speak to me then I will reciprocate the sentiment and spend the day on my own, somewhere private, somewhere I can think in peace, not in full view of her house.

The idea comes to me as I'm walking back towards Cross House. I have no idea why I didn't think of it before. My mind has been so preoccupied with finding out the answers to the questions that have been gnawing away at me for what feels like forever, that it slipped under my radar. If I want somewhere to work that provides solace and tranquillity while the house is being ripped to pieces, what better place than the disused outhouses at the far end of the garden? I thought of it a while back and then it slipped my mind. There has been so much to do since moving in that we haven't really given them a second thought. They're not our priority at the minute and besides which, they're hardly visible under the years of undergrowth. They're also set behind an old gate in a section of the garden we haven't even been in yet. All in all, the size of the land that Cross House sits in stretches to just under an acre. We saw the perimeter of the garden outlined in red on the initial plans when we purchased the place, but with the many towering trees and masses of bushes and shrubbery covering the place, it looks much smaller. It's a child's dream with loads of hidey-holes and hidden fences and gates. Aiden and Poppy have already started making a den next to the old summerhouse. According to the estate agent, there's a kissing-gate at the very bottom of the garden, the part that overlooks Brackston Woods. She only mentioned it when I asked who the land belonged to behind the house. She seemed vague about who owned it but was keen to tell us that it would never be built on due to the fact the woods are part of a conservation area that stretches the length of the village green and beyond. It was a selling point and a very strong one at that. Everybody craves privacy. Having a sprawling spread of new houses suddenly springing up at the bottom of your garden is enough to put anybody off buying when part of the appeal is not being overlooked.

I walk around the outside of the house to the back of the garden, accessing the kissing-gate through the woods, which proves trickier than I initially anticipated. There's some sort of well-worn track that leads through the trees but it quickly becomes apparent that I'm not dressed for the occasion. The path is muddy, a quagmire in places, the light blocked by overhanging branches leaving the ground saturated and unable to dry up completely.

Refusing to give in, I slip and slide my way past, pushing tree limbs aside which spring back on me, splashing water in my face and smacking me on the backside as I quickly sneak through. I look down at my shoes, not as dirty I imagined them to be, but not as clean as when I first started my foray into this small forest.

I stop and stare around. There is a crack of light coming through a nearby tree, small spots of yellow filtering through in thin streaks, highlighting an area parallel to where I'm standing. Pushing towards it, I become entangled in a knotty gathering of low-lying shrubbery. I bring my foot up and stamp on the gathering of foliage, hoping to flatten it enough for me to be able to step over into what I can now see is a clearing close to the path I'm currently on. I lean towards the trunk of a small tree and stumble, almost falling. The notebook in my hand is stopping me from getting a decent grip on anything. I lift my sweater and tuck it into the waistband of my jeans, pushing it down as far as I can, and then scissor my way across the shrubbery, slipping into a small puddle before righting myself and continuing on my way.

Just when I'm beginning to think it would have been easier to access the gate from the garden, something comes into view.

Light spreads in great waves upon a larger clearing through the trees. Looking beyond the huge conifer blocking my view, I can now see there is another much wider path.

Striding over a soggy patch of ground, I step through two towering trees into another lane. A smile spreads over my face. I suddenly feel very stupid indeed. All that struggling to get through the woods and all the time this was here – another cut running parallel to the one I was on, except this one has been cleared of any obstructions. Bushes have been hacked back and small trees felled to allow access.

Shielding my eyes against the glare of the sun, I amble through, knowing the end of my garden should come into view any second. My navigation skills aren't the best but I have a fair idea of where I am and know that in just a few seconds, that kissing-gate should be visible.

It only takes a short while to see it, an old rusting piece of wrought iron jutting out into the path. I head over to it and run my fingers over the jagged, flaking metal that has seen better days. It's surrounded by foliage and dense hedging but it's accessible, the gate moving easily as I step forward and push it open.

A feeling of exhilaration swells within me as I weave my way through the gate and into the part of my very own secret garden. I feel like a small child, ready to discover new territories and make my mark on an entirely new world. The hurt of being rejected and the sensations of mild paranoia I experienced only a short while ago are pushed to the back of my mind and all but forgotten as I edge my way forward. I am unable to ignore the childlike excitement that flutters in my belly at uncovering a virtually undiscovered piece of land; land that belongs to me. This is mine. I visualise Poppy's face when I bring her down here and think of how Aiden would plan a new den, barking orders to his sister about where it should be and what they should keep in it. I could even provide them with a couple of old sleeping bags and a picnic basket. Aiden might scoff at the idea but Poppy would practically bust a gut at the very thought of it. Now that Jeff and Todd are out of the picture I feel more confident about letting them roam down here. We could put a padlock on the kissing-gate just to be sure.

And then I see it. Just when I think we can start living our lives like normal people, the powers that be piss on our parade once again.

I end up almost standing on it, my feet becoming tangled up in each other as I do my best to avoid stepping on the basket that is sitting on the floor next to the gate. It looks relatively modern, which concerns me. Everything else about this area suggests neglect; a piece of land that hasn't been visited for many, many years. But the new-looking basket isn't the only thing that makes me feel ever so slightly sick. It's what it contains. Sitting inside the basket is a handful of empty wrappers: small pieces of foil and brightly coloured plastic scrunched up into separate balls.

I look behind me. I have no idea why, but all of a sudden, I don't feel so alone. These things are new – signs that somebody else has been here, and recently too. I think of a hundred different reasons why this basket has been placed here but cannot come up with one logical explanation.

My neurosis kicks in almost immediately. Sweat runs down my back and my stomach churns. I try to talk myself round but once I'm in this frame of mind, it's so difficult to think rationally. If somebody can get in to put a random basket down, they can get in to hurt us. I know that there is probably a perfectly innocent reason for this, but I've been through too much to trust anybody anymore, especially strangers and especially after what has happened night after night since moving here.

Reaching down, I pick it up. It's a flimsy piece of raffia, far too light and insubstantial to withstand the inclement weather of the woods, far too new to have been through the recent savage winter we encountered. Somebody placed this here recently. This is deliberate.

I rummage inside it and grab at a handful of the wrappers which end up falling on the floor and scattering at my feet. Bending down on my haunches, I pick them up and carefully open them up one by one. Most of them are chocolate bar packages. One is a crushed drink carton and another is a sandwich packet, torn up into little shreds and curled into a twisted shape that sits in my hand.

Stumbling to my feet, I pile them all back into the basket and push my way through the long grass and gnarled tree stumps. I trip and fall on more than occasion, swearing and cursing as I lug myself back up to my feet. I'm too anxious now to even think about uncovering the outhouses. What I want to do is show this to Hugh. I know what his reaction will be. He will come out with cold hard facts as to why this mini hamper was put there, and that is exactly what I want to hear. For once I want to hear my husband's clear logical thoughts. I am done with being frightened and fixated on the negatives. I am sick and tired of feeling on edge and constantly looking over my shoulder. I desperately want to hear what Hugh has to say on this subject. I want to be the old me again – the confident, self-assured me, not the bumbling wreck I've turned into.

I head back to the house, energy draining out of me with each consecutive step. The outhouses can wait. They're not going anywhere and we have more than enough time to see to them at another date. Right now, I need to hear the sound of Hugh's voice. I just want to be told that everything is all right and that my family is perfectly safe in this house. Then I can settle.

Twenty-two

'Probably somebody who's had a picnic,' he says, too distracted to take notice of how distressed I am as I wait, holding out the basket for him to look at. Hugh is standing in the kitchen surrounded by a carpet of plaster and brick dust, trying to get a decent signal on his phone.

Although this is exactly what I want to hear, it doesn't fully reassure me. I need more than that. I need his full attention and for him to say something that I haven't already thought of.

'It's hardly picnicking territory back there,' I say, a definite wobble apparent in my tone. I gulp back tears and breathe deeply to keep myself in check. No meltdowns, no crying. I promised myself as much on the way back up to the house. 'It's dark and overgrown. There's a clearing with a path but I don't think it leads anywhere that's conducive to family days out or picnics,' I say with a tone of incredulity that I do my best to curb.

'Kids then,' he replies, catching my eye and then glancing down into the basket. 'This place has been empty for years. If I were a kid living here, I'd be the first to set up camp in the garden. No adults around to bother them, nobody telling them what to do, where they can and can't go. Almost an acre of land spare for playing in. It's obvious, isn't it?'

I catch his eye and there is a moment where it's clear we are both thinking the same thing but neither of us wants to say it out loud. Local children hanging about in the garden is the explanation we want to hear. It suits our agenda. We don't have the nerve or the patience for prowlers living rough on our land. I certainly don't have the constitution to deal with it. Not after our previous dealings with Todd and Jeff. And there were a lot of sweetie wrappers in the basket. Why would a prowler choose to live on Mars bars and packets of Maltesers? Our prowler would surely steal from our fridge, wouldn't they?

I nod to show that what he is saying makes sense and empty the contents of the basket into the kitchen bin. I hang on to the basket. I shove it in a cupboard, already thinking about what I'll do with it later. I won't tell Hugh about the fact I'm going to leave a note in it, telling whoever it was that left it there that the house is now occupied and could they do us a favour and piss off. I'll place it back where I found it and see what happens. He doesn't need to know and would advise me against it anyway. Some things are best kept as secrets.

The drilling and bashing noise in the house increases, rattling off the windows and bouncing off each bare wall. I decide to go back out onto the bench. I refuse to let a moody old lady get to me and puncture my contentment, although to be perfectly honest, my mood has already been somewhat deflated by my unexpected find. If she has chosen to suddenly ignore me, then so be it. I have things to be getting on with. Cutting back the foliage surrounding the outhouses can wait. I hadn't realised just how much there was to do back there. I'll need to find the shears and gardening equipment in order to hack my way through the dense covering of trees and bushes. I imagined being able to pull a few weeds up to find them but there's at least a few days' worth of cutting back to be done before we can even begin to see what's under there. I can start putting together the questions I want to ask Zoe when we meet up tomorrow.

I leave Hugh in the kitchen, his voice raised as he tries to communicate with a customer over the din of the drilling. He barely registers my absence.

***

As expected, the bench is empty. The village appears to be deserted, everybody either at work or at school. I sit down and list the things I would like to ask Zoe.

Who was Peter?
Why did he appear to be so unwanted?
What happened to Adrian Wentworth?

I'm beginning to wish I'd never found the diaries and newspaper articles. Why are they still here? Who kept them and why? This whole thing is making me crazy.

'Now then.'

I snap my head around to see Gwen standing at her gate, her arms resting on the white painted wood that is starting to rot and crumble away. She is smiling at me as if our earlier encounter never even happened. Confusion creases my brow and I have no idea how to respond. Should I be churlish and pull her up over her rudeness and abrupt manner, or should I be the better person and greet her as if none of it ever took place? Deciding that discretion is the better part of valour, I stand up and walk over to where she is standing and greet her with a smile.

'Morning, Gwen. Everything okay?'

'Course it is,' she says a little too sharply. 'Why wouldn't it be?'

'No reason,' I say as gently as I can. A small knot of resentment still sits at the pit of my belly. She was rude to me earlier this morning and I have no idea why. I tell myself to get over it. Worse things happen. She's an old lady. She's allowed a little imprudence.

'I'd ask you in for a cup of tea but I've just cleaned a rug and it's still drying out. Maybe tomorrow?'

'Ah, thanks for the offer,' I reply softly, 'but I'm meeting a friend for coffee. Perhaps the day after?' I venture. I don't want to miss an opportunity to pick Gwen's brains. Plus, I'll have more information to go on by then. Zoe will hopefully have told me plenty and Gwen can fill in any blanks.

'That sounds great,' she says, her manner a world away from the aloof brittle lady I saw earlier this morning. I don't try to work out what the problem is. Judging by her current disposition, it's not me. I haven't done anything to upset her and have enough to worry about without taking on board the seesawing moods of an ageing neighbour.

'Can I ask you something, Gwen?'

Her eyes narrow slightly as if I'm about to delve into her deepest and darkest secrets.

'It's just a couple of questions about Cross House,' I say, keen to assuage her fears. Perhaps she knows I saw her earlier and doesn't want to divulge what the problem was. I suddenly feel a tad guilty. Not everything is about me. This is an old person we're talking about here; somebody who has seen plenty and has fears and worries of her own. I remind myself to be more mindful of others' moods and anxieties in the future.

'Ask away,' she says, a little more brightly.

'What happened to Adrian Wentworth? I know he was found up on the moors after going missing. Was it an accident?'

She puffs out her cheeks and clicks her tongue disapprovingly. 'An accident? I doubt it. The coroner's report said it was misadventure but if you ask me, he did it to get away from her.'

'His wife?' My voice goes up almost a full octave. This is what I want. Real solid information, not flimsy snippets of gossip that could mean a million different things.

'Aye, Hilary, his wife. And that daughter of his. I remember her well. A little madam she was.'

'Really?' I say, although I'd already formed a similar opinion of the girl after reading her diaries. I need to remain neutral here, however – stay completely impartial if I'm to get the full story. I'm sure Todd met people after he left our home, and spun a tale about how cruel Hugh and I were for throwing him out on the street when none of them knew the real account or knew the damaged and dangerous soul that was the real Todd.

'I was her teacher,' Gwen says, catching me completely off guard. I hadn't expected that. I surmised they were just neighbours but this revelation puts a whole new slant on it.

I take a few seconds to think about my next question. 'What about Peter?' I whisper, wondering what nugget she will come out with next. If she taught Tammy then she surely knew Peter as well?

She lowers her eyes and for a second, I fear she might be about to weep. 'Such a sweet boy,' she says in a different tone; less caustic, less cutting. 'He never stood a chance in that house.'

'I don't quite follow you?' I say. 'What do you mean, he never stood a chance?'

'Well, he didn't do any of the things that girl said he did. He wasn't capable of it. Anybody with an ounce of common sense could see that. If you want my opinion, that's why poor Adrian took himself off. Couldn't stand it in that house after his lad was sent away.'

My chest feels fit to burst at hearing what Gwen has to say. This is starting to make sense. The words in those diaries flood back into my mind with frightening clarity.

'What things did she say he had done?' My skin itches with unspent energy and a deep restlessness as I wait for her reply.

Behind her, a phone trills. I want to tell her to leave it alone. I want to scream at her to let it ring out and that this is more important. Instead, I watch as she gives me a nod and starts to turn away from me, her attention already diverted elsewhere.

'Best get that,' she says resignedly. 'It'll be my daughter. She calls me every day to make sure I'm still here and not lying dead on the living room floor. Old age, eh? Don't believe all the adages about how getting old is a blessing. Grow old along with me, the best is yet to be. What a load of old nonsense that is.' She sighs miserably. 'Believe me when I say, my dear, that growing old is actually rather shit.'

I don't know whether to laugh or yelp out loud at her words. She is certainly a character, I'll give her that. I watch as she walks away, carrying all the information I want inside her head. I need to see her again. I'll be here as soon as I can for that offer of tea, the day after tomorrow. That's if Zoe hasn't already told me the whole story. I get the feeling Gwen is the guardian of the real story, the one who has the inside knowledge. But a two-pronged approach is better than no approach at all.

I go back home to Cross House with a definite spring in my step. I'm so close to uncovering the real mystery of this house, so close I can almost taste it.

What was it Peter was accused of doing that was so bad they had to have him sent away? Myriad possibilities cross my mind, some of them too grotesque to even consider.

The turmoil that greets me as I step over the threshold is almost unbearable. Noise, dust, the shouts and grunts of overworked men and the sour face of an apprentice who quite obviously wishes he were elsewhere.

'No electricity for at least the next two hours,' he mutters, eyeing me angrily as though this whole sorry mess is all down to me.

'Okay, that's not a problem,' I say soothingly and enjoy the look of confusion and mild anger on his face as I smile and sail past him up the stairs. He's obviously used to cries of protestation from long-suffering householders who aren't prepared for what a full rewire actually entails.

I know how I'm going to spend the next few hours. I am going to grab my box of documents and take them down to the summerhouse where I will sit and sift through each and every one of them.

I don't care how long it takes, I will get them all in order ready to show Gwen the next time we meet. And then I may just get the answers I desperately crave. I will get to the bottom of Cross House and its deepest mysteries before it gets to me.

Twenty-three

Hugh doesn't attempt to stop me when he sees me brush past him on my way into the garden. I'm carrying a large box stuffed full of paper and books but he doesn't give me a second glance. His mind is on other things. Working from home during a rewire is proving tricky, especially with no electricity and a poor 3G signal. Standing in the kitchen with his arm hoisted in the air has become his default stance and his patience is wearing thin.

'Only a few more days and they'll be finished,' I mutter as I slip past him and out into the sweet fresh air, away from the incessant snarl of drills cutting through plaster.

The long grass brushes against my skin as I stumble through a maze of gnarled tree stumps and rabbit holes to get to the summerhouse. I cling on to the box and all but fall through the door onto the old wooden floor. I stand and look around. The whole place is in dire need of a good clean. Blankets are strewn everywhere, placed in here by Poppy, along with the old phone and a scattering of pens and notebooks she has used to take messages whilst playing at being a secretary. I can't help but smile. The pages are full of scribbles and drawings along with some writing that I'll read once I've sorted through these old papers. I love having an insight into how my children's minds work, being able to climb inside their heads without them knowing I'm even there.

I settle myself down on an old wicker chair that looks as if it's about ready to collapse at any time. I give it a couple of firm bounces and decide it's strong enough to hold my weight.

Opening the box gives me a fluttering sensation in my stomach as I see all those diaries. So many mysteries and secrets, so much heartache. I trail my hand over the top of them and lean in to inhale the musty scent of old paper.

I spend the next hour leafing through Tammy's diaries, most of which reveal nothing of any interest. She was clearly a confident girl who was desperate to grow up. I notice more pages have been ripped out and think back to my teenage years, full of angst and torment. They probably contained things that embarrassed her years later and she saw fit to bin them. I know I did when I accidentally found my old diaries in my mum's spare bedroom. I was in my twenties and helping my parents redecorate when I recovered them, stuffed at the back of a cupboard. Reading them made me cringe. I don't remember being that miserable but the words I put down on paper painted me as a sullen teenager who hated just about everybody and everything. My face burned with shame as I read things I had written about my parents: about how dull and dreary they were, how pitiful their lives were and how I was quite obviously superior to them if only they would realise it.

Some of the diaries even contained details of the night I lost my virginity to Robert Carmichael. And when I say details, I mean real details – intimate accounts of where he touched me and how much I liked or disliked it. At one point I even gave him marks out of ten. I shudder at the words I wrote in that diary, words that should have stayed inside my head. Instead they leaked out onto paper, giving the whole episode a feeling of permanency when it should have simply been a fleeting memory. That's the problem with saying things; once they are said they cannot be unsaid. My mother repeated that line to me over and over while I was growing up, and it stuck with me. It obviously didn't have the same effect on my sister Jan, who speaks first then thinks later.

Sometimes, she doesn't actually think at all.

Anyway, as soon as I realised what was in those childish ramblings, I threw them all away and have never regretted it. Not once. I suppose Tammy Wentworth felt the same way, which is why chunks of her journals are missing.

I am feeling more than a tad disenchanted at discovering nothing of any real interest and I'm almost at the end of the final diary when I see something that makes my stomach flip. I feel like a voyeur reading it. Such horribly private words written down and here I am reading them even though I know she wouldn't want anyone to have seen them. The other pages were ripped out but this one remains. An oversight? I would think so, judging by what it says. If anything should have remained unseen, it is definitely the things that are written down here: phrases and thoughts full of spite and such hatred it is quite literally breathtaking. I thought that I was riddled with anguish and torment as a youngster, hating everyone I came into contact with, but Tammy's diary takes teenage angst to a whole new level.

My eyes mist over and the words dance about on the yellowing paper as I pore over the page and read them again.

I've got it all sorted out. It's taken me a while but I know how to get daddy back on our side. I've seen the way Peter looks at me. I've seen the way he rubs his crotch whenever I'm about. Well, I haven't actually seen it but I can imagine it. And if I can imagine it and tell my story well enough, daddy is sure to believe me. Doesn't matter if it's true or not. And besides, Peter is too stupid to know what's going on. Getting daddy to take me seriously is going to be so, so easy. Soon it'll be goodbye Peter and then everything will be back to how it was before he came to live here. I can't wait.

A pulse hammers away in my neck. This it hideous. I hope to God it's no more than childish drivel. I hope to God this all stayed in Tammy's head and none of her plans were put into action, but as I think about what Gwen said earlier, it starts to form a picture in my mind. It would seem that something did actually take place in Cross House – some sort of grave injustice against that poor boy.

I swallow and rub at my eyes wearily. This purported event happened many years ago and doesn't involve me. I should just leave it all; walk away from it and forget what I've found. Whatever it was that took place in that house is over with. What's done is done and cannot be undone. Me digging around trying unearth new truths will change nothing.

I decide to go and see Gwen again. I'll show her what I've found and perhaps she can help me put the pieces together, tell me the full story. I don't need to go inside. She can tell me what she knows right there on her doorstep.

I have one final rummage through the box, gathering up the newspaper clippings. There's one I haven't seen before. It's tucked into the flap of one of Tammy's diaries. I open it out and am confronted with a grainy photograph of a young girl holding a trophy aloft.

Local Schoolgirl wins National Dance Trophy

It's a brief account of how Tammy Wentworth came second in a tap-dancing competition. It tells me little about the girl herself or her family, focusing on the competition and the local dance school she travelled with to London. The picture, however, intrigues me. Squinting, I stare at the photograph, trying imagine what this girl was like, wondering what was going through her head when this picture was taken. Did anybody know the secret hatred she harboured for her brother? And why did she loathe and resent him so much?

The date on the article has been cut out but the actual story tells me she was thirteen years old when this photograph was taken. She looks much older, with the thick application of make-up, including dark lipstick and nail varnish. She is wearing a leotard and her hair is tied back into a tight bun and she looks every inch the proud winner with a smile that stretches from ear to ear. There is no denying she is a pretty girl with a mature, knowing expression in her eyes. I try to associate this happy, proud girl with the malicious accusations in her diary and fail miserably. Just goes to show how easy it is to hide our true feelings, to let them fester and rot inside us, concealed from the rest of the world, masking who we really are. It's a frightening thought.

I fold up the article and place it back in the box along with the rest of the diaries, barring one. I keep it separate and grip it tightly. This one I will take with me when I go to see Gwen. I will show it to her and ask her to tell me about these words and what they led on to. Part of me is fascinated by this family's history, my curiosity piqued, and part of me dreads hearing what she will tell me. Either way, I have doubts about a positive outcome.

I shiver as the sun disappears behind a bulbous grey cloud, the temperature dropping almost immediately. I stare around at the mess that surrounds me and smile. I couldn't begin to imagine Poppy and Aiden having a relationship like Tammy and Peter's. Despite their many arguments, deep down they're pretty close and have a lasting bond that I hope will stay with them well into adulthood. And then Todd slips into my mind unbidden, blackening my thoughts. Sometimes, families can wreak havoc on one another's lives and no matter how hard we try, how much effort we put in to limit the damage caused, untold heartache will ensue. Is that what happened with the Wentworths?

Running my fingers through my hair, I scoop up the papers strewn on the floor and scattered about on the old desk. The comparison between my daughter's innocent pictures and scrawls and those of an angry resentful teenager are a world apart, emphasising Tammy's deep unhappiness and the mask of confidence that she wore for the outside world.

I flick through Poppy's drawings, smiling contentedly, if somewhat smugly, at the depictions of our family. There is a drawing of Hugh and me, two rotund figures with frighteningly spherical heads and wide staring eyes. We are linking hands and our names are underneath with a short description.

Daddy – happy and funny. Makes me laff. Mummy – smiles and makes my dinner.

I continue to browse her collection of musings. Picture of angels and butterflies fill most of the papers with the occasional unicorn which looks more like a small pig with a gigantic horn sticking out of the front of its head. There's also a drawing of Aiden which is less than flattering, giving him a protruding belly and hair like an outlandishly large haystack. I let out a loud laugh as I stare at it, making a mental note to store these for posterity once Poppy has finished with them.

Then a sickness takes hold and I feel all the blood drain out of my face as I see the last few drawings she has done. I close my eyes tight and then open them again and stare down as I struggle to comprehend what it is that my young daughter has put down on paper.

In my hands, I hold something penned by a child that has the capacity to still the air that is locked in my lungs. I struggle to release it and inhale again to keep the oxygen flowing through my body as I gape at her final few sketches.

The first picture is that of a figure, twisted into a tiny wizened shape. It resembles a gargoyle with its wide cavernous mouth and bulging eyes. It is very possibly the ugliest creature I have ever seen, its blackened body bent at a horribly peculiar angle. But it's not just the sketch that makes bile rise from the very pit of my stomach. It's what she has written underneath.

Old grunting person who lives in my room.

I'm light-headed as I try to stand up, my legs lacking in any kind of support or control. I slump back down into the chair, my hands shaking visibly as I hold the paper tightly. I stare at it for a few more seconds then, as if stung, I let go of it and close my eyes. I am almost too afraid to look at the final piece of paper that sits on the desk next to me.

Opening my eyes again and blinking rapidly to clear the film that covers them, I take in a series of faltering breaths, then steel myself and look at the last picture.

Much like the other one, this is also a drawing of a figure. Its mouth is gaping open, and its eyes are bottomless black holes set deep in its face. But there is a slight difference. And that difference chills the very marrow of my bones. The figure in this picture is sitting down. And if I'm not mistaken, the twisted sad-looking individual in my daughter's drawing is sitting in what appears to be an old rocking chair.

I cannot move. My limbs are solid as stone. Even breathing is painful. And I am freezing. My body temperature has suddenly plummeted. I have never felt so cold.

I blink repeatedly to clear my blurred vision. It feels as if a ton of grit is lodged behind my lids causing a burning sensation. I close my eyes to alleviate the awful pain. Stars burst inside my head, exploding over and over. I see a blurry rainbow that sways and merges into a fine diluted mesh of fading colours before everything suddenly goes black.

Twenty-four

My face is numb and I am shivering. My cheek is grazed where I fell onto the wooden floor and a trickle of blood runs onto my hand from my forearm. I must have put my hand out to break my fall and gashed myself on the corner of the desk as I went down.

I lie still for a couple of seconds to give myself some time to think. I was frightened. Shocked by something. I felt sick. And then I remember. It comes back to me in a rush, like a blast of cold air exhuming long-settled sediment, dragging it up to the surface, sickening me with its presence.

The pictures. Poppy's drawings.

Moving myself up to a sitting position, I shiver and cover my mouth with my hands to stem the flow of acid that is rising up my gullet. Placing my head between my knees, I breathe deeply and wait for the feeling of nausea to pass. I have to get myself looking and acting half decent before I go back in the house. I don't want Hugh to see me like this. He may have seen and heard our unwanted visitor but I have no doubt in my mind that he will still jump at any opportunity to get me back on that psychiatrist's couch. I'm not doing it. He will not get me back there. I don't care how much he has paid or how hard he tries to force me, I am never returning to Doctor Schilling's practice. Not now. Not when I know that none of this is my fault or some wild imaginings I've subconsciously cooked up. The visions I have had are definitely not some distorted version of reality or part of a parallel universe that exists only in my head. They are real.

I begin to shiver, my teeth chattering violently as the cold air bites at me. I reach across and drag one of the filthy old blankets down over my shoulders. It rests on the top of my spine, affording me a modicum of warmth in the chill of the crumbling summerhouse.

I sit there for what feels like forever, ruminating over everything that has gone on, trying to picture this house as it was. I block out the obvious thoughts, the ones that scare me, the ones that scream at me that Hilary Wentworth walks this house at night. She doesn't. She can't. It's an impossibility. I know it to be true.

So why do I feel so terrified?

Fifteen minutes pass before I feel strong enough to go back inside the house. I clean the scratch on my arm with a tissue and rub at my face, then stand up, my legs weak and wobbly. Brushing myself down to clear off any dust or cobwebs that clung to me as I fell, I step outside and stride over the lawn towards the back door, my thoughts being that if I look confident, I'll feel confident.

The noise is an assault on my ears as I step inside and close the door behind me. Part of me wishes I'd stayed out in the summerhouse as I crunch my way through the debris that litters the kitchen floor. I stumble over a large chunk of brick and almost fall onto Hugh's back.

'Three more days,' he mumbles through his teeth as he turns to face me. He is sitting in the corner of the kitchen, his elbows resting on the counter and a sprawl of papers in front of him. He looks tired. His eyes are heavy and his hair flops in front of his face. He sweeps it back with his fingers and returns his attention to his work.

'That's not so bad,' I reply. It's a pathetic attempt at injecting some enthusiasm into our current predicament; positivity in the face of adversity. Given the circumstances, it's the best I can manage.

He doesn't answer. His mind is already focused elsewhere. The noise in the house is intense, the dust as thick as the miserable atmosphere that now permeates every corner of the house, every single bit of airspace. My eyes fill up and I'm not even sure why. I do know however, that I can't stay here while this is going on. The noise is just adding to my misery and anxiety, putting me even more on edge.

Stepping away from Hugh, I go back outside and into the summerhouse where I grab the diary entry that stabbed at me, leaving a permanent hole in my festering fear and emotions. I don't read it again. There's no need. Those words have left a stain on my very soul.

I hold it firmly and make my way over to Gwen's house. I half expect her to be perched in her usual place at the white picket garden gate and am disappointed to find her not there.

My knock is a gentle tap, just loud enough to let her know of my presence but not so loud that it causes her any alarm. I want her to be in the right frame of mind when she answers – to be receptive to my probing questions.

The ensuing silence fills my head, making me feel completely isolated. I take a deep breath and knock again then wait. A raven caws above me, fluttering its huge black wings as it sits on the ridge of Gwen's rooftop, spreading its oily black feathers wide like a huge black cloak as it settles and watches me with its beady eyes.

I start to count to ten, telling myself that if she doesn't answer by the time I get to nine, then I will turn and go back home. A gunshot fires in the distance, echoing over the empty fields of corn, sending a tingle of unease down my spine. A dog barks somewhere over the other side of the village green. Then more silence.

I'm just about to walk away, having reached nine, when the door is pulled ajar. Gwen stands behind it, her hair askew, her face crumpled. She looks aghast at seeing me and closes the door to unhook the chain before opening it again and standing aside to let me in. I hesitate before stepping inside, brushing past her as I move into the shadow of the long hallway.

'Sorry,' she yawns as she shuffles behind me into the living room. 'I had a nap and must have overslept. Mind your step, it's wet,' she says as we skirt past the damp rug she spoke of earlier, the smell of wet wool filling my nostrils and making me gag slightly. I dance over the soggy fabric, its highly patterned design a bright and garish combination of clashing colours.

'I'm so sorry to disturb you,' I whisper, suddenly embarrassed at knocking so insistently and rousing her from her mid-morning nap. 'I've just got a burning question for you. Well, a few burning questions actually.'

She waves at a chair and I slump down in it like an obedient child while she makes us both some tea. There is an odd smell in the room, possibly body odour or something of that ilk; a stale, unpleasant aroma that will only be alleviated by opening a window. I presume it's the wet rug, although it seems different somehow, more pungent.

Gwen comes bustling in carrying two large cups. No fancy tray this time, no biscuits carefully arranged on a china plate. Just plain old tea. She hands me my cup and sits in the chair opposite, taking deep slurps and swallowing loudly. I study her before speaking. She seems on edge, worried about something. A line sits over her eyes, a furrow of anxiety. Guilt stabs at me. She's an old lady. I should stop this. I should leave her be and let her sleep. She did let me in though. She wouldn't have done that if she didn't want me here. Gwen may be a pleasant woman but it's quite apparent that she is nobody's fool.

'Did Tammy Wentworth accuse her brother of sexual assault?' I surprise myself at how direct I sound. There's no other way to put it, no easy way to approach such a delicate and taboo subject. I keep hold of the diary, suddenly reluctant to let her see it.

Gwen surprises me even more. There is barely a flicker of shock at my words. It's as if she's been expecting this, been waiting for me to march over here and ask her. She continues drinking her tea, the steam billowing up and concealing her features. Then she speaks, her voice filtering through the fog of steam.

'You've found something then? Something in that house?'

I nod and bite at the inside of my mouth, nipping at a piece of loose skin with my back teeth. 'Some diaries,' I croak as I take a sip of hot tea to lubricate my dry throat. 'I found them tucked away in the back of one of the wardrobes.'

There is a prolonged silence while I wait for Gwen to answer me.

'So, is it true then? Did Tammy accuse Peter of something?' I say, my voice now urgent and rasping. 'Did she actually accuse her own brother of sexually abusing her?'

'Yes, she did,' Gwen replies, her tone bitter and sharp. 'And everyone believed her. He got sent away.'

'Where?' I ask. 'Where did he go to?'

'Back to the residential unit.' She puts her cup down and for a second, I think she may be about to cry. Instead she leans back in her chair and lets out a deep breath, a long rattling gurgle as if she's been holding it in for a hundred years. 'Peter had learning difficulties. He wasn't Hilary's child. He was Adrian's child from his first marriage. He lived with his mother quite happily, then when she died, Peter went into a residential unit. That didn't sit well with Adrian. He wanted his child to live with him and his family but Hilary wasn't keen. She had her own child, her precious daughter, and didn't want anybody else's kid living with them. Hilary was what can only be described as an older mother. She didn't have Tammy till she was in her mid-forties. She'd waited that long for her that when she eventually came along, nobody else mattered. Tammy was her world and everybody else disappeared off her radar. Not that they were ever on there to begin with,' Gwen sniffs, her eyes dark with contempt.

'But it wasn't anybody else's child,' I almost roar. 'It was her daughter's half-brother!'

Gwen gives me a knowing smile and shakes her head. 'My dear, Hilary Wentworth didn't think like you or I. She was a hard woman and brought her daughter up in the same vein. The apple didn't fall far from the tree with those two, I can tell you. That girl of hers…' She stops and rubs at her eyes, bringing out her handkerchief to rub at them. 'Well anyway, the poor lad was sent back to the unit and he was miserable there. He may have had learning difficulties but he wasn't stupid. He knew right from wrong and he also knew what unhappiness and misery were. And let me tell you, that boy was miserable.'

'How do you know that?' I ask. 'I mean, I don't doubt for one minute he was unhappy at being sent away, but you talk as if you knew him really well.'

'I did,' Gwen replies suddenly, her words making my head spin. 'I used to visit him at the unit.'

I stare at my hands, giving myself some time to digest this new piece of unexpected information. She visited him? Here I was thinking she was just a neighbour, somebody who watched the Wentworth family from afar when in fact she was directly involved with them. Not only was she Tammy's teacher, she was also connected to this Peter. What else does she know? What other secrets does Gwen have tucked away in that head of hers that she is yet to tell me?

'What happened after he was sent to the unit?' My palms are damp and my stomach is a tight knot of apprehension. Something awful is coming. I can just feel it. Something even worse than the false allegations made against poor Peter.

'For a while, nothing happened. Life went back to normal in Cross House. Tammy was her usual confident self. Hilary spoilt her rotten, thinking she'd been sexually abused. Adrian was distraught. I don't suppose he knew what to do. He'd brought the boy into the house and it all went horribly wrong.' Gwen stops, her eyes flickering before she looks up at me. 'Look, I'm not even sure I should be telling you all this, but I get the feeling you're a nice lady and I can trust you.'

I nod until I feel dizzy then hold out the last page of the diary for Gwen to see. She glances at it, her eyes scanning the words written there and then looks at me, her eyebrows raised.

'Tells you everything, doesn't it? That's an admission that she lied, right there, isn't it?'

Again, I simply nod, words leaving me when I need them the most. We sit for a few seconds, the tick of Gwen's old clock the only sound in the room until a slight creak above us causes Gwen to jump up, her eyes suddenly wide as if she has just received some kind of electric shock.

'Anyway,' she says, her tone containing a forced air of conviviality, 'I must get on with cleaning this old house. Beds don't make themselves. I'll see you again as arranged – the day after tomorrow?'

I drain the remainder of my tea and stand up. 'What happened to them, Gwen? Did Peter stay in the residential unit? And what about Tammy? What is she doing now? Married I suppose,' I say, hoping for a last sliver of information before I'm led out of the house.

Gwen doesn't answer me. She walks out into the hallway and, like a small admonished child, I follow her, purposely avoiding the damp stretch of rug. She's a clever lady, I'll give her that, making sure the information she gives me is just enough to leave me wanting more. I'll be back here soon, however. I'm not giving up. Not when I've come this far.

I turn and look at her once I'm outside. She stands in the doorway and for a brief moment I wonder if she's blocking my entry back in. She seems to have grown a couple of inches, her previously diminutive frame seeming to fill the entire entrance.

'Do you believe in ghosts?' The words are out of my mouth before I can stop them. They weren't intended and I have no idea why I said it.

I'm almost on the point of apologising when Gwen smiles and reaches out her hand and places it on mine. Her skin is crisp and cool against my hot palm. Despite the ageing texture of her flesh, the feel of it reassures me in a perverse sort of way.

'My dear, I think we all pass through this world and leave a mark. Some leave positivity and good memories behind and others leave a blemish; a nasty monstrous stain. I think that blemishes unfortunately take longer to disappear, and I'm afraid some of those more stubborn ones can never be removed.' Her eyes crinkle up at the corners as she gives me a generous and warm smile and then closes the door.

Twenty-five

Hugh is standing at the door waiting for me when I get back home. He is grimy looking and covered in white dust, specks of it clinging to his dark hair, making him look like a much older man. He is wearing a self-satisfied expression as he takes my hand and leads me inside.

'Guess what we've found?'

I shake my head and feel my mouth hang open slightly, unsure as to whether or not I actually want to see what he's about to show me. Gwen's words are still echoing around my head and I try to make sense of them as we walk towards the stairs. An electrician passes us, sweat visible on his face. His shirt is dark and pitted with patches of damp as he carries a large toolbox through to the living room. He looks completely pissed off with this house. He isn't the only one.

I follow Hugh, feeling as if I'm walking on air. We get to the landing and I watch as he stands proudly next to a strip of panelling on the far wall, his hand resting on it protectively. It runs the entire length of the wall and is one of approximately a dozen panels that we have talked about stripping back and painting with an eggshell pastel paint. My bottom lip juts out to indicate my puzzlement. It's just a strip of wood and I fail to see what it is that's so appealing about it. Then I watch, both horrified and fascinated, as Hugh silently pulls one of the panels aside to reveal a space behind it.

'John found it while he was drilling here. And that's not all,' Hugh says breathlessly. 'Come with me.'

I follow him up to our study in the converted loft area. My desk has been pulled aside and behind it is another marginally shorter panel. It's a squat slightly rotten piece of wood but the width is the same and I inhale deeply as once again, Hugh slides it to one side to reveal another space behind.

Unable to resist, I get down on my knees and peer inside. It's a little cubby hole, big enough to fit in. I knock on each of the sides and on the floor. It feels solid enough.

'Go on,' Hugh says teasingly, 'sit in it. It's big enough. I've already tried it.'

I crawl forwards and crouch, my knees bunched up under my chin. It's small but not tiny and a bigger person than me could easily fit in here. An intruder. Somebody who prowls around our house at night.

Suddenly the flimsy walls of the space feel as if they're closing in on me and I half throw myself out onto the floor, my breath coming out in short bursts.

'It runs the entire length of the house,' Hugh says excitedly. 'From top to bottom.'

I fail to share Hugh's enjoyment of this find. The whole thing gives me a deep sense of doom, as if we've stumbled upon a secret place that will unleash things that are best left hidden.

'According to the boss downstairs, it probably used to be a dumb waiter that they've closed off. See in here?' Hugh says, tapping at the bottom of the opening. 'Somebody has put a solid base on it, but if we were to dig it out, you'd be able to see right through to the floor below. There must have been a pulley somewhere at one point but it looks like it's been dismantled. Shame, eh? We could have used this for lunch while we're working up here. Get the kids to send us up some snacks from below.'

He actually laughs at the idea. Laughs. That's because he hasn't realised it yet. His mind isn't focused on another obvious use for this claustrophobic hidey-hole. Hugh isn't thinking what I'm thinking: that this is a perfect person-sized space. Somewhere for a night visitor to hide. One on each floor. Ideal for anybody wanting to disappear quickly.

I try to speak but my throat feels as if it's closing up, stopping anything from escaping; the words I want to say are lodged there, solid and immovable.

I smile and calmly walk away from Hugh, and go back down to the next floor where I enter the bathroom and throw up. My stomach gurgles and churns and once I start, I cannot stop retching. My abdomen convulses over and over until it's empty and there's nothing left to regurgitate.

Strands of damp hair hang over my eyes and sweat courses down my face. I kneel there for a short while, panting and gasping for breath and when I eventually find the energy to wipe my mouth and get up, Hugh is standing behind me, aghast. His face is a sickly shade of pale, and bemusement at my predicament is written all over his face.

'You don't see it, do you?' I say gruffly, acid eating at my throat. I visualise it, hot lava corroding the soft skin in my mouth. I turn around and spit into the toilet then turn back to stare at him.

'See what?' His voice displays genuine confusion. For an intelligent man, he is sometimes so incredibly dense.

I shake my head and, were it not for the fact I feel so ghastly, I would laugh at his stupidity, at his complete inability to see what is so blindingly obvious. Instead, I place the lid down on the toilet and perch on the end of it, my legs knocking together.

'Where do you think that person went to the other evening when we searched this house, Hugh? We looked in every cupboard, every single space in this fucking house and there was nobody there! Don't tell me you hadn't thought of that when you found this – this fucking shitty hiding space?' I am gasping and struggling to breathe. I'm also aware that Hugh is staring at me, unable to take in what it is that I'm saying. Part of him will think me unstable but I know – I just know – that another small part of him will be mulling it over in his head, trying to piece it all together. He won't admit it to me immediately because Hugh doesn't like to be caught out. He likes to think he is always one step ahead, you see, and he will be furious with himself for not thinking of it before I did.

He doesn't respond, not that I expect him to, but instead closes the door and leaves me sitting there on the toilet seat, tears and snot streaming down my face.

I wipe at my cheeks and nose and sniff. I've overreacted once again, I know that, but what the hell did he expect? He acted as if the whole thing was some sort of spectacular game when in reality, discovering that shaft scared the shit out of me. This isn't a game we're playing here. This is our home, our lives, and I just wish Hugh would stop walking around blindfolded and start facing up to what is going on here.

I now have no idea what to think after this recent find. I feel foolish for even contemplating the idea that Cross House is haunted. I had been backed into a corner with no other explanation for our nocturnal visits but now, with this new piece of knowledge, perhaps we can end this once and for all. This recent find has to be the answer. It just has to be.

By the time I pull myself together and head back downstairs, Hugh is immersed in his work, caught up in a phone call with a particularly demanding customer. His voice is stiff with barely disguised annoyance and his skin is pale and waxy like putty. He taps his pen on the kitchen top, a rhythmic rattle that echoes around the room. The hammering and banging has stopped, highlighting every single sound we make. It wouldn't surprise me if he has already made another appointment for me at Doctor Schilling's clinic. That's how Hugh handles the unknown: by pretending it can be cured. Stick a plaster over a gaping wound and hope for the best. But not anymore.

I prepare a salad for our evening meal and cover it up, then put it in the fridge. I'll find something else to go with it later once all the workmen have gone. There's little I can do with limited electricity and so much mess.

Behind me, I hear Hugh sigh. His telephone conversation has ended and I get the feeling he wants me to turn and speak to him. I don't. Instead, I busy myself with cleaning up the kitchen. We have yet to converse about the other evening but now isn't the time.

'I need to go and get the kids from school,' I murmur as nonchalantly as I can.

'Okay,' Hugh replies, which takes me by surprise. I half expected him to ignore me or worse still, sit and scrutinise my every move without speaking, but he doesn't. And he even sounds light and approachable. Considering what has just happened, this is progress. 'We'll chat about everything tonight once the kids are in bed,' he says and, much to my astonishment, he gets up, wraps me in his arms and kisses me. Not a stale peck on the cheek, but a warm lingering kiss that promises so much more. I almost melt against his chest. It feels like so long since we've even been kind to each other, let alone touched or shown any intimacy, that his gentle way almost makes me cry.

I gaze up at him and nod, more tears threatening to spill over as I look into his eyes. Extricating myself from his embrace, I grab the car keys and head out of the door.

***

We spend a pleasant enough evening eating a meal of salmon salad followed by an apple pie I picked up from a local bakery opposite Poppy's school. Aiden complains about the state of the house through a mouthful of pie, which entertains us no end considering the mess his bedroom is usually in. We reassure him that this time next week, it will all be done. The walls will be plastered and we'll be well on our way to getting the whole place redecorated.

I am sorely tempted to question Poppy about her drawings as I lead her up to bed but she is distracted and tired and not in the mood for being quizzed. Her eyes grow heavy before I've even tucked her in fully. By the time I finish reading her favourite story she is sound asleep.

Flicking the light off, I sit for a short while in the darkness, perched on the edge of her bed. I'm not quite sure what I expect to happen. Do I really think an apparition is going to spring to life before my very eyes? I let my gaze roam around the room, trying visualise what it was that Poppy saw, or thinks she saw. I tell myself it was just another of her dreams, a horrible nightmare she had, and the fact that it matches what we have seen in this house and also matches the story Gwen told me, is just a bizarre coincidence. It has to be. There is no other explanation.

There is no doubt that this room has plenty of shadowy corners, lots of areas that can set a young child off with nightmares, especially if, like Poppy, they have a vivid imagination. I bite at my lip and wonder how often I'm going to do this – deny the undeniable. There is, without any doubt, something going on here, and it seems as if the more I discover, the more I try to put it all down to coincidence or chance. Perhaps it's because I've never had to deal with anything like this before. I feel as if I'm running around in circles, putting out fires only for them to start up again in a different place. And it is both disorientating and downright draining. At some point we have to do something. I don't think I can stand one more disturbed night or have to put up with my children suffering dreams so terrifying they feel compelled to put pen to paper to get it out of their system.

The bed creaks as I stand up. I lean down and gently kiss Poppy on her cheek. She is soft and warm and tiny and the very sight of her brings a lump to my throat. We are going to be happy here. We have to be. I'll make sure of it.

Hugh has poured us both a glass of wine when I get back downstairs and he is sitting watching a film that I know won't interest me in the slightest. The choice of Hugh's cerebral movies leaves me cold. In that respect we are very different indeed.

'Everything okay up there?'

'Aiden's reading and Poppy's fast asleep,' I say, scooping up my wine and taking a long satisfying gulp of it. The cold liquid travels down my throat, leaving an icy trail in its wake. I close my eyes and savour the taste before taking another sip.

Hugh pats the sofa next to where he's sitting. I drop into it and place my head back on the cushion. We are about to have a discussion that only six weeks ago would have seemed outlandish and unbelievable, and yet here we are, sitting side by side, ready to discuss what or who it is that strays through our house in the early hours. The whole thing is surreal. I think I need to be drunk in order to do this.

'You okay?' he asks, his fingers trailing through my hair. I can feel the heat of his breath on my cheek. It calms me and makes me feel as if I'm safe here. As long as Hugh is beside me, nothing can go wrong.

'So, what do we do now?' I whisper to him as he continues to stroke my hair.

'About what?' he says and then laughs, cutting in again before I have a chance to scream at him or go into a state of hysteria. 'I'm kidding, Faye. And in answer to that, I have to say, I really have no idea. Did it actually happen? It all feels a bit weird now, what with the passing of time and looking at it in the cold light of day and all that jazz.'

'It happened,' I reply tersely. 'It definitely happened, Hugh. Somebody was in this house.'

I hear him swig back his wine and listen to him swallow, watching as his Adam's apple bobs up and down. We sit in silence, neither of us sure what to say next. We don't have any solutions. We don't have any notion of what is actually going on; what it is that occurs in this house during the hours of darkness. I don't mention ghosts or anything related to the supernatural. Hugh would either laugh or tell me in all seriousness to shut up. When it comes to otherworldly matters, Hugh is a definite non-believer. Up until a few weeks ago, I was of the same mind-set, but just recently I've seen things that have begun to sway me, things that have caused me to alter my way of thinking. I never thought I would ever entertain such ideas, but here I am, the daughter of a scientist and once a facts-only reporter, wondering if my house is haunted. The whole thing is insane.

'Well,' Hugh sighs, 'all we can do is wait to see if it happens again.'

He's right. At this moment, the house is devoid of any noise: no shuffling footsteps, no rattling breaths or dripping saliva. No spilt blood. Just a couple of quiet sleeping children and us. Only time will tell whether or not our visitor will return. I pray not, but who knows? Let's see what happens tonight. Let's just see what the darkness brings.

Twenty-six

The café is small and busy. We sit at a table close to the door which affords us a welcome cool breeze every time somebody enters or leaves. Zoe is a gentle soul, perpetually on edge, eyes wide like a deer caught in the headlights. She twitches about in her seat and rubs at her face like a nervous child. I smile at her and do my best to put her at ease. She is, it would seem, deeply reserved and I get the feeling that talking about Cross House is making her even more anxious.

'Another coffee?' I say, as I attempt to catch the waitress's eye. Zoe nods enthusiastically.

She busies herself with her phone while I reel off our order to a young slim lady in her early twenties who appears visibly exasperated as she stands at our table and watches another five customers troop through the door, her pencil scribbling furiously while she writes our order down.

'So,' I sigh, as I remove my sweater, the heat in the café rising rapidly as it continues to fill up with people, 'you said your mum worked there for quite a few years?'

She nods and I make notes in my jotter, pretending to be a real journalist writing a real story.

'She loved the job but hated her.'

This catches my attention. Now she's got me. 'Hated Mrs Wentworth? Hilary?' I say, knowing full well who she is referring to.

Zoe nods. 'And her daughter. Said they were a right conniving pair. He was nice though. That's the only reason she kept on working there. Mum always had time for Mr Wentworth. He was really kind to her.'

'Tell me about the house.' I want to know everything but get the feeling this shy lady is holding something back. Something that could be important.

'Well,' she says softly, picking at her carrot cake with the utmost precision. 'Mum worked there for over ten years. She used to go in every morning to clean. It started off okay but then Mrs Wentworth's illness got worse and she became bad-tempered, shouting all the time. Nothing Mum did was ever good enough. Mind you, Mrs Wentworth was a pretty nasty piece of work long before her health deteriorated. All her declining well-being did was make her even more miserable and demanding.'

'What sort of things did she say or do?' I ask, trying to sound sympathetic when all the while my mind is focused only on getting all the dirt, finding out everything that went on in Cross House. I want every piece of filthy laundry and I want it well and truly aired.

Zoe stops and closes her eyes for a second, deep in thought. I pray she doesn't clam up or suddenly decide she no longer wants to tell me anything. She doesn't. If anything, her next words leave me reeling.

'Well, for a start, she believed that horrible bitch of a daughter of hers over the sex allegation.'

I take a deep breath and widen my eyes. 'And your mum didn't?' This is what I want to hear. This is more like it.

'She said it was awful what happened there. Apparently, the boy had the mental capacity of somebody much younger and wasn't capable of doing anything of the sort but the girl was so insistent. Put on a really good show of lying, according to Mum, and so the boy got sent away.'

'Peter,' I whisper, my heart breaking for a defenceless child I've never even met. 'His name was Peter.'

She nods and we sit for a few seconds gathering our thoughts.

'Can I ask you something, Zoe?' I sip my coffee and scribble more words down on my pad. Not that I need to. The things she has told me are scored into my brain. That poor child. That dreadful girl and her mother.

'Of course.' She seems brighter than when we first met. Perhaps she had me down as some sort of hard-nosed journalist when in reality, I'm more scared than she is.

'I know you said Peter was incapable of abusing his sister due to his learning difficulties, but was it ever proven that he didn't do it? You said that your mum seemed really certain about his innocence.'

I watch as Zoe's face flushes a deep shade of scarlet. A crimson hue creeps up over her throat and she swallows repeatedly, her mouth opening and closing as if she can't make her mind up whether or not to speak.

'I'm not sure.' She takes a slurp of coffee and winces. It is burning hot, steam billowing off it in long tendrils. Her eyes drift over to the window then back to me. The small bones and sinews on her neck protrude as she stares at me and leans forward conspiratorially, her voice low and gravelly. 'Look, I'm going to tell you something but I don't want any of it to go in your story. Will you promise me that this doesn't go any further?'

I try not to look too enthusiastic even though my heart is banging furiously against my ribcage. I nod solemnly. 'I absolutely promise, Zoe. This is just between you and me, okay?' I place my hand over hers to reassure her and let her know I'm as good as my word.

She nods at me and pulls her hand away, her fingers icy cold despite the heat of the small room we're in. 'The girl –'

'Tammy?' I add.

'Yeah, Tammy. She'd written some things in her diary about what she was going to say. Horrible stuff about how she would accuse that poor lad so he would get sent away. Awful graphic stuff apparently, going into detail about where she would say he'd put his hands and how he'd touched her. She thought it was hilarious, calling him a retard and other awful names.' Zoe's lip trembles.

I daren't move, daren't breathe. I need to hear what's coming next.

'And if you're wondering how my mum knew this, it wasn't because she snooped or went through her diary. There's no way she would ever do anything like that.'

'No, I'm sure she wouldn't,' I whisper. I'm desperate to hear the rest. The air between us feels so fragile. I'm so terrified of losing this moment, this next revelation.

'That Tammy had torn them out after the boy was sent away and they were all over her bedroom. I suppose she had intended to put them in the bin but they were scattered all over when Mum cleaned her bedroom one day, some on the floor under her bed and others shoved behind her dressing table. Mum found them. She saw all those words as she was gathering them up.'

'That's awful,' I mumble, my head spinning as I think about those missing pages. Tammy had torn them out after all, but not for the reasons I thought she had. Lies. Those pages were full of plans and schemes and the darkest most dreadful of lies. 'Your poor mum must have been horrified.' My words sound hollow and I know I'm throwing clichéd platitudes her way, but I don't know what else to say. It's all I have at the minute.

'She had to do it,' Zoe says from behind her cup as she takes another gulp. 'She had no idea he would do what he did. It wasn't her fault but she spent the rest of her life blaming herself.'

'Had to do what?' I think I know what it was Zoe's mum did but need to hear it from her. It's all coming together now. Suddenly the story of the Wentworth family is starting to make sense.

'There was no point showing those pages to Mrs Wentworth. She would have sided with her daughter and probably sacked Mum. She and my dad needed the money so she couldn't run the risk of losing her job, but she felt that she had to do something, so she gathered up all the pages and put them in Mr Wentworth's briefcase. Mum used to clean his study and he wasn't precious about his belongings. Not like Mrs Wentworth who screamed at her if she moved things and didn't put them back properly. He often left his briefcase open, so Mum slipped the diary pages in there one day next to all his papers.'

'And he read them and then he went missing,' I say, almost finishing the story for her.

Zoe raises her eyebrows, lets out a sigh and nods. 'Poor Mum. She was devastated when his body was found.'

'We don't know that the papers were the reason for his disappearance, though, do we?' I'm fishing for information here. I want Zoe to join up those few remaining dots for me.

Her lip trembles slightly as she takes another gulp of coffee. 'Some of them were tucked in his coat pocket when they found him, according to Mum. Whether or not that's true, we'll probably never know.'

I'm almost certain those diary entries played a part in his disappearance but decide to quell my impulse to speak. What good would it do to make her feel any worse than she already does? Her poor mother thought she was doing the right thing and had to live with the consequences of her actions for the rest of her life. For all we know, Adrian Wentworth may have gone for a walk to clear his head and got lost. The moors are unforgiving to the unprepared. You go walking up there in winter at your own risk.

'Well,' I say as I shrug my shoulders and chase a chunk of unwanted cake around my plate with a tiny fork, 'all I can say is, if I were in your mum's position, I would do the same thing. I think she made the right decision, Zoe.'

She smiles, a dull light beginning to glow in her eyes. I do actually mean it too. She had to make a difficult choice and many would have turned a blind eye or ignored what was going on in that house. She didn't. She did what she thought was best and that was all she could do under the circumstances.

'Is there anything else you need to know about the house?' she asks, her tone heartbreakingly innocent.

There is something that now niggles me but I doubt very much that Zoe will be able to help me with it. Her interest in the house has long since passed but I ask anyway. 'What happened to Tammy and Peter? Where are they now?'

As I expected, Zoe shrugs her shoulders and tells me she has no idea. 'After Mr Wentworth died, the old lady went into a rapid decline. She refused to get out of bed and when she did, she spent her days roaming around the house in her nightclothes. Mum tried to help her but Mrs Wentworth's chest was so bad that there wasn't anything she could do.'

Zoe's words make my face grow hot and my spine grow cold. She has no idea that what she has just said has put me on edge, made me feel as if I want to scream at her to stop talking.

'And then there was the fall.' Zoe says it so casually, as if it's an everyday occurrence.

'Do you know anything about that?' I ask, partly dreading what she may come out with. It seems to me that every new piece of information I hear about Cross House leaves me feeling either terrified or mystified. It's a house of secrets, a house with so much to hide.

'Not really. As I say, I only know what Mum told me over the years. It was a long time ago. I wish now that I'd asked more, taken more notice of her. The whole episode had such an impact on her, but growing up I got tired of hearing about it and just sort of shut off to it all. Cross House was a well-known local house in its day, you know? Both of their deaths made quite an impact locally. The papers reported on it and there was quite a bit of gossip. He was a successful businessman in the area. Employed a lot of people, he did. After he died, his business practically folded,' Zoe says, her voice going up an octave.

I think about his will and then the money his wife left after she died and wonder where it all went to.

'What did he do?' I say, annoyed with myself for not finding this out before now. And I call myself a journalist. No wonder I was the first to be offered a redundancy package. They were probably glad to see the back of me.

'Mr Wentworth?' Zoe says, mildly shocked at my ignorance. 'He owned a big hotel. The one at the far end of your village actually. You must have seen it? It's a care home now.' She shakes her head and gives me a knowing look. 'Isn't everything? Nearly every building you pass these days has been turned into a care home.'

'Oh,' I say, trying to picture the place in my mind's eye. 'I think I know where you mean. It's a right turn on the way into the Brackston. Out on its own up a country lane?'

'That's the one!' she trills. 'Used to be the place to go to back in the day. He owned a few smaller pubs as well, but that place was really big and hugely successful. Back in the days of dinner dances and business conventions, it was where you went to be seen. Anyone who was anyone visited it.'

I try to imagine it: Adrian Wentworth as the genial host, Hilary bustling around the hotel playing at being lady of the manor with Cross House as their base, a lovely home bought from the fortunes made with the hotel. And now the place that afforded them such an extravagant lifestyle is a care home and Cross House is a ramshackle old place with crumbling walls and rising damp. How times change. An eerie feeling settles on me. All those years, all those lives, gone. All the memories dissipated into the ether. Or maybe not.

My eyes suddenly feel heavy with the thought of it. I'm ready to go home now. I think Zoe is about done here too.

We sit for a few moments, not speaking, each of us locked in our own thoughts, mine full of shadowy faces from the past. I'm pretty sure unearthing these memories has had some sort of effect on Zoe as well. None of us are immune to the damage our history can cause, leaving dents on the present. Her poor mother knew all about that. I doubt there was ever a day passed without her feeling guilty for putting those papers in Adrian Wentworth's briefcase.

'Thank you for this, Zoe,' I say, and I mean it too. She has been a huge help. I stare at her, wondering how such a gentle soul can have such a boisterous child whose mouth runs away with him. Then I think about the gentleman that was Adrian Wentworth and his spiteful daughter. Sometimes, people just are what they are. Good, kind adults can spawn bad children. That's just life.

'Oh,' I say suddenly. 'I almost forgot. Here,' I whisper as I hand over a small envelope full of some recent pictures I took of the inside of Cross House. They're not the most flattering of photographs but I thought they might evoke a few memories of when her mum worked there. After what she has done, allowing me access to parts of her past that are painful to her, it's the least I can do.

She takes them and smiles brightly, thanking me profusely.

'So, when will it be out then?' Zoe asks, her eyes bright with anticipation.

'I'm sorry?' I say, too distracted to focus on her question.

'The article about Cross House?' she squeaks, her tone so full of naivety I shiver with guilt.

'Ah, sorry. Yes, the article I'm writing.' I tap my pen on the notepad to distract her attention from my face which is suddenly flushed with shame. 'I need to gather up more facts from neighbours and people in the village, so it'll be a good few weeks yet.'

'But you'll let me know when it's out?' She's sharper than I think she is. She's making sure the part she told me about the diaries her mother gave Adrian doesn't get included. I like this woman. She may be a gentle soul, but she's no fool.

I nod and tell her I'll definitely be in touch. We stand up and shake hands, the people behind us only too keen to take our seats as we vacate them and head for the door.

'I'll let you know as soon as I have a publication date,' I say, my mind already going over the idea that I could write a story after all. I could ring my old editor, see if he can find space for it. It would help raise my profile in time for the release of my book. Cross House has taken enough out of me and although we had an undisturbed evening last night, it's about time that house of ours gave something back.

Twenty-seven

'**D**id you hear that?' Hugh's voice cuts through the darkness, rousing me from a deep sleep.

I listen but hear nothing. I'm beginning to think that hearing nothing at all is more sinister than hearing something. The stillness in this house is like the calm before the storm; an indicator that something terrible is about to happen.

'I can't hear anything,' I say, and for once this is true. I don't want to think about what it is that Hugh heard while I was sleeping. I just want it all to go away. I'm tired both physically and mentally. All I want to do is sleep.

'That!' he says suddenly and leaps from the bed before I can say or do anything.

I lie still, my heart hammering against my ribcage like a trapped bird and my neck vibrating as my pulse races. Then I hear it. It's coming from downstairs – a distant tapping sound. I watch as Hugh springs into action. I'm too groggy and bleary-eyed to do anything, too fearful to tell him that this is a different noise from the other times. This actually sounds like somebody breaking into the house.

Rubbing at my face wearily, I get up and follow him. He's like a wild animal, prowling around, his face full of anger, his body stiff and tense as he makes his way downstairs.

'Wait!' I hiss as I follow him, shivering and on the verge of tears.

He turns and watches me but doesn't respond. Instead, he waits until I'm behind him then continues creeping down the stairs. Every shadow, every creak makes each and every fibre of my being howl with dread. I place my hand on his shoulder and lean in to whisper in his ear.

'Maybe we should just call the police?'

Hugh shakes his head and carries on walking. I have a bad feeling about this. It's not like the other times. This is unlike the other incidents. My stomach is clenched as we get to the bottom and tiptoe into the living room. Silence. Nothing at all. Just an empty room.

The sound is coming from the kitchen. My chest constricts, and I feel as if I'm going to throw up. I'm light-headed as we walk back out into the hallway and head towards the back door. Unsure what we're about to be faced with, I grab Hugh's arm, pure terror running through me. Something is wrong here. It's not like before. I have visions of an escaped prisoner or a dead-eyed junkie wielding a jagged blade at us, or worse still, a gun.

His steps slow down to an almost imperceptible shuffle as we creep towards the kitchen, his breath a ragged gasp as he pushes the door open.

'Fuck!' Hugh's voice pierces the silence as he launches himself forward and a struggle between two bodies starts to take shape in the darkness.

An involuntary shriek escapes me as I watch Hugh get into a scuffle with a bulky shadow who throws him to the ground with force. I hear the crack of bone against concrete and watch, horrified, as the shape exits through the open door, leaving my husband sprawled on the floor, blood seeping out of his head and smearing on the floor next to his silent still body.

I can barely breathe. Getting down on my knees, I lift Hugh's head and place it on my knee. His eyes are open and he stares up at me. I can't see his features clearly for the tears that are streaming down my face.

I look away into the darkness at a shifting shape that is meandering its way across the back lawn. Towards the outhouses. I turn back to Hugh. He's my priority. I can't think about the person who is out there or where they may be heading to. I have to get Hugh's injury sorted, make sure it's not serious.

'I'm fine, Faye,' he says, struggling to sit up. Blood is smeared on my hands as he heaves himself upright. 'Jesus,' Hugh sighs. 'I wasn't expecting that.'

'Are you sure you're okay?' I ask him, searching his eyes for any signs of concussion. I also want to get out there, to follow that person, find out where they've gone to. If I run, I could still catch them.

Hugh watches my face then speaks, voicing my thoughts. 'Don't go out there on your own, Faye. He's a strong bugger. Caught me off guard for sure.'

'I could get a torch,' I say. 'Catch up with him. You could stay here and ring the police.' I feel sure I could do it. My initial fear has gone, only to be replaced with untethered rage. How dare this person do this? Who the fuck do they think they are coming in my house and assaulting my husband? I have so much rage coursing through my body, I'm certain I could kill them with my bare hands.

'Check the door,' Hugh whispers. 'See how they got in. If the lock isn't broken, the police can't do anything.' He's right, but I would feel safer if they were informed. They could dust for fingerprints, check for footprints in the soil. They could do *something*.

I get up and turn on the light then head to the door. Hugh's right. No broken lock, no shattered glass. Apart from a small puddle of Hugh's blood on the kitchen floor, it's as if nobody has even been in.

'This is ridiculous!' I bark. 'How did they get in, Hugh? How the fuck did a stranger get into our house?'

'It's an old lock,' he says wearily as he grabs a nearby towel and presses it against the side of his head. 'We'll get a new door. That should sort it.'

'And what if they come back, get angry when they realise they can't get in and bring a knife or a hammer and start battering their way into our home? What then, Hugh? What the fuck do we do then? Can we call the police when that happens? Or will it be too late at that point?' I'm becoming hysterical, but I can't stop myself. White hot fury and terror merge into one and spill out of me, swirling and frothing up until I'm blind with it. This has gone on for too long now. I want to bring an end to it and yet again, Hugh is brushing it all aside.

'I promise you, I won't let that happen, Faye. A new door will be enough to put them off. Whoever it was has probably been doing this for ages while the place was empty. Now they know we're here, it should stop them. I'll get onto a double-glazing firm first thing in the morning and get them to come and measure up for a new door. We can do the same for the front of the house as well.'

I'm too tired to argue with him. I lean down and inspect the wound on his head. The bleeding has stopped but his hair is matted with thick red blood. I rinse the cloth under the tap and clean up the cut, then get on my knees and wipe the floor. How much blood has this house seen over the years? How much fucking blood has been spilt in this place?

Standing up, I take Hugh's hand and help him to his feet. He wobbles about before getting his balance. He watches as I drag a chair over from the table and push it under the door handle. It's not much of a deterrent but it's better than nothing. I'll feel a little easier knowing it's there.

We stagger up to bed, Hugh looking better already, me still begging him to let me call the police. He insists there's no need and that a new door will sort it. What is it with him? I know there's no sign of a break-in and we always said police involvement is the last thing we wanted when Todd and Jeff were bothering us, but surely he can see that this is a serious situation?

'We should get that cut looked at in the morning,' I say, sighing heavily to convey my frustration at his decision. We climb back into bed and I lie there, fury and fear enveloping me. I doubt I'll get back off with worrying about the intruder getting back in and Hugh falling into an unconscious state in his sleep.

'It's fine,' Hugh says sleepily. 'I feel okay. It was more a shock than anything else. Get some rest and we'll talk about it in the morning.'

He is asleep in no time. I am stock still, my arm resting over his chest, feeling the rise and fall of his breathing, a rhythmic reminder that he's still alive. It could have been so much worse. I'm not going to feel grateful for that. I'm angry that there was somebody down there at all. They had no fucking right coming into our house. What the hell do they want anyway? Perhaps Hugh's right and this house was used as somewhere for vagrants to stay while it was empty. And the back door is old and rotten. The lock doesn't work properly and can be easily picked. I'm trying to convince myself of this because the alternative is too grisly to contemplate. Tomorrow I'll inspect those outhouses. After dropping the kids off at school, I fully intend to cut everything back and check for signs of life inside those buildings. That's where that shadow was heading. I think of the basket with the empty wrappers and shut my eyes tight. Somebody has been down there. Everything points to it. Hugh is correct in one respect – Cross House being empty has provided somebody with the perfect place to reside. But not anymore. We live here now. This place is ours. Our nocturnal wanderer can go to hell. I've lived through enough fear in the past year to last me a lifetime; I don't need any more.

Closing my eyes, I don't expect to sleep and am surprised to find myself falling into a comfortable slumber within a couple of minutes.

When I awake in the morning, Hugh is already up, a dark pink smear of blood on his pillow the only indicator that anything untoward happened last night.

I slide out of bed thinking that today is the day I just may confront our unwanted visitor. Today may well be the day it all comes to an end.

Twenty-eight

Breakfast is a hurried affair. Hugh is preoccupied with an early morning phone call and the electricians arrive shortly after seven. I spend what feels like an inordinate amount of time chivvying children and screaming at them to hurry up eating and get dressed.

By the time I drop them off to school and make it back home, I feel as if I've been awake for half the day. My head aches as the drilling begins once more and I feel a growing need to get outside, where I can begin to hack back the foliage in the garden and find out what lies beneath it to find out where our visitor's hiding place is.

Hugh is busy on the phone again, his face as cheery as ever, showing no signs of distress. The one thing Hugh is, is a consummate professional. He could be dying on his feet and his customers would never know it. He turns to one side and I can see that the cut on his head is hardly visible. Were I not looking for it, I wouldn't know it was even there. He gives a slight wave, quickly scribbles a note telling me he's rung the glazier and continues with his spiel, his esoteric engineering language floating over my head, meaning nothing to me.

I leave him in the kitchen and head outside. The gardening tools are in the garage. I unlock the side door and step into a faceful of cobwebs. Grabbing at what I need along with a thick pair of gloves, I brush my hands around the frame to clear a path back out and slam the door shut. If there is one thing that sets my nerves jangling, it's spiders. I expect I'll find a few of those when I start to cut back the bushes and greenery that surround those buildings, but I've dealt with worse in the past few months. If I can handle being assaulted by workmates and drooled on in my sleep by perfect strangers, I can handle a few creepy-crawlies.

I march down to the bottom of the garden and set to it with a vengeance. All the anger and terror I've been subjected to over the last year spews out of me. I tear and hack at a lone growth of something half dead that looks like it used to be a tree, until I can begin to see the real shrubbery behind it.

Standing back to take a breather, I try to work out how long it will take me to cut through it all. A swarm of insects' buzzes about my face as I stare at the enormous mass of foliage and gnarled branches in front of me. This is a much bigger job than I anticipated.

I wipe at my face with my sleeve, figuring the longer I stare at it, the longer it will take to cut it all back. I take the shears and start to cut and snip, leaves falling and fluttering over my head and shoulders and down to the ground. Tiny flies flutter out from each branch as I continue to slice through the mini forest in my garden. I have no idea how many years of growth this is, but it may as well be a century's worth. Why would anybody let a garden get in this state? This kind of outside space is an asset. It could be turned into something pretty astounding given some time and care.

I don't stop, my arms burning with the exertion as I reach up to the higher branches, pulling them apart, hacking and cutting at them until I start to see signs of crumbling red brickwork beneath. It occurs to me that if I can't access these buildings without a fight, then nobody else can get to them either. So, where did our intruder go to last night? Where the fuck did he disappear to?

Stepping back to catch my breath, I stumble and fall to my knees, landing on the hard earth with a solid bump. I stay there for a couple of seconds to catch my breath. I'm not sure I can do this. It's going to take forever and a day to get to those outhouses.

As I do my best to get up, my hands press down onto the damp soil. Something solid juts up from the ground under my palm. I touch it and recoil, scrambling backwards to get away from it. After the past few weeks, I can't bring myself to think what it might be. With this house, anything is possible. I've very probably unearthed something that has been concealed for decades and I can't bring myself to even guess at what it might be.

I look down and swallow the acrid flow of vomit that is doing its best to make a quick exit out of my body. I place my hand over my mouth, pressing hard to suppress it, to stop the tide of sickness that is threatening to erupt out of me.

I can see what it is now. It's patently obvious, even to me, what it is that's protruding out of the earth next to my feet. The sight of it is so clear and lifelike that I have to close my eyes.

A bone is sticking out from a clearing where I've cut back the shrubbery. A grubby-looking bone sits there next to me. The soil and foliage surrounding it has been moved, leaving it visible, and now, despite not wanting to look, I can't tear my eyes away from it.

I have no idea what to do next. I sit for a couple of seconds, letting it sink in. After the last few weeks, this shouldn't surprise or frighten me but every time I think I have the secrets of Cross House sorted in my head, this mysterious old property throws something else my way, blindsiding me.

Crawling forward, I reach down and tentatively pluck the sliver of dirty bone from the ground, brushing away the dirt with my trembling fingers. I shouldn't be touching it, I know that, but I have to be sure it is what I think it is before I start to really panic. It comes up with surprising ease, the ground I take it from crumbling away to reveal a small pile of more bones buried underneath. I let out a shriek and drop the one I'm holding. I fall backwards, away from my find, unable to breathe properly. Dear God, is this really happening?

My heart pumps madly and I feel as if my neck is about rupture under the pressure. I give myself time to calm down. Sweat covers my face and yet I feel so very cold. I just need a couple of seconds to think what to do next. I let out a juddering gasp and concentrate on controlling my breathing. I know all of these techniques and yet in times of real stress my memory lets me down, blocking out rational thought and allowing blind panic to take hold of the reins and drag me away.

My heart begins to slow down as I take unhurried deep breaths, exhaling through pursed lips. I can do this. I have to do this.

Wiping at my face with my sleeve, I take one final deep breath and sit upright. Leaning towards the mound of earth, I tentatively pick up two of the small bones and stare down at what sits beneath them in the shallow burial place, my eyes fixed on what the tiny makeshift grave contains. Lying at the bottom, probably only seven or eight inches down, is a skull. I don't know whether to laugh or cry. It's clearly the bones of an animal. I have inadvertently stumbled across the place where a family once buried their beloved pet.

As carefully as I can, I gather the other bones back up and lay them all back in the hole. I drag soil back over to cover it up, using my hands as shovels to claw at the damp earth. I press it down in place and stand up, stepping back, away from the recently shifted mud. Somebody's pet. A feeling of utter sadness weighs down on me. This place is riddled with somebody else's memories. We are not in the least bit acquainted with this house. I get the feeling we're going to have to work damn hard to become a part of it, for Cross House to finally accept us as its new residents.

It becomes apparent that uncovering the outhouses is beyond my strength and capabilities. I spend another two hours cutting and shearing and yet I barely make a dent in the mass of leaves and algae-covered branches that conceal the brickwork beneath.

I step back to survey my work and let out a short bark of laughter. Apart from a small opening that reveals a partial rotten window and a small portion of wall, there is very little difference – nothing to say I've spent the morning out here tearing the area apart.

A huge pile of foliage and broken branches sits behind me on the lawn. We'll need a bonfire to rid ourselves of this lot. At least Aiden and Poppy will benefit from my efforts. They like nothing better than watching a roaring fire and toasting marshmallows on the flames.

I decide I've done enough. It's quite clear that nobody is hiding out in these crumbling buildings. Whoever it was that escaped from our house last night didn't use these as somewhere to hide.

They must have got through the gate at the back of the garden and made their way out through the woods. Either that or they clambered through the small gap in the hedge that leads onto the main road through the village.

Stumbling over the pile of leaves, my limbs trembling with exhaustion, I head back over the lawn towards the house. I pass the summerhouse and something stops me. It looks different somehow. The place is a mess. It's a kid's playhouse with toys and papers scattered far and wide, but something else catches my eye. Footprints. Dirty great footprints cover the floor and a pane of glass is broken. My stomach flips. This is it. This is the place our nocturnal visitor has been using to hide out. Why did I not think of it before now?

I run back up to the house gripped by both excitement and terror. Hugh will need to board the summerhouse window up and put a padlock on it. The sooner the glazier fits a new back door to the house the better. Bit by bit we're blocking the intruder's entry points.

'Somebody's in a hurry.' Hugh is standing at the back door as I practically throw myself at him.

'I've found it!' I blurt it out, my face alight with realisation. 'The summerhouse. He's been in the summerhouse, Hugh. We need to put a lock on there.'

Hugh arches his eyebrows and slowly smiles, his words dashing my hopes. 'You mean the broken window? That was me, I'm afraid. I went in there yesterday looking for some of my tools and accidentally smashed a pane of glass as I lifted a hoe out of the way. I swept it up and told the kids to stay clear until I made sure I'd got all the shards of glass cleared away.'

Frustration and disappointment overwhelm me. 'What?' I stammer, my voice rising in pitch until I'm almost screeching at him. 'Why didn't you tell me this?'

'Why would I tell you? It was a minor thing, Faye. The house is getting ripped to pieces and you're worried about a broken window in an old summerhouse that's probably about ready to collapse?'

'Because I saw it and thought that was where he went, Hugh!' I'm panting now. Anger balloons in my chest. 'Did you make the muddy footprints as well?'

'Probably,' Hugh laughs. 'Jesus, Faye. Look, I had no idea it would upset you this much. And as for last night, I'm convinced it was a junkie who's been using this place while it was empty.'

'A junkie?' I shout. 'A fucking junkie, Hugh? Christ almighty, are you blind? Did you see the size of that person? That was no drug-addled junkie. They were bigger than you! For fuck's sake, Hugh, when are you going to wake up to what is going on in this fucking house?'

A cough behind us stops me, my words ringing in the air around us.

'We need the keys to get into the garage.' The chief electrician is standing in the doorway, an embarrassed flush creeping up his neck.

'Sure,' Hugh says lightly as if I haven't even spoken. He leads the way to the garage, leaving me feeling deflated and empty.

I stare down at my clothes. I'm filthy. I need a shower and then a walk to get out of this house and clear my head. I also need to be away from Hugh. Once I'm cleaned up, I'm going to call in on Gwen and talk to her about it. She made me an offer of coffee and I'm going to take her up on it.

I head upstairs, not caring if we have no electricity, not caring whether or not I'll end up standing under a stream of freezing water. I grab a pile of clean clothes and head into the bathroom, slamming the door behind me.

Twenty-nine

'You're very harassed looking, my dear,' Gwen says as she hands me a biscuit and sits down, her knees cracking loudly like a gunshot in the quiet of the room.

'I've been working in the garden, cutting back all that overgrown shrubbery.' I keep my voice as low as I can. I don't want her picking up on my near hysterical mood.

'Ah yes, well it's been a while since anybody tended to that old place. It's so lovely that you've moved in with a young family. You're breathing new life into it. Exactly what it needs.' She crunches on her biscuit and nibbles at it noisily.

'I found some old animal bones in the garden. Must have been somebody's pet they buried out there. Who lived in it after the Wentworth family moved out?' I already know the answer to this. If it had been occupied, the diaries would have been found and disposed of. Nobody would keep another person's documents and detritus. I just want to hear it from Gwen, to have it confirmed.

'I'm afraid nobody lived there, my dear. The people who bought it after the Wentworth family never came near the old place. They were going to use it to visit their family but the lady became ill and flying back was impossible. Or at least that's what I heard.'

'So, it was empty for all those years after Hilary died? That's an awfully long time to have a house with nobody living in it. Why was that?' And then I think of Tammy. Did she continue living in it on her own?

Gwen falters and I speak for her: 'Tammy lived there for all those years after her parents died? Did she marry? Have children?'

'No children. No marriage either. There was a partner but it didn't last long. He went abroad, leaving her to wallow

204

in her own pit of misery.' Gwen takes a silent sip of tea and watches me carefully. 'It was impossible for anybody to live there in comfort. She had the place decked out like a shrine to her mother. Ghastly pictures of Hilary Wentworth all over the house. That's the last thing anybody wants to see when they get home on an evening, isn't it? A large framed photograph of your mean old mother-in-law staring out at you. It's enough to make anybody run a mile.'

'And what about Peter? Where did he end up living?' I think about his predicament: a man with learning difficulties, orphaned at a young age. He will have spent his life in an institution, possibly being moved from place to place. So many homes and, I'm willing to bet, so little love. Could this story get any worse?

'Oh, he managed. Went from unit to unit and ended up living with a distant cousin who was kind to him and took him in.' This last piece of information pleases me. It's a tiny chink of happiness amidst a storm of sorrow and misery. At least he ended up somewhere half decent. At least he had a home.

'Do you remember a cleaning lady that used to work there while Hilary was alive?' I watch Gwen's reaction carefully. I don't want her to hide anything from me. I'm almost there with this story. So very close to finding out the Wentworth secrets. There can't be much more left to disclose.

If Gwen is lying, she is adept at it. She narrows her eyes and thinks for a moment before speaking. 'I do vaguely recollect a lady who used to call in from time to time. Tiny quiet thing as I recall. Helped out around the house. Didn't speak much.'

I picture Zoe, how reserved and delicate she appeared to be and nod. Like mother, like daughter. 'So where did Tammy move to when she sold up?' I think of the vast fortune she inherited in today's terms and how it wouldn't buy much of anything, certainly nothing on the scale of Cross House. She possibly bought a cottage somewhere – less maintenance – or a flat perhaps. That's the answer when you're on a budget and living alone. Pay a service charge and let somebody else do all the work.

'Not far at all. She's still local.' Gwen raises her eyes and smiles a wry smile. 'Bit of a shame really, where she ended up, but then sometimes you get out of life exactly what you put in.'

My stomach tightens a notch. She lives nearby and all this time I didn't know? I've been sitting reading her teenage diaries while she has been just a few doors away? Somehow, that makes my snooping and secret investigative work feel so much worse. I feel like a cheat. She may have been no angel but those journals are hers. If she lives close by, I intend to return them to her, to their rightful owner.

'Where?' I almost gasp. 'I have her diaries. She can have them back. They don't belong to me. I could take them to her.'

'Well,' Gwen says as she brushes a handful of imaginary crumbs off her lap and onto her plate, 'by all means take them to her, my dear, but don't expect her to thank you or even recognise them.'

I widen my eyes and shake my head to indicate my confusion.

'She has early onset dementia. That's why the house was sold. She couldn't maintain it. Never could really. Looking after things was never Tammy's way. The only thing she ever cared about was herself. By all means pay her a visit, but she won't be able to hold a conversation. She's developed speech dysphasia and communication is more than a little difficult. She's in the care home on the outskirts of the village, but you'll not get any sort of response from her. She may understand you but she won't be able to speak to you. Not in words you'd understand anyway.'

'Millview?' I splutter, almost choking on my tea. 'Tammy Wentworth is in Millview Care Home? The one that used to be the hotel that –'

'That her father owned?' Gwen finishes my sentence for me. 'Yes, that's the one. Quite sad really, isn't it? But then, some people really do deserve their comeuppance and Tammy definitely deserves hers.'

I sit for a while, trying to process it all. For a wise old lady, Gwen's words sting. Does anybody warrant getting such an illness, especially before they reach old age? Tammy was a teenager when she made that accusation. Everybody makes mistakes. Nobody deserves to end their days a drooling husk of their former selves being fed and toileted by strangers.

Gwen reads my thoughts, sees the look of mild disgust in my expression, and speaks. 'I'm not a cruel person, Faye. I realise I may come across as such but let me tell you a few home truths about Tammy Wentworth. The bones you found buried earlier? That was the dog that young Peter brought with him. It was found with a nail in its head at the bottom of the garden. Peter was distraught. He'd had it since it was a puppy and only a few weeks after going to live with his father at that house, the poor thing was found in agony after somebody had hammered a nail into its head.'

My eyes fill up as I think of the small cracked skull, buried out there for all those years. I think of the furore and heartbreak that would accompany such an event, then take a deep breath and shut my mind to the agony that animal must have suffered.

'They put it down to the dog falling on it. How many animals do you know that fall onto the sharp tip of a rusty nail? And don't forget, I was her teacher. I saw how she went on at school and was privy to the things she said and did and believe me, that girl was bad through and through.'

I don't ask what the other things were that Tammy did. I don't want to know. If what Gwen is saying is true, I may just throw those diaries on the bonfire we are going to have to get rid of the branches. All the rubbish can go up in flames together. Can anybody really be that bad? But then, why would Gwen make these stories up?

We sit for a short while, sipping our tea and listening to the distant chime of birdsong outside the window. I try to assimilate these new pieces of information, to put them in order in my mind. So much mystery and intrigue in one family and one house, yet none of it helps me work out who it is that wanders the place at night.

I bite at my lip before speaking, not sure if I really want to hear the answer to my question. 'Another thing's happened to us since we've moved in, Gwen.' Shen watches me so closely, I begin to feel hot and uncomfortable. I swallow and stare around the room, breathing in its musty stale odour, wondering how long it's been since this house has had a lick of paint. Never mind Cross House, Gwen's cottage is in dire need of a makeover. 'We've had somebody wandering around the house in the early hours. Has Cross House ever had squatters while it was empty?'

I wait and watch Gwen's face as her eyes crease and darken and am taken aback at what she says and does next.

'No. Never. Now if you don't mind, I'm ready for my nap.' She stands up, snatches the cup out of my hands and strides off into the kitchen. I'm left ashen-faced and wondering if I'm just expected to leave while she bustles about in there washing pots and tidying up. What on earth just happened between us? Did I say something wrong?

I wait a couple of seconds, half expecting her to walk back in and give me a wide smile, apologising for being so abrupt. It doesn't happen. Instead, she opens the back door, picks up a small watering can and begins to water the plants, heading further down the garden away from the house. She shuffles along, not glancing back until she disappears through a foliage-covered archway and out of view.

Feeling more than a little embarrassed and mildly annoyed, I start to leave the room, but not before I spot something that makes me feel as if a furnace has been lit inside my head. Leaning down to stare at it, I squint just to be sure it is what I think it is.

Lodged in a tight, dark corner, behind the chair I was sitting in, is a photograph. It's old – an image printed long before digital cameras were the norm – and it's grainy and blurred, but even without picking it up to inspect it closely, I can see who it is.

My heart is a tight fist in my chest as I stagger backwards. Why is it here in Gwen's living room? Has she been lying to me all this time? I stare outside at her long stretch of garden. She's still nowhere to be seen. For a brief second, I consider taking the picture, slotting the entire frame into my pocket and going home, but what would that achieve? She would know it was me. I've never seen any other visitors here. Except for the shadow I thought I saw in the window. That shadow. Who was it? It certainly wasn't Gwen; tiny frail arthritic Gwen. It was somebody larger, a bulky frame. Ridiculous thoughts bounce around my head, too outlandish to entertain as being even remotely feasible. She is bound to have family and friends visit from time to time. She has a daughter; that much I do know. A daughter who rings her every day. I'm sure there was once a husband that Gwen has outlived. But that day of the shadow – just a few days back – was another time when Gwen acted differently. She was distracted, sharp and on edge. Much like she was in here just a few minutes ago. There's some kind of link, I just know it, but it's still out of reach. I can't quite work out what the connection is to Gwen and the Wentworths, although finding this photograph is edging me ever closer to the answers I need.

I heave a sigh of resentment and annoyance. I have no idea what to make of this recent find. Gwen, the sweet old lady with sage advice and wise words, is obviously hiding something from me. She may not be telling me outright lies, but neither is she telling me the whole truth, such as what her involvement with the Wentworth family actually is. It would appear that it's a whole lot closer than she's letting on. Why would she keep this photograph for all these years if it means nothing to her? None of this makes any sense.

On impulse, I squat down onto my haunches and snatch the photograph up, stuffing it deep into the pocket of my fleece sweater. I don't give myself any time to change my mind. Gwen has lied to me. Even if she hasn't lied, she is certainly withholding information from me. Well, sweet old Gwen isn't the only person in this village who's good at playing games. It's becoming clear to me where her hatred of Hilary Wentworth comes from.

I stand up and make to leave the room, anger slowly building in me at Gwen's deceit and am stopped in my tracks by a voice behind me.

'I think you've forgotten to put something back where it belongs, my dear.' She is standing behind me, her voice cool and detached.

I spin around, suddenly furious. I feel foolish for lots of reasons: for being left to see myself out, for being caught stealing, but most of all, for being lied to by somebody I hoped I could trust, somebody I was starting to think of as a friend.

I pull the photograph out of my pocket and wield it in the air, waving it about furiously. 'Why, Gwen? Why have you got this picture of Adrian Wentworth in your house and why haven't you been telling me the complete truth?'

Her face is like stone as she reaches up and snatches the photograph out of my hand. 'That,' she says frostily, 'is my business and definitely none of yours.'

Her other hand pushes the small of my back, directing me towards the front door.

'Come on, Gwen!' I half plead. 'What exactly is it you're hiding? Why have you got that photo here? And who was the person that was in your house the other day? Because there was definitely somebody here. I saw them!'

She stops pushing me and for a fleeting second, I hope she may soften her resolve and tell me what's going on. But if she was even considering it, the moment disappears and with one final quick thrust that's surprisingly powerful for somebody so small, I'm propelled out of the hallway and onto the street. The door is closed with a resounding bang and I'm left standing there wondering what the hell just happened.

Thirty

The noise melts into my dream. I'm with Hugh and Todd is there. Jeff is standing close by, watching us, a twisted angry expression on his face. Todd and his father are in the middle of a heated debate, their voices raised and growing in crescendo, full of years of accumulated anger and bitterness. I can hear Hugh's grunts of protestation as Todd accuses him of being a shit absent father and abandoning him. The argument gains traction and their voices boom around me. Todd lifts one of his huge fists and knocks Hugh sideways, laughing as his father's head hits the floor and cracks open on the hard surface. I watch, horrified, as a pool of viscous blood gathers around Hugh's head. I let out a scream and then listen to the sound of my husband's heavy breathing as he slowly lapses into unconsciousness. The rattling gasp continues, booming in my ears and echoing around me. Everyone disappears from view until there are just the two of us left, me rooted to the spot and Hugh lying there on the floor, struggling to breathe.

And then I wake up with a start. A shape is looming over me. Breath in my face, hot and sour. Grunting and gurgling. I scream and the shape is gone, moving away from me out of the room, disappearing into the shadows of the darkness.

'Shit!' Hugh sits up, his outline a stiff silhouette in the darkness. He sits for a few seconds trying to get his brain into gear and then jumps up and races around the side of the bed, pulling on a T-shirt and slapping at the wall to turn on the light. An ochre glow slowly spreads over us, the energy-saving lightbulb taking an age to fully illuminate the room.

'Outside on the landing!' I shriek and hurl myself off the mattress, my body weak with shock as I follow Hugh. My legs feel like liquid as I stumble behind him.

'The panels!' My voice is a scream as I throw myself at the wall, ripping the rectangular piece of timber to one side. I feel Hugh's hand drag me back and try to shake him off. He's stronger than me and is roaring at me to not do it.

'They're empty, Faye. We cut through the wood on each level. It's back to being one long chute again. For fuck's sake, whatever you do, do NOT lean in or you'll fall straight through!'

I feel a blast of cold air hit me full in the face as I kneel down and stick my head through the opening. I am met with a wall of complete darkness. Before I can do anything else, Hugh wraps his arms around my waist and pulls me away, my body pressed firmly against his as he holds me tightly. He places me back down on the landing floor and tugs at my hand, pulling us both away from the gaping darkness.

'Christ almighty, Faye! Close that panel. It's a fucking death trap!' His eyes are wild and his skin is pale under the yellow flood of light from the unshaded bulb overhead.

'Well, why has it been left like that?' I shriek. 'We could have found them hiding in there! Now where are they going to go to? Where the fuck have they escaped to now, Hugh?'

'Mummy!'

My eyes bulge and I feel as if I'm going to pass out as Poppy's scream reverberates around us. Everything swims in front of me and the floor tilts violently as both Hugh and I race to her room, my body so heavy I can barely stay upright.

The door slams into the wall as Hugh launches himself through it and I bang the wall with my outstretched palm to turn on the light. Without stopping to look, Hugh grabs Poppy out of her bed and holds her tiny body close to his, her limbs flailing about as she shrieks at him and pummels his back with her small fists.

'Stop it, Daddy! You're scaring me.'

'Hugh!' I shout. I can see he's hysterical now and Poppy is terrified. 'There's nobody here! She's fine. Put her down, you're making her even more frightened! Please...'

His eyes scan the room. He looks like a crazed feral animal, his movements sharp and the sinews in his neck stretched to capacity as he continues to hang on to her.

'Give her to me. Please, give her here to me!' I hold out my hands and he slowly passes our screaming daughter over to me, her hot limbs wrapping tightly around my neck. She clings on to me and sobs into my shoulder as Hugh slumps down onto her bed and runs his fingers through his mop of dark hair.

'They're not here, Hugh. They've gone,' I whisper, tears biting at the back of my eyelids. He doesn't reply, just sits there silently, shaking his head over and over.

'You and Daddy were shouting,' Poppy says, her warm tears smearing my neck as I continue to keep her pressed close to me.

'I know,' I say softly, trying to placate her. 'I'm sorry, sweetheart. I'm so sorry we woke you and scared you.'

'Why were you shouting?' She hiccups, her tone becoming calmer as begins to regain control and slowly composes herself.

I gently stroke her back as I speak, my voice a whisper in the now silent room. 'I had a nightmare, Pops, that was all it was, my darling. I just had a bad dream and Daddy was helping me.'

'What was it about?' she asks, and I do my best to think of something quickly, something that won't frighten her even more.

'Oh, I just dreamt about a bad man who was chasing me, that's all. But it was just a dream. It wasn't real.'

She releases herself from my grasp and pulls back to look at me, her eyes glassy with tears, her skin blotchy and wet. 'A bad man? Did you really dream about a bad man?'

I nod, thinking she is trying to help me. I expect a wet kiss to be planted on my face, for her to tell me not to be scared because dreams are just dreams and they can't hurt us; all the phrases I use to soothe her back to sleep. That's what I imagine will happen. It doesn't. Her words slice through me. She may as well have taken a knife and cut me in two. I struggle to hold myself together as her tiny sibilant voice rings around the room.

'Was it like the person who was here earlier in my bedroom? Did you dream about them?'

I can't hold in my shriek and watch, horrified, as Hugh springs to his feet and runs out of the room bounding across the floor like a wild animal on the prowl for its prey. I hear his feet as he all but leaps down the stairs.

'Stay there, Poppy!' I try to remain calm but it's so fucking difficult. Her eyes widen as I lean forward and tuck her back in bed, smothering her in kisses. 'Everything's fine, sweetheart. Daddy's just going to make sure the door is locked. I think I may have left it unlocked accidentally.'

'Is he looking for the person?' she asks in such a level and easy voice I almost want to weep.

'No, sweetheart,' I utter through gritted teeth, my desperation and terror almost at an all-time high, 'I told you, he's gone to check the doors downstairs. It was just a dream. There is nobody else in the house.'

Poppy shakes her head and juts out her chin defiantly. Her mouth purses into a determined oval shape as she speaks. 'Yes there is, Mummy. There is definitely a person here and they were in my room earlier, before you and Daddy started shouting.'

'Sweetheart,' I say, my voice almost pleading for her to believe me, 'there's only me and you and Aiden and daddy in this house. There's nothing for you to be frightened of, I promise.'

Her eyes widen and she frowns. 'Yes there is! There's a lot to be scared of. Especially the person in my room. They told me they live here with us in this house.'

The walls close in and my throat becomes a tiny pinhole, stopping enough oxygen from getting through.

'What?' I manage to gasp as I cling on to my throat and sink onto the bed. Acid rises up my gullet, burning my throat. I swallow hard and take a deep rattling breath. 'Poppy, what are you saying? Please stop this! There is nobody else here in the house with us.'

'Yes, there is!' She crosses her arms and straightens her back. Her lip is stuck out and her eyes are no longer wet with tears but ablaze with anger.

'Poppy, take a look around you,' I wheeze, my voice reedy and desperate as I stare at her in horror. 'There's nobody else here with us, is there?'

'Not now there isn't!' She laughs, as if I'm some sort of imbecile unable to fully comprehend what it is she is saying.

'But there was somebody here earlier? Like when you were asleep but you thought you were awake? That's what happened to me too, Pops. That's just a dream, my darling.'

She lets out a high-pitched giggle and covers her mouth with her small, pale hands. 'No! That's silly. I wasn't asleep. They've been here again since then.'

'When?' I bark, fully aware I'm becoming hysterical. 'When were they here? Please tell when you saw this person?'

She points at me and continues to laugh, her voice thin and soft like silk in the cold night air. 'Just a few minutes ago!'

'A few minutes ago? A few minutes ago?' I'm almost screaming now. I don't care. I can't stop it. 'Where exactly was this person just a few minutes ago, Poppy? Where were they?'

Her finger wobbles about and her crisp childish voice rips through the room as she speaks, sealing this awful unthinkable situation with her precise, well-thought-out words. 'Right behind you, Mummy. The person who was in my room and wants to live here in our house, was right behind you all the time.'

Thirty-one

Aiden and Hugh are standing over me. The colour has seeped out of Aiden's skin and all I can focus on is the concerned look on Hugh's face, the horrified expression that is present as he strokes my forehead and places his other hand on my back. It sits there, warm and reassuring. Embarrassment and shame balloon inside me, my insides twisting and turning with the thought of what I have just done.

My screams and cries alerted them. I lost control and sent everyone into a frenzy. Aiden looks as if he's about to cry and Poppy is next to him, huddled under her bedsheets, the cotton tucked tightly beneath her wobbling chin. All this time, after all we've been through, I've tried so hard to protect them from what Todd and Jeff put us through, and now it's me who has scared them the most, subjected them to an ordeal they shouldn't be witnessing. I've made a spectacle of myself and more importantly and more horrifying than that – I have frightened my own children. Worse than that, I've terrified them. This is a memory they may well struggle to forget.

'I'm sorry,' I mutter feebly. 'I'm really, really sorry.'

'Ssh, it's fine,' Hugh murmurs softly.

I didn't expect this from him; all this compassion and concern and sympathy. I expected a backlash for being so irrational and thoughtless, for waking Aiden up and scaring Poppy half to death. I expected him to tell the kids to go back to bed while I was led away like a selfish child and given a good telling off for waking everybody up and making this whole thing all about me. Instead, I'm being comforted and told to stay calm. I'm being offered cups of tea and having my hand held while I regulate my breathing and attempt to stem the flow of tears that don't seem to want to stop.

'Aiden, tuck your sister in, will you? I'm going to help your mum back to bed and then go downstairs to get us both some tea.'

I smile as Aiden puffs out his chest and nods. We can always rely on his maturity at times like this. He may be boisterous and sometimes belligerent, but underneath it all, he's a good kid – a caring thoughtful boy who loves his family and always puts them first.

I listen to the rustle of bed linen and the soft murmurings of siblings behind me as Aiden sorts Poppy out, whispering to her to lie down and close her eyes, telling her that yes, he'll stay with her until she falls asleep and no, she can't have a story as it's too late. Hugh takes my hand and leads me to our room. I perch on the edge of the mattress, my head dipped, while he stands over me. A miasma of despair hangs heavily in the air between us, its intensity too great to ignore. Or perhaps I'm imagining it. I am no longer sure of my own feelings or anything that goes on inside my own head. Everything is askew and out of kilter. Am I really going mad? Maybe all this time Hugh had the right idea sending me to see a doctor; maybe I should have just gone with it instead of railing against it.

I press the heel of my hands into my eyes, suddenly exhausted. I'm too tired to do this anymore. I don't want to go over any of it in my head. I no longer want to think about nightly visitors or ghosts or anything at all. I just want it all to stop.

'I'll only be a minute,' Hugh says quietly as he backs away from me. 'Get yourself into bed and I'll be back up in a short while with a cup of tea.'

I want to tell him not to leave me and to stay with me and hug me. I want to tell him that I'm frightened, so very, very frightened, but I'm all too aware how needy and childish it would sound, so I simply nod meekly and watch him go, my blood rushing around my veins, my heart slamming against my ribcage like a battering ram.

Clambering into bed, I feel like a young girl again, my legs quaking as I swing them in and cover myself up. I pull at the quilt and wrap it around my freezing body, not daring to glance around

217

the room. I don't want to look into the shadowy corners, to imagine what might be lurking there. I don't want to make spectres out of innocuous objects, to imagine the undead staggering out at me from the darkness. I want to live a life where my family and I are safe and happy. I'm tired of living in terror.

Downstairs, Hugh shifts around the kitchen. Every now and then I hear the dull crack of a cup and the shuffle of his footsteps. In the bedroom I hear nothing but the pulsing throb of my own heartbeat. It crashes through my ears, making me dizzy and sick. The voices in Poppy's room have died down. Aiden is moving back to his own bed. I imagine what he must think of me, his hysterical mother who is fast losing the plot, and quickly block it out of my mind.

I lie back on the pillow, my eyes dry and gritty, my neck aching. I could sleep for a hundred years and yet ironically, sleep in this house is when the living nightmares really begin.

The sound of Hugh coming back up the stairs helps to still my thrashing heart. He silently enters the room carrying a tray with two mugs perched on it. 'I thought a cup of cocoa would have more of a soporific effect than tea. There you go,' he says, handing me the drink with the utmost care and precision.

I take a sip, the sugary taste hitting the back of my throat immediately. My mouth is instantly coated with a silky film of hot milk and chocolate. It doesn't take me long to finish it. Hugh slips into bed beside me and we sit in near silence as we both drink our cocoa and ruminate over what has just taken place in our home.

'Why did you take the wood out of the old dumb waiter?' I think about one of the kids climbing in there and falling. My stomach judders.

'I thought about what you said the other day, you know? About it being somewhere to hide? So I hammered out the bits of timber that separated the whole chute. I didn't want any compartments that could be used as a hidey-hole.' Hugh's voice is a steady calming force in the room. Visions of Aiden or Poppy toppling through the thick blackness to the concrete floor below still fill my mind.

I reach over and grasp Hugh's hand. He laces his fingers through mine and squeezes gently. 'You need to nail the outer panels in place so the kids can't clamber in and fall,' I say as I stare straight ahead and drain the last of my drink.

'Shit, yeah. I hadn't thought of that. Christ almighty, how did I not think of it? All the health and safety regulations I have to go through every day with my job and I completely forgot about nailing it up.' His face is pale as I turn to look at him.

'We've had a lot to think about. Don't beat yourself up over it.' I put my mug down on the bedside cabinet and lean over to him, snuggling into his chest. A musty odour emanates from him, a combination of fear and exhaustion that is pulsing out of his body in regular waves. I close my eyes and feel myself begin to drift off on the crest of a deep and welcome slumber.

***

I awake to the sound of hammering coming from the landing area. I squint at the clock, waiting for the numbers to come into focus: 7am. Hugh's fear of the kids inadvertently finding the panels and falling through them is our alarm call since I forgot to set the clock. Leaping up, I drag on a pair of joggers and an old shirt. Breakfast will be whatever I can lay my hands on without creating too much mess. The kitchen is in a state as it is and I don't think I can face the thought of more debris on top of what's already there.

Aiden and Poppy are already downstairs by the time I get down and are helping themselves to cereal and juice. I hope they're too groggy to converse. The one thing I don't think I can face is a barrage of question about last night. Fortunately, they also are too exhausted to speak and we sit, eating our breakfast in near silence. The sound of Hugh's hammering punctures the quiet every couple of minutes, causing Poppy to cover her ears with her hands. Neither of them asks what he's doing. After all the work that has gone in this house in the past week, they have probably become inured to it, deducing it's just part of the building work. That's good. I don't want them to ask. Truth be told, I don't want to talk about it.

We finish eating and pile our pots in the old dishwasher that has seen better days.

'Right, get your things together, guys, we're setting off as soon as I've showered and dressed. Poppy, your uniform is laid out on your chair. Make sure you button your shirt up properly today. Remember to start from the top and then you won't get so muddled up.'

I give her a sly wink and blow her a kiss. She blows one back and smiles. Aiden gives me an unexpected hug that brings tears to my eyes. I really do have the best children. At this point, despite everything, I feel like the luckiest person alive. It's people that makes places, and my people are, without doubt, the best.

We all head upstairs, a definite bounce in our step as we reach the top. We can do this. We can overcome this thing together. We'll get through it. I can somehow sense it.

Aiden and Poppy step over Hugh's array of tools that are sprawled across the floor, and head into their respective bedrooms. I'm just about to do the same when Hugh reaches up, grabs my hand and pulls me down to him, his voice close to my ear as he speaks. 'We need to talk when you get back from dropping the kids off.' His voice is a hoarse whisper and makes me go cold.

'About last night?' I venture. I needn't have asked. What else is it going to be about? There's an edge to his voice that I don't care for. A look in his eyes that scares me. All of a sudden, I don't think I want to hear what it is he's got to say. I want to block my ears and run away from it all – get as far away from it as I can and return when it's all over. 'It's going to be hectic in here by the time I get back. The electricians are going to be here. We won't be able to hear ourselves think, Hugh, never mind have a serious conversation.'

I hope this is enough to put him off, to make him shake his head and tell me it was nothing, that it can wait and that it's not really important.

He doesn't. Instead, he pulls me even closer, his eyes bulging as he utters the words I don't want to hear. 'I didn't want to tell you this last night, not when you were so upset. But you need to hear this. It's really important.'

I almost stagger back away from him. I don't need to hear it. I don't want to hear it – whatever it is he's about to tell me. I can just about deal with all the facts as they are; I don't need more worry heaped on top of the nightmarish things currently roaming around in my brain. Surely, he can see that?

He keeps tight hold of my hand as I try to move away, his large fingers clinging on to me, keeping me rooted to the spot. My knuckles crunch and grind as I twist my body to escape from whatever it is he is about to reveal.

'Please, Faye,' he whispers. 'It's something you need to hear. I think it's one of our neighbours.'

'One of our neighbours?' I reply incredulously. 'What on earth are you going on about? What is one of our neighbours?' I almost laugh but his face is so serious, so stone-like that I don't have the heart and remain quiet instead.

'Last night,' he hisses, pulling me closer, 'I followed whoever it was that was creeping around up here. I followed them out of the back door. I watched them as they snuck around the front of the house. The big gates were locked and they couldn't get out. I thought we had them then, Faye, I really did. But then I stood and watched as they ducked through a gap in the hedge, limped over to one of the houses opposite.'

My chest bangs furiously. My face grows hot even though I suddenly feel freezing cold. I know what he's going to say. I don't want to hear it, but I know exactly what Hugh is going to say. This is a small village with only a handful of houses close by. It's only too obvious where the intruder went.

I gulp loudly and speak. 'Did you see them? What did this person look like?'

Hugh shakes his head and stares at me. 'I didn't get a close look but I'd say it was a man – somebody older. They looked pretty out of shape, a bit arthritic with some sort of limp.'

I ask the next question even though I already know what he's going to say. 'Which house did they go to?'

He narrows his eyes before speaking and rubs at the bristles on his face with the back of his hand. 'Not sure of the number. It was the one with the white fence and gate. Got a gravel path leading up to the door.'

I don't need to hear any more. An old man? Is Gwen hiding somebody in her house? Is that why she was being so furtive last week? It would explain her behaviour but it doesn't tell me who she is hiding and why. I'll find out though. As soon as I get back from dropping Aiden and Poppy off at school I am going to march over there and knock on her door until she opens it. I don't care how upset she is about me trying to take her photograph, I am not leaving her doorstep until she starts giving me some answers. I'll stay there and shout my questions through the letterbox if I have to. Gwen, our sweet old neighbour, is definitely full of not-so-pleasant surprises. She knows exactly what's going on in this house and by the end of today, so will I.

No more living in fear. I'm going to demand the truth, a full disclosure of who this person is and why they keep breaking into my house. Gwen may not know it yet, but the secrets she is hiding are all about to come tumbling out into the open.

Thirty-two

I watch as Irena bustles her way through the crowd at the school gates and heads over to where I'm sitting in the car. Aiden has taken Poppy and walked her to the school gate to save me getting out and having to find a proper parking space. I am just waiting until she is safely on the premises before I drive off. I rarely see Irena at the school. My perplexed expression at her presence must say it all as I wind the window down and she leans in, her musky perfume filling the small space as it wafts around us, a cloud of welcome sweetness in the stale air.

'Oh!' she says, waving her hand about dramatically and rolling her eyes. 'Don't ask why I am here, Faye. I am having the most terrible morning. First, childminder, she ring saying she is ill and then Bianka, she sick everywhere and then would you believe it, work, they ring as well asking me to do longer hours today. I tell them, no! I am having traumatic day. Worst of all days ever. In the end, I put last-minute holiday in. Work not pleased, in fact they furious, but what can you do? Family first every time.'

I indicate for her to get in, feeling a need to speak to her. Irena doesn't have to be asked twice. Wrestling with the door handle, she slides in next to me and turns to face me, her face full of sincerity and compassion. 'You are looking pale, Faye. The house is difficult at the minute, yes?'

She has no idea. Irena thinks the decorating and building work is what is causing me to look so drawn and washed out. She doesn't know the half of it.

'I am parked in good place. No yellow lines,' she says cheerily. 'Why don't you drive to more convenient place in your car and we will talk?'

I slip the key into the ignition and pull away from the traffic, cruising along in first gear until we find a space away from the hubbub of school parents. I park up, turn the engine off, spin around to look at Irena and burst into tears. Without a word, she rummages in her handbag and produces a tissue which she passes over to me with the greatest of care, her watchful gaze sweeping over me as I dab at my eyes and heave a huge trembling sigh.

'So, my dear, you have much to tell me and I'm guessing it's not all good?'

***

We sit for half an hour and between the sobs, which seem determined to control me, bursting out of me unbidden despite my best efforts to keep them under wraps, I tell Irena all about the goings on in Cross House. I tell her about the Wentworth family and the diaries and the information I've found out about them. I tell her about Poppy's drawings and what she said last night. Finally, I tell her about the nocturnal visitor and Gwen and how I've recently discovered that they are somehow linked. Then I sit, drained of all energy, and watch for her reaction.

I don't have to wait for long. Irena's words explode out of her like magma bursting out of its chamber. 'Oh my God, Faye! Are you being mad? Why have you not called in police? Please tell me you have rung them?'

I lower my eyes and bite at my lip, humiliation and awkwardness gripping me.

'Why, Faye? What will it take for you to be thinking you need help? First you are having those bad men at your door in your old house and now this in your new home and still no phone call to 999! Think of your children's safety. Think of your babies, Faye. They are needing protection. You cannot be having strangers in your house where children sleep. Heaven's sake, woman!' Irena leans forward and grasps my hand in hers. Her fingers are warm and comforting. 'Get this sorted, please. Get in police and they will arrest this person.'

I nod and sniff, dragging the tissue over my face.

'And also, if you not mind me saying it, you look like shit.' Irena takes me by the shoulders and hugs me tightly. I half laugh and half cry into her soft warm neck.

'Oh God, Irena, I've ruined your jacket!' We both laugh as she pulls it down and stares at the snotty wet smear spread over the suede fabric.

'Ah, that is nothing. I have children. Seen far worse!' She brushes it with her hand and smiles a broad smile then looks at me with a serious expression on her face. Her voice is solemn and low as she speaks. 'And can I be saying, you do know there is no such thing as ghosts? This shadow you are seeing is not spirit from the hereafter. You do know that, yes?'

I nod and sniff, tears misting up my vision.

'Good! As long as you know this. You also need to get out, meet people. Live a little. One old woman is no good as a friend. You are young. You need youthful friends. Get out, drink wine, eat cake, laugh till you are giddy.'

I tell her about Allison and meeting Zoe. She raises her arms and congratulates me. 'Good, good! And once you are done with building work, Stefan and I will visit with our children. Will be good to see you all again.'

I almost cry out at the idea. The thought of having them all round almost makes me light-headed with happiness. I picture us sitting in the garden, drinking wine, Stefan roaring with laughter as Hugh tells one of his smutty jokes and nudges Stefan in his ample belly. The kids will play in the summerhouse or run through the vast sections of unexplored land beyond the main part of the lawn. It will be perfect; something to look forward to. Something to keep me going.

'But not until all workmen gone and your house is newly decorated,' Irena says, her mouth tilted upwards slightly. 'We don't want to drink in any old shithole.'

***

I can barely control my laughter all the way home. Irena is the tonic I needed. I wish I had her passion and common sense. She is right about one thing: in a bid to protect my children, I've actually put them in danger. Whilst not wanting them subjected to a police presence in the house, I've left them wide open to all kinds of threats and peril. So stupid and thoughtless of me. So utterly selfish. That will all change when I get home. I've turned into some sort of frightened shrinking violet in the past year. I've allowed people to terrify and dominate me. But not today. Not ever again. I've learnt my lesson the hard way. Things are about to change. I don't care what Hugh says – if we get another visit, I will be straight on the phone to the police.

The passing foliage is a blur of distorted green in my peripheral vision as I wind my way through the country lanes back into Brackston. Gravel spits around the drive, spewing far and wide as I pull up at speed. I feel fully energised for what I'm about to do. Seeing Irena has helped me put everything into perspective. It's not entirely clear to me what is happening in this house, but it soon will be.

I step out of the car and don't bother going inside. There's too much work and noise in there anyway. Even from here, I can hear the boom of the electricians' radio and the whirring of their drills as they scrape away yet more of my walls and tear my house to pieces. I definitely don't want to go in and watch the destruction taking place inside. We're still at the 'getting worse before it gets better' stage. I just want it all to be better more rapidly than this. And anyway, I've got more important matters to attend to.

I tuck my keys deep into my pocket and head straight over to Gwen's house, my heart pattering out a strong steady rhythm as I cross the road and crunch my way up her path.

My knock ricochets around the vacant air of an almost empty village. With a population of just over a hundred, everybody is either at work, school or still in bed. Even the birds seem muted. In the distance, the hum of farm machinery kicks in. For some strange reason, this comforts me. I don't feel so alone.

226

My knuckles ache as I rap again, this time more forcefully. I'm not leaving until Gwen speaks to me. She owes me. I deserve to have my questions answered. I stand waiting, the words I plan on saying rushing through my head in an angry indecipherable stream. I need to calm down first, however. I don't want to appear flustered. I have to show her that I'm completely in control. I muster up my best authoritative air, pushing my shoulders back and smoothing down my hair with trembling fingers.

I take a step closer to the door, listening out for any signs of life on the other side. She's in. I know Gwen is in there and I'm pretty certain she knows it's me out here knocking. The fact that she's not answering adds fuel to the raging fire of anger that licks at my belly.

I decide to take a different tack and stick my fingers through the letterbox, letting it slap back, metal against metal, making a sharp tinny echo. I do this several times and then lean down and shout through to let her know that I'm not going to give up. I'm not going anywhere until she answers this fucking door.

'Gwen! Open up. I need to speak to you.'

I can't be certain but I think I hear something on the other side – a distant shuffle or some kind of movement from deep within the house.

'Come on, Gwen. You don't want your neighbours hearing this, do you? You know exactly what I mean.'

I start to count, telling myself that if she doesn't open by the time I get to forty-nine, then I'll threaten her with the police, shout it out loud enough for any nearby residents to hear. She arrives just as I get to ten. I can't help but smile. I do like feeling empowered. It's all about taking back control. I've cowered for too long now. It's time to get back on my feet and start walking unaided.

The door opens a crack. Gwen's tiny eyes peer through as she stands inside saying nothing. I sigh and place my hands on the frame. I don't do it to appear bigger but the fact I am now towering over her gives me the kick I need to get inside.

'Take the chain off. We can't talk out here on the street.'

'Yes, we can. I don't have to let you in. You tried to steal my photograph. I don't trust you anymore.'

I almost laugh out loud. She doesn't trust me? Who the hell is she kidding?

'Okay, Gwen, we can do this out here if really want to, but I don't think you're going like what it is I have to say, and I'm almost certain you won't want the neighbours hearing about how you're allowing an intruder to enter my house on a night and then letting him back into your house. I think the police might just want to listen to what I've got to say though, don't you?'

My words have the desired effect. There's a slight clanking sound and a low creak as she unhooks the door chain, pulls it open and steps aside to let me in.

I stare down at her. She suddenly looks tiny – this harmless-looking woman who has so much to hide, so many secrets salted away she is practically bursting at the seams with them. Her white hair hasn't been combed and sticks out at various strange angles and she is still in her dressing gown. Maybe she wasn't ignoring me. Maybe she was still in bed when I was knocking. Either way, I need to speak to her and it's going to be here and now, on my terms, not when she decides. I'm done with the secrecy in this village. I'm done with having somebody creep around my house on a night, but most of all, I'm done with living in fear. I've endured enough to see me through a hundred lifetimes.

'Put the kettle on, Gwen. Get dressed if you want to. I'm not going anywhere,' I say loudly as I march through to her small living room and sit down in one of the overstuffed antique armchairs. 'We need to have a conversation and I'm not leaving until you tell me everything you know.'

Thirty-three

Her face is pale as she sits in a wingback chair opposite me. She hurriedly went upstairs while I waited and came back wearing a pair of dark-brown crimplene trousers and a white blouse. Her hair had been combed and she looked marginally better as she pulled the curtains open and slumped down, a defeated look on her face.

'Okay, we can dance around this issue or I can just come straight out with it. Which would you prefer?' My voice is clipped as I stare at her. I can't rein myself in. I feel so fucking angry. All this time I've been so worried and scared about the person who roamed my house at night and I'm guessing that all this time, she knew.

She doesn't respond. Her shoulders sag slightly before she rights herself and sits bolt upright, a useless attempt at trying to act innocent. I can see beyond it. I know what her game is. Actually, I don't. That's why I'm here, but I do know she'll try to deny any connection. I won't let her. I'm not leaving until she tells me the complete truth and I'm satisfied with her answers.

'Right, well since you're choosing to remain silent, let me spell it out for you. We've had somebody coming in our house in the early hours, creeping around, coming in our bedrooms while we're asleep. My children's bedrooms, Gwen! Can you begin to imagine how frightening that is?'

Still no response from the diminutive pensioner. She's stubborn, I'll give her that much. I continue, determined to break her silence. 'And then last night, Hugh gave chase while I stayed upstairs with our children. And guess where our intruder went to? Can you guess where he snuck back to?'

It's barely imperceptible, but I see it – a slight twitch in the corner of her eye as my words begin to penetrate the steel bars she's surrounded herself with. She slides down in the seat a fraction and her knuckles are white as she clasps her hands together tightly in her lap. I'm winning. I'm actually getting there. Very slowly, I'm breaking her down.

'He came over here, Gwen, into your house. Now why would he do that? Why would somebody who keeps coming into Cross House come back here? I'd like an answer, and I'd like it quickly because if I don't get it, then I'm going to go straight to the police and report everything that's gone on. I'll give them your name and address and tell them you're involved in a case of trespassing and harassment. And perhaps even stalking. I'm not completely up on how the law works and what somebody can and can't be prosecuted over, but I'm almost certain it's illegal to aid and abet a person who has entered somebody's else's house and been in their bedrooms without their consent.'

I watch the colour leech out of Gwen's face and feel a certain amount of gratification. My entire body feels as if it's on fire. Flames burn their way through my veins, revitalising me, making me lose my fear. No longer the victim.

'So, what do you have to say about it, Gwen?'

She doesn't respond, her posture shrinking before my eyes as I hear a sound behind me. It extinguishes the raging fire inside of me. I recognise the noise. I know that shuffling sound only too well. The powerful fire that pulsed through my veins is replaced by a sliver of ice that skewers my innards, twisting and turning as it travels through me. My bowels threaten to open as the sound grows closer.

I want to turn around and face them – this person who has terrorised me and my family – but raw fear grips me, holding me hostage. I hear Gwen scream and then listen to three words that penetrate my brain before pain takes hold and everything goes black.

'No, Peter. NO!'

***

I drag my eyes apart. I'm propped up by cushions and Gwen is sitting next to me dabbing at my face with something wet. I try to move away but everything sways and my stomach churns.

Closing my eyes again, I swallow hard and let out a trembling sigh. I'm freezing. I can feel Gwen's body heat close to me. I want to move away from her but everything is unclear. I feel tired and unsteady. Why do I feel so exhausted and why does my head hurt so much?

I can't seem to think straight. I try to get my thoughts in order. I'm in Gwen's; that much I do know. I'd gone to see her. I was angry.

And then I remember.

It dawns on me suddenly, exploding into my consciousness like a bomb detonating in my head.

I scramble to get away from the wet flannel that's being placed on my forehead. This whole thing is insane. I need to get to a phone, to call the police. I need to –

'Stay still, Faye. You're hurt. I just need to clean you up. Please don't move.' Gwen's voice is calm and measured but determined. No longer the tiny shrinking pensioner, she is back in the driving seat. Gwen is back in control. Not for long.

I pull away from her, the walls and floor leaning and sloping as I jump out of her grasp. 'Get the fuck away from me! You're a maniac. Don't touch me. Don't fucking touch me!'

She widens her eyes and shakes her head as if I'm the mad one. She actually looks frightened. What in God's name is going on? My eyes are misted with fear and confusion.

I need to get a grip here. I've got to get out of this madhouse. Her words reverberate around my head. Peter… the same Peter I've been pitying? The same Peter I've been doling out sympathy to?

Stumbling to my feet, I look down at a splattering of blood on the carpet and at the object beside it. It's a small metal lampshade, red with my blood. Christ almighty… I struggle to breathe as I stare down at it. My blood.

'I'm so sorry, Faye. He's gone. I made him leave. Please don't blame him. He doesn't know what he's doing.' Gwen is sitting on the edge of the sofa, her body rocking back and forth. She looks fragile, as if she could snap in two at any time. Under normal circumstances I would feel sorry for her, would even want to take care of her. But not today. Not after what has just happened.

'He could have killed me,' I whisper, my voice hoarse with disbelief and white-hot rage. My hands form fists as I stare at her. She's tiny. I could give her one firm push. She would collapse onto the floor, her old bones hitting it with force, doing her untold damage. A broken leg or hip would probably be enough to see her off. A couple of infections as a result, or a bout of pneumonia, and she wouldn't have a strong enough immune system to fight them off. Her age is against her.

I stop myself and shut my eyes tight. Christ almighty, is this what I've become? Am I really considering killing off an old lady? I honestly don't know whether to laugh or cry. I really am losing my mind. What little bit of sanity I had when I came in here has been eroded by a knock on the head from a person I thought was a gentle creature. All this time I've had it all wrong. There is no ghost. There's just Peter, the wrongly accused boy who has grown into a violent man.

'He won't hurt you again, I promise. Please sit down and I'll explain everything.' Gwen sounds genuine but I no longer know who I can trust. What if she's lying? What if this Peter guy is hiding around the corner with a knife or a hammer or any number of objects he could use to hurt me? A piece of wood, a chair leg, the old metal poker sitting by Gwen's fireplace; any of those everyday objects would be enough to split my head open and put me in my grave.

She pats the cushion beside her and shakes her head at me. 'I know what you're thinking, that he could come back any second. He definitely won't. You're just going to have to trust me.'

I don't how to respond. I'm torn between wanting to run as far away from this house as I possibly can, screaming for Hugh to call the police and get this mad old bitch arrested, and sitting down begging her to tell me exactly what's going on. Eventually I opt for the latter. I've come this far. I'm in pain but thankfully not seriously injured, although I can feel a small trickle of warm blood as it continues to trail down the side of my face.

I slump down next to her, aware I may be making the biggest mistake of my life, but I have to find out. Not knowing is killing me.

She faces me, her skin pale and liver-spotted. I stare at her, wondering what sort of things she's going to come out with – what terrible atrocities and secrets she is about to tell me.

Words fail her. She sits silently, opening and closing her mouth, her eyes filling up with tears until I step in and speak for her. 'Is Peter your son? You had an affair with Adrian and Peter was the product of that relationship. Am I right?'

This seems to stir her into action. 'No! Absolutely not. Peter is definitely Adrian's son. His mother died. But you're right about one thing. I did have an affair with Adrian.'

I almost laugh out loud and clap my hands together. At long last, I've got a small part of it correct. Unexpectedly, tears fill my eyes and a lump rises in my throat. My head throbs where I was hit as I swallow to fight back the sorrow that threatens to overwhelm me. I have no idea why I want to cry. Grief for the past perhaps? Or more likely a sense of mourning for a family so fractured, they all ended up dead or damaged in some irreparable way.

'Can I get us some tea and finish cleaning you up before we go any further? Then I promise, I'll tell you the whole story.'

Tea does sound good. My throat is dry and I can feel the warm blood as it continues its journey out of the wound on my head and down my face. I stare down at my top, now stained dark pink with blood, and nod at Gwen as she stands up.

'Right,' she says brightly, as if nothing has even taken place. 'I'll get some clean warm water and put the kettle on. Won't be a minute.' And with that she's gone, buzzing about in the kitchen like a busy little insect.

I stare out of the window, shake my head at the absurdity of it all and let the tears flow freely.

Thirty-four

The texture of the warm fabric against my head soothes me. I feel like a child being nursed back to health by one of my elders. Gwen gave me a couple of paracetamols which I took with a swig of hot tea. She dabs at my temple as she surveys the wound, scrutinising it closely with her dull rheumy eyes.

'There. The bleeding's stopped.' She puts the cloth into the bowl of water and swills it about. I watch as the water blends with my blood, turning it a sickly shade of pink. She stands up, goes into the kitchen and pours it all down the sink then dries her hand on a nearby tea towel. No disinfectant or rubber gloves. No need for all that sterile nonsense in her world. Gwen is old school. She was probably brought up on a diet of red meat and lard and slept four to a bed with her siblings. She's made of stern stuff. But then, so am I. Despite feeling scared and permanently tired, when it comes to being resilient, I think we're an equal match.

'Okay,' I say, my voice still gruff with exhaustion and shock. 'I think you owe me an explanation.'

She seems to shrink a little as she slides down next to me, her miniscule body ice cold and fragile looking. I feel like a giant compared to her. If she gets any smaller, she'll disappear altogether.

'Yes, you're right. It's the truth you want then?'

'Of course, it's the truth I want,' I reply. 'Why would I not?'

'Okay,' she says with a sigh, 'but bear in mind it all happened a long time ago and my memory isn't what it used to be.' Gwen's tone has suddenly sharpened. She's on the defensive. What exactly is she hiding? I decide to pre-empt her. If I ask the questions, I keep control. That way she can't leave anything out.

'How long had you been having an affair with Adrian?' It comes out like rapid gunfire. I expect her to look rattled by my words. I've usurped her, jumped in before she could speak, but she doesn't. If anything, there's a look of resignation in her countenance, as if she's been expecting this all along.

'Almost two years. My first husband had died the year before it began. I'd spent six months nursing him through cancer. I was working full-time as a teacher and had a young daughter. They were tough times and Adrian was kind to me. It started off as neighbourly friendliness but then one thing led to another. His marriage wasn't working and we were both lonely.'

I want to intervene and tell her it sounds like one big cliché but instead sit silently, my expression and body language impassive. I need to hear more before I can start to form any real opinions.

'What about Peter and Tammy?' I ask, keen to keep the story factual and not be drawn in by her emotive language and descriptions of her life that paint her as the victim in all of this.

She lets out a juddering breath and for a brief moment, I fear she might cry. She doesn't. She sits up straight and continues. 'Well, as you know, Tammy accused Peter of sexual assault and everyone believed it. It was her word against his. She was able to give a good account and he wasn't. He was confused, frightened. He had no idea what it was he had even been accused of.'

'This is the same Peter that's just hit me over the head? Smashed a heavy lamp into my skull with absolutely no provocation whatsoever?' My voice threatens to fail me as my words turn into a half shriek. I take a deep breath and adjust my posture, sitting bolt upright. I can't lose it now. Got to keep everything together, be the stronger person here.

I can see that I've disturbed her. A slight flicker takes hold in her cheek, a small pulse that taps out a rhythmic beat on her lined skin. She shakes her head and purses her lips.

'He didn't mean it. He was horrified when he realised what he'd done.'

'So why did he do it?' I'm shouting now, my voice filling the room. I'm incensed. How can she possibly defend his actions?

She brings her hands up to her face, rubbing her fingers over her eyes and shaking her head over and over. 'It was a mistake, a complete mistake. He was frightened. He's been though such a lot. It was just an awful mistake.'

'That doesn't answer my question, Gwen!' I no longer care if I'm shouting. He could have killed me. 'Why did he do it? Would you still be defending him if I were laid out on your living room floor, with my brains spilling out all over your recently cleaned carpet?'

'No! Definitely not. Like I said, it was a ghastly mistake. Just a terrible error.' Her lip is trembling and she is pale, her skin suddenly waxy and sallow looking.

'So why? Why has he been creeping round my house and why has he just tried to kill me?'

I hear her small, trembling breaths as she gulps and speaks softly. 'He thought you were Tammy. That's why he's been in the house those couple of times. He's been looking for her. When she was living there he used to try and visit but she always turned him away. He's angry and upset.'

I close my eyes and try to piece it all together. There are holes in Gwen's story. Either she's lying to me still, or she's withholding information.

'Firstly, he's been in my house more than a few times. He's crept around there repeatedly since we moved in. And if he wanted to see Tammy while she still lived there, why didn't he do it then? How has he been getting into Cross House, Gwen? How?' And then I understand. I fix my gaze on her and feel myself go cold as it hits me, a slow dawning realisation. 'You gave him a key. You gave Peter a key to my house. Why, Gwen? Why would you do that?'

She doesn't try to deny it. If anything, she sits up straighter and I can't swear to it, but I feel sure there's a hint of a smile as she speaks. 'I tried to take it off him once the house sold and you moved in, but he wouldn't give it back.'

'How did you get a key in the first place?' My heart is starting to batter around my chest. It feels like a fish thrashing around on dry ground, slippery and uncomfortable. I take a few steadying breaths and clasp my hands together until the skin on my knuckles feels so tight, the bones so rigid, it causes me physical pain.

'I asked you how you got a key to Cross House, Gwen. If you don't answer me I'll report you to the police for breaking and entering.' I have no idea if she is even breaking any laws but right now, I'll throw any threats her way to get her to speak up and start telling the truth.

She blinks repeatedly and smiles as if we're discussing the weather. This lady definitely isn't all she appears to be. A veil of fear slowly descends over me. I'm on unfamiliar territory and I don't like it. Not one little bit.

'I stole it, my dear. How else do you think I got it? Oh, don't look so shocked. I didn't steal it from you.' She stops and picks at a piece of imaginary fabric on her trousers. 'I took it from Tammy's belongings when she went into the care home. She shouldn't have had it really. She was meant to hand them all over to the solicitor when the house sold but she couldn't do it. Deep down, she couldn't let go either. Cross House does that to you. Once it gets its claws into you, you become a part of it.'

I ignore her last comment, designed to frighten me. 'You visited her?' I don't know why I'm asking. It's quite apparent she did. Despite hating Tammy, Gwen was in on it from the very outset.

'Oh yes,' she says, her eyes now twinkling.

Jesus, what sort of woman is she? What the fuck is going on here?

'I helped the carers at the home to settle her in. She had nobody else, you see. I was a close friend of the family, a neighbour, her old teacher. They trusted me. In fact,' she says quite proudly, 'they seemed only too glad to see me. Tammy can be a lot to handle since getting dementia and she was getting feisty with them, lashing out and hitting them. I helped to calm her down.'

She sits back, a smug expression on her face. I can hardly believe what I'm hearing. I suppress the urge I have to slap her hard across the face. One swift movement from me would knock her clean to the floor.

'Why did you give it to Peter? It was no longer his house. It had been sold.'

'No longer his house?' She quickly loses her self-satisfied poise like a snake shedding its skin, and morphs into an angry old lady, a savage creature ready to pounce. 'He deserved that house! After that old bitch Hilary died, everything went to Tammy while Peter was shuffled from institution to institution. It was only when his mother's cousin decided to house him in her little cottage in the next village that he finally had a home; somewhere decent to live. How is that fair?'

I try to think of something coherent to say. A million questions scratch at my brain. I clutch at one that keeps pushing its way forward and bark it at her. 'Why would any of this bother you, Gwen? It's not your family, nothing to do with you. You're a neighbour, for God's sake, not a family member.'

She grimaces and narrows her eyes, spitting the words out at me, full of poison and bitterness. 'We had plans, Adrian and me! He couldn't wait to get away from that wife of his. We were going to move away from here, sell both houses. He would have given half to Hilary. The daughter could have stayed with her and we would have taken Peter with us. Me and my daughter and Peter and his son. It would have been perfect, and then that wayward daughter of his went and made those accusations. It ruined everything. Adrian couldn't function properly afterwards. He wandered around in a daze after Peter was sent away.' She stops, her chest heaving up and down as she struggles to catch her breath.

'And then Adrian disappeared,' I murmur, finishing the story for her.

'And then Adrian, the love of my life, disappeared,' she echoes, tears now streaming down her face.

I'm torn between feeling pity for this woman and wanting to take her by the shoulders and shake her, this Miss Havisham character who is still clinging on to the past. All these years and she still harbours a grudge against a grown woman who did something terrible when she was a teenager. Not just any grown woman, a demented woman with a debilitating disease that's currently eating away at her brain, leaving her in an almost vegetative state. I can almost understand Gwen hating the wife of her lover, but to keep this thing going for all these years? It's complete lunacy.

'You said earlier that your first husband passed away? I take it you married again after Adrian's death?' She winces as I say the words. So many years ago, and yet it's as fresh in her mind as the day it happened.

'Yes, and what a waste of space he was. Only lasted a few years. Left me for another woman. Never heard from him since.'

I stop myself from thinking that what goes around comes around. Cruel and unnecessary. Even if it is true. A sudden thought spears into me. 'The basket of food. That was you, wasn't it?'

She shrugs listlessly and stares at me. 'I could hardly leave it on the front doorstep, could I?'

'Why, Gwen? Why?'

'Look, I don't expect you to understand any of this. To be perfectly honest, my dear, I'm not even sure I understand it myself. I just know that Peter liked to go back in there, thinking Tammy was still around, and I think he deserved that much. He's had a rotten life. He didn't go in often. Sometimes he would just hang around in the old shed. I used to worry about him, and he isn't always the most communicative of people, so I did what I could to help him out. I did it for Adrian. It's what he would have wanted.' She sounds unhinged with her childish reasons, forcing inexcusable activities to fit her warped ideas and way of thinking.

'So, when he's not roaming freely around my house, where does he go to?' I want to add that perhaps Peter isn't as unclear in his thinking as Gwen makes him out to be. He always managed to come at night when he was less likely to be caught.

She sighs loudly and enunciates as if I'm too stupid to understand the finer details of what's been going on. 'Look, I said earlier, he spends a lot of time living with a distant cousin in the next village.'

'And when he's not there, he's here with you?' I know it to be true. The shadow at the window, her lies to keep me out of the house, it all fits. 'That day,' I add suddenly as I remember. 'The day you said a rug was wet? What happened? What were you looking for in the bushes outside your front door?'

She lowers her head then stares out of the window, her eyes glassy. I suspect this is to allow herself some thinking time. I'm in no hurry. I've got all day to hear what it is she's got to say.

'Peter had come over in the early hours –'

'After fleeing from my house,' I add. Gwen turns to look at me and at least has the decency to look shamefaced. Her pale cheeks become tinted with a hit of pink.

'Yes. He was in a bit of a state. One of his shoes had come off and he had stood in some mud, dragging it through the house.'

I want to laugh. At least some of her story was true. She had cleaned the rug. Unfortunately, she omitted to tell us the part about hiding our intruder in her house. So many lies. So many secrets.

I hold my hand out to her. She stares at my palm and gives me a quizzical look.

'The key, Gwen. I want my key.'

She shakes her head and looks away from me. 'I don't have it. I told you, Peter won't give it back. He's very stubborn. He's convinced Tammy is in there and wants to see her.'

'Well, it hardly matters anyway,' I say a little too loudly. 'All the locks are getting changed in the next day or so.' This may not be strictly true. We don't have an actual date for getting new doors fitted but I can tell that she has taken on board what I've said. It may just be enough for him to surrender them without a fight. 'And if he tries to break in once they're fitted, I'll call the police straightaway and tell them of your involvement in all of this.'

She looks suitably frightened. Even if she's deranged, Gwen still recognises the seriousness of a possible arrest for being involved in a case of breaking and entering.

'He has had a terrible time of it, you know,' she says in a childish manner, a pout evident as she speaks. 'Over the years he hasn't always received the medical care he should have. He has terrible chest problems and some mobility issues. He does his best to stay agile, walking and going outdoors. It isn't easy for him.'

I think of his rattling breaths and dripping saliva as he leaned over me, and shiver. 'He's active enough that he always managed to escape whenever we went looking for him,' I say bitterly. 'I'd like to know exactly how many times he came snooping around. Too many for my liking.'

Gwen shakes her head and sighs. 'I told you already, he only went in your house once or twice. Twice that I know of, three at a push. Definitely no more than that.'

'How would you know that?' I'm shouting now but I don't care. I want her to stop lying. 'Gwen, how do you know that?'

'Because he told me. And I trust him.'

I almost laugh out loud. Can she not see any irony in any of this? I let out a deep breath and stare at her, my voice icy with contempt and disbelief. 'You've said yourself he has learning difficulties. Do you not think it just the tiniest bit possible he's misjudged how many times he's been in? Come on, Gwen, wake up! Think about what you're saying here.'

She looks at me as if I'm mad. 'Think what you like, my dear. I know what I know, and Peter may be many things, but he's nothing if not loyal and true to his word. If he says he's only been in there twice, then that's what I know to be the truth.'

I don't have the energy to argue any further. I look behind me, worried that he may have crept up again and is standing right next to me holding something heavy, a manic glint in his eyes. Not that I even know what he looks like. It's incredible really – this man has stalked me while I slept and knocked me out no more than an hour ago, and yet I wouldn't recognise him if I passed him in the street.

'Who is he?' I ask, looking around for any photographs that she may have scattered around the place. 'I mean, what does he look like?'

She screws up her eyes and smiles one of those enigmatic, smug smiles that makes me want to drive my fist into her face. Her voice is laced with sarcasm as she speaks. 'Oh, dear me, there are none so blind as those who cannot see. Or those who don't want to see.'

'Gwen,' I say wearily, rapidly tiring of her power games. 'I really can't be bothered with all of this. Like I said earlier, I could go straight to the police. Or you can start being straight with me. Your choice.'

Her smile fades away and she moves her gaze over to the window. For one awful minute, I fear he may be standing there staring in, but then she shifts her eyes back to me and speaks again, her voice serious, the sickly-sweet tone now absent. 'You've seen him before. Out there that time you were sitting on the bench.'

I shake my head and think back to that day that feels like a lifetime ago and suddenly feel faint at the memory. The old man who passed by me. That was Peter? That was the prowler who terrified me night after night? I don't know whether to laugh or cry. My head feels too heavy for my body as I stand up, thinking of how I'll explain this wound on the side of my face to Hugh when I get home. This whole thing is surreal.

'I need to leave now, Gwen. I might be back for that key. Or maybe I won't. It's in your best interests to get it off him though. If you don't want the police knocking at your door, that is.' I enjoy seeing all the colour bleed out of her face at my words. Sometimes it feels good to be mean, to have the upper hand. It's not very often the scales of power tip my way. I'm making the most of it.

I think of the Wentworth family as I head into the hallway towards the door, and stop. Something that's been niggling me while she was speaking now causes me to turn around. 'The fall down the stairs? Hilary's fall. Could that have been Peter?'

'No, definitely not,' Gwen says, her lips thin and puckered with certainty.

'How do you know that?' I say, feeling slightly light-headed as a throb takes hold in my temple. 'I mean, he was probably angry and upset at being wrongly accused and sent away. You said yourself, he's had an awful life. How do you know it was an accident? How do you know it wasn't Peter who broke in and pushed his stepmother down those stairs?'

'Because,' Gwen says, her voice sending a deep chill right into the centre of my bones, 'it was me. I pushed Hilary Wentworth down the stairs. But like many things that happened in that house, nobody can prove it. Now if you don't mind, my dear, I'd very much like to be alone.'

Thirty-five

I can't quite put my finger on the all-pervading smell that fills my nostrils as I stroll along the corridor at Millview Care Home. I would say it's akin to rotting flesh but that would be completely unfair. The place is immaculately set out and clean to the point of being clinical. The smell, however, isn't pleasant and no matter how hard I try, I can't seem to switch off to it. I long for that point when my olfactory system becomes resistant to it, but it doesn't seem to be happening just yet.

The flowers in my hand drip water onto my jacket. I stick my nose closer to them to attempt to block out the strong odour that I'm pretty sure is urine. I remember when my poor old dad had a water infection and I had been just outside his room while the nurses changed his catheter. That's the type of smell that is present in this place, pungent and impossible to ignore.

I head towards the lift at the bottom of the corridor, my legs suddenly feeling weak. A carer smiles at me as I pass. I reciprocate, wondering if they can see through my flimsy façade. I told them I was a distant relative, gave them a few facts about mine and Tammy's lives – fabricated obviously. I needn't have bothered. They seemed only too glad for her to be receiving a visitor. From what I can gather, Tammy Wentworth lives a fairly solitary existence. She has the other residents here at Millview, familiar faces she sees every day, but when it comes to visitors, according to Olwyn, the manager of the place, Tammy rarely sees anybody from one month to the next. I mentioned Gwen's name to her, casually dropped it into the conversation, mainly to see what sort of reaction it provoked but there was none. She seemed nonplussed as I described Gwen's occasional visits to see Tammy but she also mentioned that she has only been the manager here for the last four months.

The lift is thankfully empty as I step inside. My claustrophobia is always heightened when I'm surrounded by other people in a confined space. I press the button and feel my stomach tighten as I'm elevated to the second floor where Tammy's room is.

The doors swish open and I step into a wide area with low coffee tables and lots of brightly coloured modern art adorning the walls. I try to imagine what the place looked like as a hotel. I expect the interior was ripped apart and completely redesigned once it was bought for the purpose of caring for elderly people. I would love to have seen it back then with its brightly patterned carpets and state-of-the-art fixtures and fittings that were in keeping with that era.

Hoisting my overstuffed bag onto my shoulder, I slowly walk into the main lounge and try to look less nervous than I actually feel. I have no idea of what I'm about to be faced with and feel a buzzing in my head as I edge ever closer. It's a wide airy room, half filled with elderly people who are sitting watching the TV. One old gentleman is being helped out of a chair by two carers who look as if they've just finished school. I'm pleased to see that they chat to him softly and handle him with what seems to be the utmost care as he stands upright with a slight wobble.

It all seems very calm and surprisingly orderly until one of the residents turns and points a bony finger at me, her bare thin lips pursed into a firm tight line. 'You're not my mother so don't go saying you are!' A fine spray of spittle bursts into the air and dissipates around her face, tiny droplets of liquid evaporating into the ether.

I smile and nod, hoping to placate her, then turn away and scan the room for somebody I think may be Tammy. I'm gripped by a sense of mild apprehension as it suddenly occurs to me I have no idea what she looks like.

Slowly making my way around the room, I scrutinise everyone, hoping her face will jump out at me from the sea of sad-looking people. I feel as if I know her so well and yet in reality, we are perfect strangers. I spot a lady slumped in the corner and instinctively know that's it's her. She's younger looking than anybody else here and something about her features reminds me of the picture I have of her when she won the dancing trophy all those years ago. The same picture that's tucked into my bag along with all of her diaries and newspaper clippings. They're not mine. They belong to Tammy and no matter what she did all those years back, she deserves to have them back.

I don't go straight over to see her. I stand for a short while watching her, assessing her if I'm being honest. I've been told she can get testy if suddenly approached. The last thing I want is for her to fly into a rage. If I can, I'd like to sit with her a while and explain who I am; she deserves that much. She deserves the truth. We all do. There has been enough deceit and duplicity lately to last a thousand lifetimes. I don't want to come across as an imposter. I want to explain to her where I've come from and why, and hope that somewhere deep in her damaged brain, there is some sort of recognition.

When I called to tell them I'd be visiting, I was told it was highly unlikely she'd recognise me or understand anything I was saying. Well, one part of that is true at least, but as for her understanding what it is I've got to say – I'd like to give it a try. Who knows exactly what she can hear or comprehend? There may be some small part of her mind that's still functioning properly. Studies into dementia have shown that sufferers have moments of clarity, flashes of pure normality that get snatched away as fast as they appear. I'll talk to her, tell her about Cross House, explain to her that I'm living there now and that I found her old diaries and hope that somewhere in my words she hears something, some message or thought that spurs her brain into one of those rare moments of understanding. I can only try, can't I?

I feel the bulk of Tammy's journals in my bag and readjust the strap that's digging into my shoulder. It's as if the weight of the world is on my back and I long to be relieved of it. A line of perspiration sits around my hairline. Why is it so hot in here? And why doesn't anybody else seem to notice it?

Tammy looks deflated by life, as if all the air has been sucked out of her and all that remains is her outer skin, a shapeless pallid vessel where her body used to be. I stand and watch her, both fascinated and horrified by how cruel life can be. When it comes down to it, we are all just mass of bones and flesh and blood, DNA and our life experiences defining who we really are. I once asked a friend who was a GP what the key to longevity was and he replied, *Everything in moderation and choose your parents carefully.* If Tammy's parents were alive today I wonder how they would be. Would they be as fit as Gwen, or like their daughter here, unaware of the world around them and completely incapacitated?

I take a step closer, keen not to alarm her. She doesn't flicker. She doesn't seem to register anything that's going on around her. This is good, isn't it? Better than her being aggressive and trying to push me away, something the manager explained she has done in the past if people in the room get too close.

Her clothes are at least two sizes too big for her and her greying hair has been flattened down, her parting combed thoroughly flat with little or no thought to appearance. She's clean, but as far as fashion statements go, Tammy is dressed like a ninety-year-old woman. Wearing a bright yellow cardigan and pale-blue cotton trousers, she looks as if she's just stepped out of a 1970s catalogue.

Grasping the strap of my bag, I take another step closer to her, my hand outstretched as if I'm trying to tame a wild animal. 'Tammy?'

She doesn't respond. Not even an eye flicker, but then, what did I expect? I move again, ever so slowly, my feet shuffling along the thick carpet, my legs beginning to shake slightly. I'm nervous. I have no idea why. What's the worst that could happen?

I'm almost standing over her as I say her name again. 'Tammy.'

Her head snaps up, her eyes suddenly locking with mine and for a fleeting second, too finite to measure in terms of time, I could swear there is a moment of recognition, some sort of lucidity as I say her name.

Then it's gone. Her eyes cloud over and she stares at the wall, a sullen expression on her face. I decide to press on, to go ahead and say what it is I've got to say anyway. I'm here now. It would be cowardly and foolish to turn around and leave just because I'm feeling somewhat apprehensive and Tammy is non-responsive. This is what I expected. This is how I knew it would be.

As gently as I can, I slide down next to her, our arms touching. I can feel her bones and cool flesh through the thin fabric of her cardigan. I move away slightly and rest my bag on my lap. It sits there, bulky and distorted, crammed full of her teenage diaries. They're hers. I don't want them anymore. A pulse taps against the side of my neck as I softly touch her arm and lean forward to look into her eyes. 'Tammy,' I whisper in a voice so taut and full of unease, I sound more like a child than a fully functioning adult. 'I'd really like to talk to you if that's okay? I've got something that belongs to you, something from a long time ago that you might like to see.'

Thirty-six

She remains in some sort of catatonic state, her shoulders hunched forward, her face totally indifferent as I talk to her about the contents of my bag.

I lay the diaries out on the small coffee table in front of us and watch to see if she recognises them. The room has all but emptied around us, people either wandering around aimlessly or being led to other rooms by carers. I raise my voice and crane my head to stare into Tammy's eyes. They are a piercing cobalt blue but vacant; nothing to indicate she is aware I am present. It's as if somebody has reached into her soul and extinguished whatever light was shining there. Tammy Wentworth now lives in a dark place deep within her own body, unreachable and alone.

'These are all yours, Tammy. Do you recognise them? I found them in a wardrobe in Cross House.'

She doesn't move. I trace my hand over one of them and lift it up before placing it on her knee. She moves her head and gazes down at it then turns to look at me. I daren't move for fear of breaking the spell.

Very slowly, she drags her hand over the paper, her fingers white and skeletal as she traces the lines of writing with her long yellowing nail.

'Me.'

My heart almost stops. I nod and smile at her, barely able to conceal my excitement. 'Yes, Tammy, this is yours. You wrote it! Do you remember?'

A line of saliva trickles out of the corner of her mouth. I rummage in my pocket for a tissue and wipe at her face. She must only be fifteen years older than me and yet our age gap may as well be a hundred. The human body can do remarkably cruel things to itself.

She sits, rigid and unmoving while I dab at her face, her eyes set like stone as she stares straight ahead once more.

'Here, Tammy,' I say excitedly as I shove the tissue back in my pocket. 'Do you recall writing this?' I point to a large crudely drawn heart that declares her teenage love for Rod Stewart.

I wait for what feels like an age as she slowly turns to look at it, lifting her hand over the page and letting it hover there before dropping it back onto her knee.

Feeling desperate for another positive response, I dip my head and search in my bag until I find what it is I hope will catch her eye and maybe even stir her, cause her to snap out of her current inert state.

Unfolding it with the greatest care, I hold the grainy picture up to her face and watch her closely to see if there's any flicker of recognition. Very slowly, her mouth turns upwards into a half smile. She looks at me and turns back to the photograph, a low gurgling sound coming from the back of her throat. 'A – ammy.'

'Yes!' I almost shout, 'That's right. It's you, Tammy. You went to London and won a dance trophy. Do you remember?'

I feel like punching the air with my hot clenched fist. I'm so excited, so carried away with the whole situation that I inadvertently let my guard down and give her a quick hug. It's the worst thing I could do. Her reaction is instantaneous. Tammy lets out an unearthly shriek and lashes out at me, her arms thrashing around wildly, her long, ridged nails clawing at me, catching my neck and face. A sudden biting sting on my skin tells me she's drawn blood. I try to back away but she pushes herself closer to me, her face knotted with anger and confusion. She scratches and hits, pummelling at my body, slapping at my face. I would never have thought it possible that somebody so small and emaciated could inflict so much pain.

I snap my eyelids shut, not wanting to see her contorted features or to stare into her cold dead eyes. I bring my arms up to defend myself against her blows although I fear it's probably too late. I'm cut and will probably have an enormous bruise on my face in the morning. I try to stand up but she has hold of my shoulder and is pinning me down in the seat. I take a deep breath and steel myself for further hits but suddenly feel a waft of cold air as the pressure on my shoulder is released and I'm helped to my feet.

'That's enough, Tammy! Beatrice, take her to her room, will you?'

When I open my eyes, I recognise the face next to me. It takes a couple of seconds to place her. Then I remember. The young mother with the toddler who refuses to sleep is standing opposite me, helping me out of the room, her arm slung around my back, her hand cradling mine.

'I'm so sorry about that. Tammy can be quite volatile if the mood takes her. Here,' she says, lifting my face up for her to inspect, 'let me clean up that cut for you.'

I try to protest but she insists, reeling off all sorts of rules and regulations about safeguarding and health and safety and hygiene. She leads me to a small office that has a sink in the corner. I watch as she grabs a handful of paper towels and runs them under the tap, scrunching the wet paper into a tight dark ball.

'I know you,' I murmur as she puts her face close to mine and cleans the wounds on my cheek and throat.

'I know,' she replies, her breath smelling of toothpaste and coffee. 'I saw you come in and remembered our conversation.'

I don't say anything. She was so tired when we spoke that day, she was close to tears. I don't ask whether or not things have improved for her. Some things are best left alone.

'I brought Tammy some items that I found in Cross House. I think I may have upset her.' I feel wracked with guilt and marginally silly. I should have known it would evoke some dim and distant memories. I just hoped they would be positive ones. Looks like I was wrong on that score. All I've done is dig into the past and unleash a mountain of misery.

'Ah, don't worry about it. I doubt it was anything you did or said. I'm afraid that's just how she is. It's part of her condition. A lot of dementia patients get quite aggressive.' She laughs and dabs at my face. 'Sorry, I was going to say don't beat yourself up over it but that's a poor choice of phrase considering, isn't it?'

I start to laugh. I don't know whether it's mild hysteria setting in, an outburst of mixed emotions, but before I know it, tears are streaming down my face and I'm hanging on to my sides.

'I'm Bryony, by the way,' she says, smiling as she continues to attend to my cuts and bruises. 'You have to laugh, don't you? If you take things too seriously in here, you'd end up losing your bloody marbles.'

'You probably won't remember my name. I think I told you but you were past yourself with exhaustion that day. I'm Faye.'

'Faye,' she whispers softly, her hands soothing my stinging face. 'Faye of Cross House.'

'For my sins,' I add and roll my eyes dramatically.

'Don't knock it,' she says with a slight tone of envy. 'We live in the tiny terraced house at the end of the village. Your place is absolutely huge.'

And that's when I tell her. Before I can stop myself, I give Bryony the whole sorry tale, only leaving out the part about Gwen and her admission.

'You're kidding me!' she shrieks, her gloved hand poised mid-wipe. I glance at the bloodied paper towel and begin to wonder just how damaged my face is. 'The old guy who sometimes wanders around the village green? You mean him?'

I nod and wonder if I've done the right thing telling her. The whole sorry tale came tumbling out and now I'm regretting it. 'Please don't tell anybody,' I say. My voice sounds tinny and embarrassingly desperate as I plead with her to keep it to herself.

'Don't worry, I won't,' she says in such a calm and measured voice, I have no choice but to believe her. Besides, who is she going to tell? Not Tammy, although if she did talk to her about it, it wouldn't matter. Brackston is a tiny village. I suppose she could gossip to her neighbours, but even if she did, what's the worst that could happen? I block it out of my mind and think about other things, like the completion of the rewire and the new kitchen that's getting fitted shortly afterwards. Good things, positive things. That's what I need to focus on now.

'There,' Bryony says, her tone peaceful and gentle. 'All done.'

I thank her and just stop short of giving her a hug. 'I'll probably see you around next time we're both out and about.'

She nods and touches my arm softly. 'We should get together sometime for a coffee and a chat.'

I tell her that I'd like that very much and head out of the room before stopping and turning back around, remembering something. 'Those pictures and diaries that I was showing Tammy before she... well anyway, they're hers. I brought them here for her to keep.'

Bryony nods and hitches her dark arched eyebrows up at me. 'You do realise she won't look at them or even understand what they are?'

'I know,' I say to her, 'but they're hers all the same.'

'I can go through them with her, if you like?' Bryony's voice is softer now. 'You know, wait until she's in a more receptive mood and sit with her explaining where they came from.'

'I'd really appreciate that,' I reply.

'She used to talk about Cross House when she first came in here, before her speech became too difficult to understand.' Bryony is watching me as she snaps the rubber glove off and throws it in a nearby bin. 'I know she and her mother were really close. Apparently, she didn't have Tammy till she was a lot older. In her forties I think.'

I get the feeling she wants me to ask what it was Tammy used to say, to talk about what went on in that house. I'm not sure I can. Not here, not today. Perhaps when we meet up at a later date. Instead I thank her for her help and tell her I'll be in touch about that coffee, then head towards the lift and press my hand on the button.

It's only as I step outside that I realise I no longer noticed the stench of stale urine. I guess I did get used to it after all. Just goes to show what we are able to adapt to if we set our minds to it and really try.

Thirty-seven

I'm awake and I have no idea why. I suppose my body clock has become accustomed to waking up in the early hours, listening, being permanently on edge. Did I hear something? Is that what woke me? I'm not entirely sure.

I think about Peter and what he did and then I remember Gwen's reaction when I asked her for the keys back. Anybody would think I'd asked her to sever one of her own limbs and hand it over to me. Not that it matters now. The new doors are getting fitted in the morning. Soon we'll be completely secure. Perhaps then I'll start to sleep a little more soundly.

A distant rustling sound permeates the near silence. An uncomfortable ache sets deep into my bones. My chest rises and falls in panic until I realise it's Aiden getting up to go to the bathroom. I listen to the flushing of the toilet and the gush of the running tap and close my eyes with relief as he pads his way back into his room and settles himself back in bed.

I'll be glad to be rid of this feeling, this constant sense of dread that's so deeply embedded in me it's become a part of my make-up and is starting to define who I am. I won't miss it when it's gone.

I turn on my side and stare at Hugh's slumbering shadow, listening to the comforting sound of his breathing. There was a time, not so long ago, when I thought the problems this house threw at us would send us both on our separate ways. I'm pleased to say we're stronger than that. I took great delight earlier in tearing up Doctor Schilling's contact details, shoving them in the kitchen bin and emptying the leftover food from our dinner plates on top of the tiny scraps of paper. Hugh laughed. Then I joined in and in the end, we couldn't control ourselves. It was probably the relief that did it. The rewire is almost complete and our intruder has been banished. I feel as if a great pressure has been lifted.

I managed to disguise the cut on my head by wearing my hair up in a messy bun, teasing strands out to conceal the scar. The last thing I want is for Hugh to go over to Gwen's and start demanding to see Peter and getting into a conversation with Gwen that could lead anywhere. I explained to him that I'd been to see Gwen about the man who went towards her house. I told a few white lies, saying it was a distant relative of hers who had learning difficulties and was prone to wandering in the early hours. I said he had only been staying over for a short while and was returning to his care home in a few days. I also told him that Gwen was a dizzy old lady and it was best to leave her be and not mention it to her if he sees her out and about in the village. I'm not sure Hugh was fully on board with my tale. He eyed me with a great deal of caution while I was speaking but eventually nodded and exhaled loudly, saying there's nothing as queer as folk. When it comes down to it, we all believe what we want to believe, don't we? Like me, Hugh dreads the thought of police involvement. It's a last resort. Part of me thinks he wanted to be fobbed off with some cock and bull story about a harmless individual who will soon be gone from our lives.

I realise many men would have acted differently, shouted, been aggressive, marched over there to confront this intruder and made all kinds of wild threats. But not Hugh. That's one of the things I love about him: his reserved ways and quiet dignity. And anyway, after dealing with Todd and Jeff, a couple of disturbed nights barely registered on Hugh's radar. It registered with me, almost sending me into another major meltdown, but it's over and done with now. All in the past. Just a part of our history; another event that adds to life's rich tapestry.

The thought of Gwen still makes me shiver. She may not even be around for much longer if the police take any notice of the anonymous letter I sent them this morning. I pondered over it for a good while, wondering what I should do after hearing her admission of guilt. In the end, my conscience forced me into doing the right thing. Hilary Wentworth may have been a particularly unlikeable lady, hateful even, but she didn't deserve to die. And I also want to sleep at night. Keeping it secret would have made me feel permanently uncomfortable, dragging me into the whole sorry mess when my only sin was to discover those diaries, so I typed up a letter, telling them exactly what she told me. I didn't sign it. I don't want any involvement in it. I guess if the police really want to, they can find out where the paper and envelope were purchased, perhaps eventually trace the letter back to me, but I doubt that's going to happen. They may not even take it seriously. There's no evidence linking Gwen to the crime. All they have are her words. Hilary Wentworth's death wasn't considered suspicious at the time; any possible incriminating evidence is long since gone. The police have nothing to go on. Just an anonymous note sitting on a desk in a village police station; a small white envelope nestled among the rest of the recently delivered post.

I heave a sigh and stare at the clock: 3am. Time I got some proper sleep instead of lying here mulling over things I can't change. I close my eyes and drift off, the deep surrounding silence music to my ears.

Thirty-eight
Two weeks later

I'm glad the weather has held out. It feels good to be outside. It feels even better to be socialising in a garden we can move about in. After two days of back-breaking work, Hugh and I saw fit to hire a team of people to clear the entire area and I'm glad we did. With hindsight, there's no way we would have been able to get it looking like this. Two of the large conifers had to go, a decision we didn't take lightly, and all the knotty shrubbery was cut back and disposed of. A decorative arch now separates the garden into two large sections, allowing lots of light in. Hugh is determined to put the back part of it to good use and wants to get his own orchard going. He's talking about having apple and pear trees and perhaps even a few cherry trees as well. I'll leave it all up to him.

The crumbling old summerhouse went the distance and has been replaced with a brand-spanking new one. We kept the Bakelite phone.

I've not seen Peter around. I haven't seen much of Gwen either. Whenever I pass her house on my walks, she bustles back inside and slams the door behind her. I think both of them have decided to maintain a healthy distance from me and Hugh. Should I ever bump into him, I'm not entirely sure how I would react. I doubt he would even recognise me. I'm pleased to say he hasn't been back over to Cross House in search of Tammy. I've even more delighted to report that our new doors have a triple locking mechanism and it would take a bulldozer to open them once they're secured.

I sip at my gin and tonic and watch as Zoe keeps a careful eye on Bailey. There's no need. He and Aiden have grown pretty close over the past few weeks. They've discovered a cycle track that runs

257

parallel to the three fields that separate our villages and both of them use it regularly to visit one another. Aiden has learnt how to manage his new friend, and Bailey is learning how to think before he speaks. They've moulded together as friends often do and are good for one another. Yin and yang and all that.

Irena bounds towards me, an empty bottle of wine swinging from her hand. Her lips are moving and she's saying something to me but her words are drowned out by the music and screams of children as they tear around the lawn chasing each other with water pistols. I point her towards the garage where a rack of chilled drinks stands. She nods and gives me a beaming smile before disappearing in through side door. Allison catches my eye, gives me a quick wave then turns and follows Irena to refill her glass.

'Now then, gorgeous. You come here often?' Hugh spins me around and plants a kiss on my mouth. He tastes of beer and beef-flavoured crisps. He still has a post-coital glow about him after our brief but outrageously pleasurable early morning lovemaking session. He takes a swig of beer, his face positively beaming with happiness.

'I just might, if you hang around, mister.'

He brushes his hand over my backside and gives it a little squeeze before waving over to Stefan and moving off, the drink in his hand sloshing from side to side as he weaves his way across the garden, dodging the army of children who spray him with their loaded guns.

'They make a good pair, don't they?' I say, pointing to Aiden and Bailey. I sit down next to Zoe who's looking a little lost among the surrounding melee.

'Don't they just?' she replies, taking a sip of wine and shuffling along the bench to make more room for me. 'Lovely garden, Faye. I'd spend all day out here if I was you.'

'Oh God, you should have seen it when we first moved in. It was completely overgrown. It was in a worse state than the house, if that's at all possible.' I lean down and inhale the sweet scent of the peach China rose that is in the flowerbed next to our seat. We discovered it hidden behind an old tree stump and a gathering of bindweed that had all but strangled it. I have no idea who planted it, but I like to think that either Adrian or Hilary Wentworth placed it here in happier times before their marriage turned sour. Before everything turned sour.

'Still,' Zoe says softly, 'at least once you've finished decorating, you'll have a lovely grand old house in a gorgeous village. It's a dream come true, isn't it?'

'It is.' I nod and remind myself how lucky I am. There've been many ups and downs in the past year or so – and I mean many – but we've worked our way through them. Todd and his father are back on speaking terms and Todd is even planning a visit back to the UK later in the year. Whether or not I'll join them is another matter entirely, but at least the lines of communication are open again and from what I can gather, Todd is still clean. No drugs and only the occasional drink, or at least that what he's told Hugh. Only time will tell on that score.

Jeff, from what I've heard, is still receiving medical care for his mental health issues. There's been no contact and that's the way it will stay as long as I have breath in my body.

I smile at Zoe and lift my glass to chink against hers. 'I'm a very lucky lady indeed.'

'Mummy, can me and Bianka have more cake?' Poppy's face is flushed with excitement. Her eyes glisten and sparkle with childish delight. She gives a small twirl and dances about in front of us, hopping from foot to foot as she practises her routine for the school concert. Zoe smiles at her and turns to smile at me, the look on her face telling me she is smitten by Poppy's cute ways and absolute innocence. Bianka links her arm through Poppy's and they both squeal with pleasure when I nod and tell them that they can.

'But not in the house!' I yell after the two girls as they clap their hands and jump about. Poppy moves away from me and is oblivious to my cries. 'And especially not in your room, young lady. Not now it's been decorated and has new curtains and bedsheets in it.'

She stops and turns to look at me, her hands pressed onto her hips indignantly, a look of utter disgust on her face as she steps towards me again and speaks. 'I wasn't going to go into my room anyway, Mummy. I hate it in there.'

Zoe catches my eye, shakes her head and chuckles, giving me the look of solidarity recognised by mothers everywhere, the look that we share when children decide to humiliate us in public without doing anything untoward except be brutally honest.

I'm torn between smiling sweetly at my daughter's cutting reply, and wanting to pull her aside and give her a stern talking to for being rude to me in front of friends.

'Don't be silly, sweetheart,' I say through slightly gritted teeth. 'It's a lovely room. There's no reason to say such things. Once you've had your cake, you and Bianka can play up there. You can show her your new bookcase and the doll's house grandma bought you.'

'No,' Poppy says, her face beginning to grow pink with anger. 'I've just told you, I don't want to. And I don't want to see her. She's horrible.'

'Poppy!' I shriek, horrified at my little girl's words. 'That's a mean thing to say. You need to apologise right now or I'm going to –'

'I don't mean her,' Poppy says swiftly, pulling her friend near to her. She leans up and twirls a strand of Bianka's luscious brown hair loosely around her finger. 'I wasn't talking about Bianka, silly.' Both girls lean in even closer, their faces almost touching.

'Then who,' I ask, the words sticking painfully in my throat, 'are you talking about?'

'The lady,' Poppy says sourly, her mouth pursed and suddenly pale. 'It's the lady up there in my bedroom who's horrible. She's a nasty lady and I hate her.'

Time stops. My breath is suspended in my chest. I'm not hearing this. I want somebody to step in and tell me it isn't happening, that's it's a bad dream. But they don't. And I know that this is reality and it's no dream.

I want to curl up in a ball and block it out. Zoe's eyes watch me, scrutinising my every move, waiting for my response. I can't seem to say or do anything. The earth is soft under my feet, tilting wildly, spinning out of control. Still I don't speak. I'm not even sure I can. I don't have the energy to form the words. And I definitely don't want to ask Poppy who the lady is. But I know I have to. I just have to know. In a perverse sort of way, I think I've always known. I just need to hear it said out loud.

'What lady?' I croak wearily. My voice comes from another place far away from here. It doesn't belong to me. It echoes around me, eerie and lifeless. 'Who is this lady you're talking about, Poppy? Who is she?' My throat is raw, each word uttered causing me pain.

I don't know why I'm asking. I already know the answer. It's been locked in my subconscious since moving in, since that first day when I pulled up the driveway of Cross House and a sense of doom settled heavily on me. I had doubts then. I should have taken notice of the voices in my head, listened to my inner fears and taken heed. I ignored them at my peril.

The ground rushes up to meet me, a powerful malodorous fusion of wet soil and vomit covering my face as I hear my child's words, crisp and clear. True and inescapable.

'The nasty ill one in the rocking chair. That's the lady I'm talking about. She's awful. She's spiteful and mean and I'm scared of her. I've asked her to leave but she won't. She says she lives here with us and that this is her house. It's not though, is it, Mummy? It's our house, isn't it?'

I continue to listen to my daughter's voice as it cuts through the cold air above me, telling me what I knew, what I've always known from the beginning but chose to ignore. Poppy begins to cry and shriek, kneeling down next to me, begging me to get back up. Her cries are drowned out by my own wails of protest and fear as I curl up into a ball, close my eyes and weep.

THE END

Acknowledgements

As always, I owe a great deal of gratitude to everybody at Bloodhound Books for their support. I would like to thank Betsy and Fred for continuing to publish my work and to Heather Fitt for her kind words and helpful emails. Believe me, they help my flagging confidence!

A huge thank you to my ARC readers and a big thanks to Dee Williams, Gail Shaw, Donna Wilbor, Theresa Hetherington, Craig Gillan, Livia Sbarbaro, Michelle Ryles, Caroline Maston of UKCBC, Sarah Hodgson and Charlie Pearson for their ongoing support. Also a massive thank you Emma Welton and a big apology to anybody I may have missed out! You're a marvellous bunch.

This book deviated slightly from my usual genre, with a sprinkling of the supernatural in there. I hope I've managed to pull it off.

Last but not least, a big thank you to family and friends who have supported me on my writing journey over the past few years. Here's to quite a few more.

J.A. Baker

Printed in Great Britain
by Amazon